Punk's Not Dead

Punks Versus Zombies, Volume 3

Jon Cronshaw

Published by Wyvern Books, Ltd, 2025.

This is a work of fiction. Similarities to real people, places, or events are entirely coincidental.

PUNK'S NOT DEAD

First edition. September 1, 2025.

Written by Jon Cronshaw.

For Axel.

1. Bottles to the Ground

The van rumbled along the highway, the endless stretch of asphalt unfurling before them. Tommy stared out the passenger window, his eyes tracking the barren landscape without really seeing it. His mind was elsewhere, lost in a maze of grief and guilt that seemed to have no end.

Zero sat behind the wheel, his jaw set and his gaze fixed firmly on the road ahead. In the back, Roxy and Jimbo made small talk, their voices a low murmur beneath the hum of the engine. But there was a heaviness to their words, a forced levity that couldn't quite mask the sorrow.

Laila was quiet, withdrawn in a way that made Tommy's chest ache. She sat huddled against the window, her arms wrapped around herself as if she could somehow hold in the pain that threatened to consume her.

They were halfway to Columbia, Missouri, the miles falling away beneath their wheels. But the fuel gauge dipped low, the needle edging towards empty with each passing minute.

"We need to find a gas station soon," Zero said, his voice cutting through the silence. "We're not going to make it much further on fumes."

Tommy nodded, his fingers drumming a restless beat against his thigh. He scanned the horizon, searching for any sign of civilisation amidst the endless fields and farmhouses.

1

Ahead of them, a small town loomed, its streets choked with the shambling forms of the undead. They filled the main road like a dam, blocking their path forward.

"Damn it." Zero slammed on the brakes, the van lurching to a stop just shy of the horde. "We can't go through that."

Roxy leaned forward "Is there another way around?"

Zero consulted the map spread across his lap, his finger tracing the spiderweb of back roads. "Maybe. If we cut through the residential area, we might be able to bypass the worst of it."

Tommy chewed his lip. Every blind corner, every overgrown lawn could be hiding a fresh horror, a new threat waiting to leap out at them.

But what choice did they have? They couldn't go back, couldn't risk running out of fuel in the middle of nowhere. They had to press on, had to find a way through.

"Do it," he said. "Just...just be careful."

Zero grunted his assent and eased the van into gear, steering them away from the main road and into the labyrinth of side streets.

The houses stood dark and silent. Cars sat abandoned in driveways, their doors hanging open and their interiors stripped bare. It was as if the entire neighbourhood had vanished, swallowed up by the apocalypse.

"I don't know about you guys," Jimbo said. "But I'm not sure I have another fight in me. Not today."

Roxy nodded, her hand straying to the hilt of her machete. "Same here. I'm sick of this, you know? I just want to curl up somewhere safe and binge-watch something mindless."

Tommy understood the sentiment all too well. The constant fear, the never-ending struggle to survive...it wore on a person, grinding them down until there was nothing left but raw nerve endings and a bone-deep weariness.

But they couldn't afford to give in to that exhaustion, couldn't let their guard down even for a moment. He reminded himself why he was still doing this, why he was set on getting back to Philly, getting back to Niamh and Sean.

"If we have to fight, we will," Zero said. "We don't have a choice."

Roxy sighed. "I know. But that doesn't mean I have to like it."

Jimbo attempted a weak grin. "Hey, at least with Micky gone, we can focus on getting back without having to search for meds every five minutes, right? Silver linings, and all that."

The words hung in the air.

Tommy felt them as a knife twist to the gut.

Laila made a small, pained sound.

Jimbo's face fell. "Too soon?"

Laila shook her head, turning to stare out the window once more. Tommy reached back, squeezing her hand.

They drove on in silence, the only sound the low rumble of the engine and the distant moans of the undead.

Tommy scanned the streets ahead, a pulse pounding in his skull with each turn, each blind corner.

But they encountered no resistance, no fresh horrors lurking in the shadows.

They emerged from the residential streets, the open road stretching out before them once more.

Tommy let out a breath, his shoulders sagging. They had made it through, had avoided another pitched battle.

But their gas tank was still running on fumes, the needle dipping lower with each passing mile. They needed to find a station, and fast.

Zero consulted the map once more, his brow furrowed in concentration. "There's a town called Boonville coming up in about twenty miles. Might be our best bet for fuel."

Tommy nodded, his jaw tight. Twenty miles. It might as well have been a thousand, with the way their luck had been going.

He leaned his head back against the seat, letting his eyes drift shut for a moment. He was exhausted in a way that sleep could never touch.

But he couldn't rest. Not now. Not with the image of Micky's dying face haunting his thoughts.

So he focused on the road ahead, on the miles falling away. His mind kept drifting to thoughts of Micky, of the laughter and the music and the bonds that had kept them going.

Abandoned cars and wrecks littered the road, forcing Zero to slow down.

"What the hell happened here?" Jimbo gestured to the abandoned vehicles. "It's like everyone just vanished."

Zero shook his head, his eyes never leaving the road ahead. "Could be anything. Zombies, raiders, military evacuations. Doesn't matter now. All that matters is that we keep moving." The van lurched and spluttered to a stop.

"What's happening?" Jimbo asked.

"We're out of gas." Zero slammed a hand down on the steering wheel.

"We need to find a station," Tommy said. "There's got to be one around here somewhere."

Roxy leaned forward, her brow furrowed. "And what if there's not? What if everything's been picked clean already?"

He met her gaze. "Then we find another way."

They gathered their essentials, stuffing food and water and weapons into their packs. Tommy made sure to grab the gas can from the back of the van

And then they set out, leaving the van behind.

They walked in silence. Tommy scanned the road ahead, taking in the scattered debris and abandoned cars.

Bullet casings glinted in the fading light. Dark stains spattered the road.

Behind him, Laila lagged, her steps heavy and shoulders slumped.

The others shot her worried looks. But Laila brushed them off, her gaze fixed on the ground.

As the hours passed and the sun began to sink towards the horizon, the group grew increasingly fatigued.

"We can't keep going like this," Roxy said. "We need to find somewhere to hole up for the night."

Zero nodded. "There's got to be a house or a barn or something around here. We just need to keep looking."

"We could go back to the van," Jimbo said. "At least we know it's secure."

Tommy shook his head. "No. We keep going. We've come too far to turn back now."

He squinted through the gathering dusk, his eyes straining to pierce the shadows.

"Over there." Zero pointed to a house set back from the road, its windows dark, its front yard bordered by a sturdy-looking fence.

"That could work," Tommy said.

"I'll go check it out. Wait here." He unslung his rifle and moved off towards the house.

Tommy and the others waited in silence, their eyes scanning the surrounding darkness for any sign of movement.

After a minute or so, Zero reappeared. "It's clear. No corpses, no sign of anyone living. Looks like it's been abandoned for a while."

"Alright," Tommy said. "Let's get inside, shore it up as best we can."

Tommy made his way up the path, his bat at the ready, and followed Zero through the front door.

Inside, the house was dark and musty,. They moved through the rooms, flashlight beams cutting through the gloom.

In the kitchen, Tommy found a few cans of food in the cupboards. It wasn't much, but it was better than nothing.

He joined the others, barricading the entrances as best they could, pushing heavy furniture against the doors and covering the windows with whatever they could find.

With the house as secure as they could make it, they gathered in the living room, huddling around a small fire Zero had built in the fireplace.

As they ate canned beans and stale crackers, Jimbo rummaged through the kitchen drawers, his eyes lighting up as he pulled out a handful of drinking straws. "Hey, who's up for some cocktails? I make a mean Zombie Sunrise."

Zero looked up from his can and slapped his forehead. "How could I be so stupid?"

Jimbo frowned. "Huh?"

Zero rose to his feet. "Straws. We can siphon gas. Why the hell didn't I think of that before?"

"You're right," Tommy said. "We've been passing abandoned cars for miles."

Roxy nodded. "Beats wandering around on foot, that's for sure."

As the night wore on, they took turns keeping watch, peering out through the gaps in the barricades for any signs of trouble.

Laila curled up on the couch, her eyes drifting shut.

Tommy sat by the dying fire, his gaze distant. Beside him, Roxy shifted, her shoulder brushing against his.

"Hey. You okay?"

"Yeah. Just thinking about Micky. All the crazy times we had together back in Philly." Tears pricked at the corners of his eyes, blurring his vision. He blinked them away, but more followed.

Roxy reached out, her hand finding his in the darkness. She twined their fingers together, her thumb brushing over his knuckles in a gentle, comforting motion. "I'm so sorry, Tommy. I know how much he meant to you."

Tommy nodded, not trusting himself to speak. He leaned into her, resting his head on her shoulder as the grief washed over him in waves.

They sat like that for a long time, the silence broken only by the crackle of the dying fire.

Roxy sat up and cleared her throat. "Tommy, I need to tell you something."

He lifted his head, meeting her gaze in the flickering light.

"I care about you, Tommy. As more than just a friend. And I know you feel it too, even if you won't admit it to yourself."

He thought back to that moment in Kansas, the electricity that had crackled between them as they stood together on stage, the sound of the crowd fading to a distant roar.

He had felt it then, that undeniable pull, that sense of connection that went beyond mere friendship. And he had felt it again after the show, the growing closeness between them taking on new depth and meaning.

But he had pushed it down, had buried it beneath the weight of his grief and his guilt and his desperate, aching hope that somehow, someway, he would make it back to Niamh and Sean.

"Rox...I can't. I'm sorry, but I just can't."

He saw the hurt flash across her face, the way her shoulders slumped and her hand went slack in his.

She pulled away, her eyes shimmering. "I knew you'd say that. You're still holding out for Niamh, even after everything we've been through together, everything we've lost."

He wanted to reach out to her, to pull her back and tell her that he did feel something for her.

Instead, he nodded, his gaze dropping to the floor. "I'm sorry."

Roxy stood. "Yeah. So am I." She turned and walked away, disappearing down the hallway.

Tommy sat there for a long time, staring into the dying embers, his mind a whirl of conflicting emotions.

Finally, he stood, his joints aching from the long hours of walking.

He made his way into the kitchen, rummaging through the cupboards in search of something, anything to dull the pain that throbbed in his chest.

His fingers closed around the neck of a bottle, and he pulled it out, squinting at the label in the dim light. Whiskey, the cheap stuff that burned going down.

He hesitated, staring at the bottle in his hand.

The push. The pull.

The revulsion. The desire.

He had sworn off drinking years ago, had embraced the straight edge lifestyle with a fervour that bordered on religious.

The bold black Xs tattooed on the backs of his hands were a constant reminder of that commitment, a symbol of his dedication to a life free from the temptations of alcohol and drugs.

The music was more than enough.

Or, at least, it was.

Now, with the weight of Micky's loss and Roxy's rejection crushing down on him, the thought of Niamh and Sean still being out there, and the thought of them not—that dedication seemed like a hollow thing, a flimsy shield against the darkness that threatened to overwhelm him.

With shaking hands, he unscrewed the cap, the sharp scent of alcohol reaching him like an old friend. He raised the bottle to his lips, hot tears stinging his eyes as he took a long, burning swallow.

The whiskey seared his throat.

He took another swallow, then another, feeling the numbness begin to creep over him, dulling the edges of his pain.

He let the tears come then, let them spill down his face in hot, silent tracks as he drank, drowning his sorrows in the comfort of the bottle.

And as he pulled his sleeves down over the Xs on his hands, he couldn't help but wonder what Niamh would say if she could see him now.

The morning sun cast a dull, hazy glow on the horizon as Tommy emerged from the house, his head pounding and his mouth dry. He squinted against the light, shading his eyes with a hand as he surveyed the area.

The others were already up and about, gathering their gear and checking their weapons.

Zero crouched beside an abandoned car, a length of rubber tubing in his hand and a look of grim determination on his face.

Tommy made his way over, trying to ignore the way the world seemed to tilt and sway with each step. "What's the plan?"

Zero glanced up, his eyes narrowed. "We siphon what gas we can from these cars, then we head back to the van. With any luck, we'll have enough to get us to Columbia."

Tommy nodded, his gaze sliding to Roxy. She stood a little apart from the others, her arms crossed and her face unreadable. The events of the previous night hung between them, a barrier that he didn't know how to breach.

He took a deep breath, steeling himself, and made his way over to her. "Rox, about last night..."

She cut him off with a sharp look. "Don't, Tommy. Just...don't."

He swallowed hard, his throat tight. "I'm sorry. I didn't mean to hurt you."

Roxy let out a brittle laugh, shaking her head. "You didn't hurt me, Tommy. I'm a big girl, I can handle a little rejection." She uncrossed her arms, her hands clenching into fists at her sides. "But I won't be anyone's second choice."

"I know. And I'm sorry for making you feel that way. I just...I can't give up on Niamh. On Sean. They're my family."

"I get it, Tommy. Believe me, I do. But you can't keep living in the past. You have to focus on the here and now, on the people who are still with you." She reached out, laying a hand on his arm. "We're your family too, you know."

"And I'm grateful for that, more than you can imagine."

Roxy gave his arm a squeeze, then pulled away, her nose wrinkling. "God, your breath reeks. What did you do, gargle with a bottle of Jack last night?"

A flush of shame creeped up his neck, and he ducked his head. "It won't happen again."

Roxy snorted, shaking her head. "Sure it won't."

He flinched at the words. But he knew she was right. He had let his grief and his guilt get the best of him, had let himself slip back into old habits that he thought he had left behind long ago. "I mean it, Rox."

She studied him for a long moment, her eyes searching his face. "Alright, Tommy. But you have to prove it, not just to me, but to yourself."

With that, she turned and walked away, leaving Tommy standing there, his head pounding.

He watched as she joined the others, watched as Zero showed them how to siphon gas from the cars, the tube held between his teeth as he sucked.

They worked quickly, moving from car to car, filling up their gas cans with the precious fuel. Laila was quiet and withdrawn throughout, her eyes distant and her movements mechanical.

After what felt like hours, they had filled the can, the weight of it dragging at Tommy's arms as they made their way back to the van.

His head throbbed with every step, the hangover a constant, nagging reminder of his weakness.

Jimbo fell into step beside Tommy. "Everything alright with you and Roxy?"

Tommy shook his head, not trusting himself to speak.

"Come on, dude. Talk to me. What's going on?"

Tommy sighed. "I don't know, man. Everything's just so screwed up. Micky's gone, and I can't stop thinking about Niamh and Sean, wondering if they're even still alive. And then there's Roxy..." He trailed off, shaking his head. "I don't know what to do. I don't know how to make it right."

"You can't make it right, T. Not really. All you can do is keep putting one foot in front of the other. We've all lost people. We've all got regrets. But we can't let them define us. We have to keep fighting, keep holding onto the hope that somehow, someway, we'll make it through this."

Tommy nodded. "Thanks, Jimbo. I needed to hear that."

Jimbo grinned. "Anytime, dude. Just don't go getting all sappy on me now. We've got a reputation to uphold."

Tommy chuckled, shaking his head, and together they walked on, the sun beating down on them.

It was late afternoon by the time they reached the van, the shadows lengthening and the air cooling as the sun dipped towards the horizon.

But as they drew closer, Tommy froze. A lone zombie shambled towards them, its movements jerky and uncoordinated.

Roxy roared, her machete blade slicing through rotten flesh like it was nothing.

The zombie crumpled to the ground, its head rolling away into the dirt.

Tommy and the others approached cautiously, their weapons at the ready. But the zombie lay still.

Roxy wiped her blade on the leg of her jeans. "Let's get the hell out of here."

They piled into the van, Roxy taking the wheel as Tommy slid into the passenger seat beside her. Zero and Jimbo climbed into the back, Laila following close behind.

Roxy turned the key in the ignition, the engine sputtering to life with a cough. She glanced over at Tommy, her eyes unreadable. "You ready for this?"

He nodded, his jaw set. "As I'll ever be."

2. The Library

Tommy's eyes fluttered open, the harsh sunlight filtering through the van's windows, and he winced as he sat up.

He expected the familiar pounding in his head, the sour taste in his mouth, but the hangover had cleared.

"Where are we?" Tommy asked.

"Just entered the campus," Roxy said. "Figured it was worth a shot to look for supplies here."

"What campus?"

"Missouri. We're in Columbia."

Tommy nodded, taking in the stillness of the surroundings. The buildings loomed silent, their windows dark and empty.

Roxy steered the van towards the central quadrangle, parked, and killed the engine.

"Alright, everyone," Zero said. "We don't know what we're walking into here. So stay sharp, stay together, and if you see anything suspicious, don't hesitate to speak up."

There were murmurs of agreement as they gathered their weapons and supply bags, preparing for the task ahead.

Tommy's gaze lingered on Laila, who had barely spoken a word since they'd left Kansas City. Her face was drawn, her eyes haunted.

Zero took the lead as they made their way towards the cluster of administrative buildings. "We check the registration office first. Could prove a potential goldmine of keys and maps."

"Good thinking," Tommy said.

Reaching the building, they found the doors unlocked. They filed inside, flashlights sweeping over the desks and filing cabinets.

"Check everywhere," Zero said. "Desk drawers, cabinets, anywhere they might have stashed something useful."

Tommy set to work, rummaging through the abandoned office.

"Guess they didn't keep a stash of snacks in here," Jimbo said.

They moved on to the science and technology department. The sound of their footsteps echoed off the bare walls.

Zero entered the lab first and gestured for Tommy and the others to follow.

Roxy made a beeline for the cabinets, her machete at the ready. "Jackpot." She held up a bottle of rubbing alcohol. "Found some bandages and antiseptic, too."

They moved from lab to lab, their haul growing slowly but steadily.

"Let's keep moving," Zero said. "We've got a lot of ground to cover."

Zero led them to the student union. But as they approached, a sense of unease settled over the group.

The building was darker than the others, the windows boarded up from the inside. It was clear that it had been used as a shelter at some point, a refuge for those fleeing the horrors outside.

once more. "Each of you will be assigned to work with one of our new allies. We're all in this together, and the only way we'll survive is by working as a team."

A few of the students shifted uncomfortably, their gazes darting between Tommy's group and Dr. Jameson.

One young man raised his hand. "Are you sure this is a good idea? We don't know these people. How can we trust them?"

Dr. Jameson fixed the student with a stern look. "I understand your concerns. But we've discussed this before. Our survival depends on our ability to adapt, to forge alliances with those who can help us."

The student nodded, his expression still uncertain.

Dr. Jameson turned back to Tommy, a small smile tugging at the corners of his mouth. "Thank you for your patience, Tommy. I know this isn't an easy situation for any of us. But I truly believe that together, we can create something extraordinary here. Something that will endure long after the last of the monsters have fallen."

Tommy wiped the sweat from his brow as he hefted another heavy wooden desk, his muscles straining with the effort. Beside him, a student grunted as she adjusted her grip, her face set in a determined grimace.

"On three," she said. "One, two, three!"

Together, they lifted the desk and carried it across the library floor, navigating the maze of desks and shelves.

Around them, the other survivors worked in teams, hauling furniture to shore up the barricades.

Dr. Jameson stood at the centre of the chaos, barking orders, and directing traffic. "You there." He pointed to a lanky young man with a mop of curly hair. "Take that shelf and wedge it against the front doors. We need to reinforce the entrance."

The young man nodded and hurried to drag the shelf across the floor with the help of another student.

As Tommy and his partner set the desk down against a window, Zero appeared at their side, his eyes narrowed as he examined the barricade. "No, no, no. That's not going to work, Tommy boy."

Dr. Jameson looked up, his eyebrows raised. "Is there a problem?"

Zero gestured to the desk "This is too flimsy. One good hit from a zombie and it'll splinter like kindling. We need something sturdier, like metal or concrete."

Dr. Jameson frowned, his hands on his hips. "We're working with what we have. We don't exactly have a surplus of building materials lying around."

Zero shrugged, his eyes scanning the room. "Maybe not, but we can improvise. See that metal shelving unit over there? You could dismantle it and use the pieces to reinforce the windows."

"Alright, fine. But we need to work quickly. We don't know how much time we have before the next attack."

"Leave it to me, Doc."

Over the next few hours, Tommy lost himself in the work. He hauled desks and chairs, dismantled shelves and bookcases, and hammered nails into boards until his fingers ached and his arms trembled.

As the last of the barricades fell into place, the survivors stepped back to survey their handiwork.

The library was far from impenetrable, but it was a damn sight stronger than it had been just a few hours before.

Dr. Jameson clapped his hands together as he looked around at the assembled group. "Well done, everyone. You've all worked hard today, and it shows "

"Don't mention it, Doc," Zero said. "We're just doing what needs to be done."

Dr. Jameson nodded. "But still, we couldn't have done this without you. You've given us a fighting chance, and that's more than most people have in this world."

The sound of shattering glass and splintering wood echoed through the library.

Tommy whirled around to see a group of armed raiders pouring through the shattered barricades. "Everyone, get ready to fight!"

The library survivors scattered, some grabbing weapons while others fled deeper into the stacks.

Dr. Jameson shouted orders.

Zero was already in motion, his rifle raised and his eyes hard. He moved with a fluid grace, weaving between the shelves, and taking aim.

A man charged at Tommy, a knife glinting in his hand.

Tommy swung his bat with all his strength, feeling the satisfying crunch of bone as it connected with a raider's skull.

The man crumpled to the ground, his knife clattering to the floor.

Tommy caught sight of Roxy, her machete flashing as she carved a path through two men. And Jimbo, hurling books with reckless abandon.

Tommy gritted his teeth. They had to fight, had to stand together against this threat. There was no other choice.

He charged forward, his bat swinging in a wide, vicious arc. The impact of each blow shuddered up his arms.

They were quicker than the undead, prone to dodges and feints.

A scream pierced the air.

Tommy whirled around to see Dr. Jameson crumpling to the ground, clutching his side as blood seeped between his fingers.

There was nothing anyone could do.

Tommy's gaze fell on Zero, who was crouched behind an overturned table. Tommy sprinted over, dropping to his knees beside him.

"We need to do something. We can't let them overrun us."

Zero glanced at him, his eyes hard. "We need to force them into a bottleneck. If we can lure them to the main entrance, we might have a fighting chance."

"Okay."

Zero grunted, already moving. "I'll take the left flank, you take the right. The others can hold the centre."

Tommy sprinted back into the fray, his bat swinging with renewed vigour. "Everyone, fall back to the main entrance. We'll make our stand there!"

The others responded with shouts, falling back towards the towering wooden doors.

Tommy could see Laila in the midst of the fighting, swinging the tyre iron with a savage efficiency.

He skidded to a halt, spinning around to face the oncoming raiders.

"Hold the line!" Zero said. "Don't let them through!"

The others fanned out beside Tommy, their weapons at the ready.

And then the raiders were upon them.

Tommy swung his bat with all his strength.

Beside him, Zero smashed his rifle butt against a raider's jaw, sending the man sprawling.

Roxy was a blur of flashing steel, her machete carving through the raiders' ranks. Jimbo swung his golf club in wide, crushing arcs.

Movement flickered at the edge of his vision as a pair of raiders broke away from the main horde, circling around to flank them from the side. "Zero! On your left!"

Zero whirled around, his rifle snapping up to his shoulder.

A cry struck Tommy's ears, high and sharp with pain.

Roxy staggered backwards, clutching her arm.

"Roxy!" He tried to push forward, to reach her, but the raiders were too many, too strong.

A sudden sharp blow exploded against the back of his head.

The world spun, his vision blurring as he stumbled forward.

He heard shouts, screams, the harsh bark of gunfire. And then the ground was rushing up to meet him, hard and unyielding.

Darkness engulfed him.

Tommy awoke to the sound of muffled voices, the acrid scent of smoke and blood thick in his nostrils. He blinked, wincing at the throbbing pain in his head as he struggled to sit up.

He found himself on a pile of blankets, his clothes sticky with sweat and grime. Around him, the shattered remains of the library stretched out in all directions.

"Easy."

Tommy looked up to see Zero crouching beside him, his face streaked with soot and blood. "You took a nasty blow to the head. Might have a concussion."

Tommy reached up, gingerly probing the back of his skull. His fingers came away sticky with drying blood. "What happened?"

"We drove them off. But not before they did their damage."

Tommy looked around. "Is everyone..."

"We're good, Tommy."

Tommy's gaze found Laila sitting apart from the others, her knees drawn up to her chest and her face buried in her arms. She rocked back and forth, her shoulders shaking.

Tommy tried to push himself to his feet, his head spinning with the effort. But Zero held him back.

"Give her space. She's been through a lot."

Roxy sat against a nearby wall, her arm bound in a makeshift sling. Jimbo lay sprawled on the floor nearby, his golf club clutched to his chest, his eyes staring blankly at the ceiling.

And the library survivors, lay scattered among the debris, injured but alive.

Tommy let out a shuddering breath, his chest tightening. This was his fault. People were dead. People were wounded.

He pushed himself to his feet, ignoring the throbbing in his head and the protests of his battered body. "We have to go. We can't stay here. It's not safe."

Zero nodded. "We'll gather what supplies we can, bury the dead. And then we'll move on."

Tommy looked over at Laila, still huddled in on herself, lost in her own private hell of grief and trauma. His heart ached for her, for the pain and the loss that she carried with her.

But there was nothing he could say, nothing he could do to ease her suffering. All he could do was keep moving forward.

He wandered through the shattered remnants of the library, his feet crunching on broken glass and splintered wood. The once pristine halls were now a war zone, the books and shelves torn and scorched.

His mind reeled with the images of the day, the screams of the wounded and the dying echoing in his ears. He'd seen death—too much death.

But this was different. This was human violence, raw and brutal and senseless.

He found himself in one of the offices, the door hanging off its hinges and the windows shattered. The room had been ransacked, the desks and filing cabinets overturned, their contents strewn across the floor.

He drew the bottle of whiskey from his pack, its amber liquid glinting in the fading light.

He unscrewed the cap. He raised the bottle to his lips, the liquid burning his throat as he swallowed.

It was a mistake, he knew. A momentary weakness, a surrender to the darkness.

But in that moment, as the warmth of the whiskey spread through his veins and numbed the sharp edges of his pain, he couldn't bring himself to care.

He drank deeply, the bottle growing lighter in his hand with each swallow. The world around him began to spin, the shattered remnants of the library blurring into a kaleidoscope of shadows and light.

He stumbled out into the hallway, the bottle clutched tight in his fist. He could hear voices in the distance, the low murmur of conversation drifting through the empty halls.

He followed the sound, his feet carrying him towards the library's main atrium, the bottle sloshing in his hand.

Laila looked up at him, her eyes widening. "Tommy?" She glanced at the bottle. "What are you doing?"

He shrugged, a bitter laugh escaping his lips. "What does it look like? I'm celebrating our glorious victory."

Roxy got to her feet and glared at Tommy. "You're drunk."

He laughed again and raised the bottle to his lips, taking another long swallow. The whiskey burned his throat, but he welcomed the pain, welcomed the numbness.

Zero stepped forward. "That's enough, Tommy. You're not thinking straight."

Tommy rounded on him. "Oh, I'm thinking just fine, Zero. For the first time in a long time, I'm seeing things clearly." He gestured around at the shattered remnants of the library, at the haunted faces of the survivors. "This is what we've been reduced to. Scavenging and fighting and killing, just to stay alive another day. What's the point of it all? Tell me, Zero. What's the point?"

Laila reached out to him, her hand gentle on his arm. "Tommy, please. We need you sober, now more than ever."

He shrugged her off, his grip tightening on the bottle. "You don't need me. You never did. I'm just a liability, a weak link in the chain." He gestured to Zero. "Follow him. He knows what he's doing. I'm just a useless punk."

He raised the bottle to his lips once more, but before he could take another drink, Zero's hand shot out, knocking it from his grasp. The bottle shattered on the floor, the whiskey spilling out.

Tommy stared at it for a long moment before sinking to his knees.

Laila knelt beside him, her arms wrapping around his shoulders. He could feel her tears soaking through his shirt as she held him close.

They stayed like that for a long time, huddled together on the cold, hard floor. The others kept their distance.

As the minutes ticked by, the others drifted closer. Jimbo approached first, a steaming mug of coffee clutched in his hands. He crouched down beside Tommy, offering the mug. "Here, dude. Get this down you. Clear your head."

Tommy stared at the mug for a moment before reaching out with a shaky hand to take it. "Thanks, man."

Jimbo squeezed Tommy's shoulder. "No worries, T.."

Tommy managed a weak nod, sipping at the coffee.

Roxy appeared, a plate of food in her hands. It was a simple offering - a few cans of beans and some crackers.

She set the plate down beside him. "Eat."

Tommy hesitated, glancing between the food and Roxy's face. He knew he didn't deserve their concern. But the gnawing emptiness in his gut won out, and he reached for the plate with a mumbled thanks.

"We should stay here," Zero said, his voice firm. "Get some rest, regroup, and head out in the morning when we've got the daylight on our side."

The others murmured their agreement, and Tommy found himself nodding along. As much as he hated the idea of staying in this place, he knew Zero was right.

Laila's arms tightened around him as she leaned in close. "It's going to be okay, Tommy. We'll get through this."

Tommy swallowed hard. He wanted to believe her, to cling to the hope and comfort her words offered. But he had failed them, letting his own weakness get the best of him. How could he ever hope to lead them, to keep them safe, when he couldn't even control his own demons?

"Thanks, Lai. For everything. For not giving up on me."

"That's what family does, Tommy. We stick together, no matter what."

The morning sun cast a pale light over the library grounds as Tommy and his group gathered with the survivors to bury their dead. The air was heavy with the scent of smoke and decay.

Tommy's head throbbed with the aftereffects of the whiskey, his stomach churning with nausea and guilt. He stood at the edge of the makeshift gravesite, his eyes fixed on the shrouded form of Dr. Jameson.

Beside him, Laila and Roxy stood in silence, their faces etched with grief and exhaustion. Zero and Jimbo flanked them, their weapons held at the ready, ever vigilant even in this moment of mourning.

One of the students, a young woman, stepped forward to stand at the head of the grave. "Dr. Jameson was more than just a professor. He was a mentor, a friend, a leader. He believed in the power of knowledge, in the idea that by preserving the lessons of the past, we could build a better future. And that's exactly what we're going to do."

Tommy thought of all the people they had lost along the way. Dr. Jameson was just the latest in a long line of casualties, another name to add to the ever-growing list.

The student turned to face Tommy and his group. "We owe you our lives. Without your help, we would all be dead. You gave us a fighting chance, and for that, we will be forever grateful."

Tommy wanted to tell her that they didn't deserve her gratitude. But the words wouldn't come, trapped behind the lump in his throat and the pounding in his head.

Instead, he simply nodded, his gaze dropping to the ground at his feet.

As the last shovelfuls of dirt were placed on the grave and the survivors began to disperse, Tommy felt a wave of exhaustion wash over him. His body ached with the aftereffects of the battle and the alcohol, his mind spinning with the events of the past few days.

He turned to the others. "We should get moving."

Zero nodded. "Tommy's right. We need to put as much distance between us and this place as we can. Never know when those raiders might come back for another go."

They made their way back to the van in silence.

As they loaded the last of the bags into the back of the vehicle, Roxy leaned against the side. "If the roads are clear, we can make it to St. Louis in a couple of hours. From there, we can figure out our next move."

Tommy climbed into the passenger seat, his head falling back against the headrest.

Zero slid behind the wheel and turned the key in the ignition, the van sputtering to life. He glanced at Tommy. "You gonna be okay, Tommy boy. You're looking a bit green there."

"I'm fine."

Zero nodded. "Well, if you need to hurl. Shout up. This van stinks enough as It is."

Tommy wrinkled his nose. "Don't worry about me. I'll be fine."

3. Blame

As the van rumbled down the highway, leaving Columbia behind, a sombre silence settled over the group. The weight of their recent losses hung heavy, a palpable presence that couldn't be ignored.

"We can't keep going like this," Zero said, his voice rough. "Our weapons, our supplies...they're not enough. Not anymore."

Tommy looked up from where he sat hunched in the passenger seat, his head throbbing with the remnants of his hangover. "What are you saying, Zero?"

"I'm saying we need to stock up on weapons and ammo, on anything that can give us an edge out there." Zero's gaze swept over the others. "First chance we get, we hit up any place that might have what we need. Military surplus stores, gun shops...anything."

Tommy nodded, his jaw tight. "You're right. We can't afford to be caught off guard again."

Zero grunted, his hands tightening on the steering wheel as he guided the van towards the distant horizon. "St. Louis isn't far from here. Big city like that, there's bound to be places we can scavenge for gear."

Roxy leaned forward from the backseat. "You want us to go back into a city? After Denver?"

Tommy turned to her. "We can't keep running forever, Rox. We need supplies, and a big city like St. Louis is our best bet."

Roxy shook her head. "It's too dangerous. We barely made it out of Denver alive. What makes you think St. Louis will be any different?"

Zero scoffed. "We don't have a choice. We're running low on everything, and we need to restock if we want to survive."

Roxy leaned back, her arms crossed over her chest. "There has to be another way. Smaller towns, rural areas. Somewhere safer."

Tommy sighed, rubbing his temples. "Look, I get it. Going into the city is a risk. But we can't keep scavenging in the sticks and expect decent results."

Jimbo leaned forward, his elbows resting on his knees. "I'm with Zero. We need better weapons, dude. I don't know about you, but I'd feel a whole lot safer with a real gun in my hands instead of this stupid nine iron."

Roxy shot him a look. "Guns attract attention, Jimbo. The sound, the flash. It's like ringing the dinner bell for every zombie in the area."

Jimbo shrugged. "Maybe. But at least we'd stand a better chance."

Tommy held up his hands, trying to calm the rising tension. "Okay, look. How about a compromise? We go into St. Louis, but we keep it low-key. Stick to the outskirts, scout around a bit. If things look dicey, we bail out. No heroics, no unnecessary risks."

Zero gave a nod. "Fine. But we need to move fast. In and out, no dawdling."

Jimbo leaned back in his seat. "I'm cool with that. Zombies are one thing, but it's the humans that really scare me. At least with the dead-heads, you know what you're getting. But people? They're unpredictable. Dangerous."

Roxy sighed. "Not all of them. We've met good people too, Jimbo. People who helped us, who took us in when we needed it most."

Zero sniffed. "And look how that turned out. Those 'good people' at Haven? They were a bunch of psychos. And the library? They couldn't even protect their own."

Roxy opened her mouth to argue, but Zero cut her off with a sharp gesture. "Face it, Rox. In this world, you can't trust anyone but yourself and your own. Everybody else is just a liability waiting to happen."

A heavy silence settled over the van.

Tommy glanced over at Laila, who sat huddled against the window, her gaze distant and unfocused. "What do you think, Lai?"

Laila didn't respond, her eyes never leaving the landscape outside. After a long moment, she gave a slight shrug, her shoulders barely moving.

Tommy sighed, turning back to face the road ahead. He understood Laila's silence, her withdrawal. After everything they'd been through, after all the losses and the horrors, it was a miracle any of them could still function at all.

Roxy sank back into her seat. "Do whatever you want. I just want to get back home. That's all that matters now."

Tommy nodded, his chest tightening. Home seemed like such a distant concept now, a fading memory of a life that no longer existed. But still, the thought of seeing Niamh and Sean again, of holding them in his arms and knowing they were safe...it was the one thing that kept him going.

But as the miles fell away beneath the van's wheels, his mind drifted to thoughts of Dr. Jameson, of the way the man had welcomed them into his community, had fought and died to protect the knowledge he held so dear. He thought of the survivors they had left behind, the men and women who had chosen to stay and continue the professor's work.

And he thought of Micky, lying cold and still in a makeshift grave, his life cut short by the cruel whims of fate.

The guilt and the grief threatened to overwhelm him, to drag him down into the dark abyss that yawned at the edges of his consciousness. But he pushed it away, forcing himself to focus on the present, on the challenges that lay ahead.

There was only survival, raw and brutal and unrelenting.

They were broken and battered, scarred in ways that might never fully heal. But they were still alive.

Still breathing.

Still fighting.

It was late afternoon by the time they reached the outskirts of the city, the sun casting long shadows.

"There." Zero pointed towards a low building set back from the road. "Police station. Looks abandoned."

Tommy peered through the windshield, his eyes straining to make out the details of the structure. It was a squat, unassuming thing, its windows dark and its parking lot empty. "You sure about this?"

Zero shot him a look, his eyes hard. "Without taking a closer look, I'm about as sure as I can be, Tommy boy."

"Alright, you don't have to be a dick about it. It just looks very quiet."

"Quiet is good. Means there's less chance of running into trouble." Zero brought the van to a stop, the engine idling as he surveyed the police station. After a long moment, he shook his head and threw the vehicle into reverse, backing up until they were facing the road once more.

"What the hell are you doing?" Roxy asked.

"Making sure we have a clear exit strategy if things go south in there." He killed the engine and turned to face the others. "Alright, listen up. Stay alert, stay focused. Check your corners, watch each other's backs. Anything looks off, you speak up. Clear?"

They gathered their weapons and filed out of the van, Zero taking point as they approached the police station.

Tommy fell into step beside him, his bat gripped tight in his hands.

Zero held up a hand and cocked his head. After a moment, he gestured for them to fan out, moving in a slow, cautious arc around the building's perimeter.

Every shadow seemed to hold a threat, every rustle of wind a potential warning of danger.

Zero paused at each window, each doorway, his rifle at the ready.

They completed their circuit of the building, meeting back up at the front entrance. Zero held up a hand, his eyes narrowing as he studied the heavy metal doors. "Looks clear. But there could be a whole horde of zombies waiting for us on the other side."

Roxy shifted her weight, her machete glinting in the fading light. "So what's the plan? We just go in blind, hope for the best?"

Zero shook his head. "No. We do this properly. Tommy, you're on point. I'll be right behind you. Roxy, Jimbo, you cover our flanks. And Laila..." He glanced over at her, his expression softening for just a moment. "You stay in the middle, keep an eye on our backs. Anything moves, you shout out."

Laila nodded.

He turned back to Tommy, his jaw set. "You ready for this?"

Tommy took a deep breath. "Ready as I'll ever be."

Zero gave a curt nod, then reached out and grasped the door's handle. "Alright. On my count. Three, two, one..."

He yanked the door open, the hinges shrieking in protest.

Tommy darted through the opening, his bat at the ready, his heart pounding in his ears.

The lobby loomed dark and still, the air heavy with the scent of dust and stale coffee. Tommy swept his flashlight beam across the room, its beam catching on overturned furniture and scattered debris.

On Zero's signal, the others fanned out, each taking a different section of the room, their weapons at the ready.

Tommy's eyes strained to pierce the gloom, his muscles tense. But there was no sign of life or unlife in the abandoned station. Just the oppressive weight of silence, broken only by the soft creak of their footsteps on the dusty floor.

"We check every room," Zero said. "Every closet. And stay quiet."

As they moved through the station, Tommy half-expected a zombie to come lurching out of the shadows at any moment, its jaws snapping and its eyes glazed with hunger.

But the station remained still and silent, the only sound the soft rasp of their own breathing and the occasional clatter when someone kicked aside debris.

Tommy led the way through offices and hallways, his flashlight cutting through the blackness. Desks and filing cabinets lay overturned, their contents scattered across the floor. Bullet holes pockmarked the walls.

His torch lingered on a sign. He glanced back at the others. "The armoury."

"Jackpot," Jimbo said.

Tommy nudged the door with his bat and waited.

Nothing.

He gave a nod and pushed the door open fully.

Inside, the racks and shelves stood empty.

"Looks like it's already been picked clean."

"Wouldn't be so sure about that, Tommy boy." Zero's torch beam lingered on a small open box tucked under one of the shelves. He picked up a bullet, turning it over in his fingers. ".223 Remington."

Tommy raised an eyebrow. "How many?"

"Enough to make a difference." Zero began scooping the bullets into his pack, his movements quick and efficient.

Roxy rattled the handle of a metal locker, cursing under her breath. "Jimbo, give me a hand with this."

Jimbo grinned and hefted his golf club. "Stand back." He swung hard, the metal denting under the force of the blow.

It took a few more swings, but finally the locker door gave way.

Roxy reached inside, rummaging through the contents.

"Anything good?" Tommy asked, moving to join her.

Roxy emerged with a police baton and riot shield. "Not much, but better than nothing." She tossed the baton to Jimbo and handed the shield to Laila.

Laila took it, her fingers running over the scuffed surface. "I don't know if I can use this."

"You don't have to fight with it," Tommy said. "Just hold onto it for now, protect yourself if things get hairy."

Laila nodded, slipping her arm through the straps.

Zero finished loading the bullets into his pack and straightened up. "Alright, let's keep looking. There might be more scattered around."

They fanned out again, each taking a section of the armoury. Tommy moved down the aisles, checking each shelf and drawer for anything of use.

Roxy appeared at the end of the aisle, a handful of pistol magazines in her hands. "Found these in a desk drawer. Looks like nine millimetre. Might be good for trade if we can't find anything to use them in."

As they regrouped near the entrance, Zero did a quick inventory of their haul. "Okay, so we've got a couple hundred rounds of .223, maybe fifty shotgun shells, and a handful of nine mil mags. Plus the baton and the shield."

Jimbo hefted the baton, giving it an experimental swing. "Not bad for a quick smash and grab."

Roxy snorted. "Speak for yourself. I was hoping for a grenade launcher, at least."

A low, guttural moan, echoed through the halls.

Tommy's head snapped up.

They weren't alone anymore.

Zero moved to the door, his rifle at the ready. He peered out into the hallway, his head cocked.

The moan came again, louder this time. Closer.

Laila clutched the riot shield to her chest. Jimbo and Roxy moved to flank Zero, their weapons drawn.

Tommy gripped his bat tighter. He forced himself to take a deep breath, to push down the fear and focus on the task at hand.

Zero glanced back at him. "We move fast and quiet. Stick together, cover each other's backs. Anything gets in our way, we put it down hard."

He led the way out into the darkened hallway, Roxy and Jimbo falling into step behind him.

Tommy took up the rear, Laila just ahead of him with the shield held before her.

The moans grew louder. The scrape of feet on tile, the rustle of clothing.

They rounded a corner and a dozen or more of the undead shuffled towards them.

Zero dropped to one knee, his rifle snapping up to his shoulder. He fired once, twice, three times in rapid succession. Three zombies dropped, their heads exploding in a spray of blood and brain matter.

Tommy charged forward, his bat whistling through the air as he closed the distance. He felt the impact shudder up his arms as he connected with the first zombie's skull.

Beside him, Roxy hacked and slashed at the reaching arms and snapping jaws. Jimbo attacked with the baton, the heavy steel rod pulping flesh and shattering bone with each brutal impact.

And Laila stood her ground, her tyre iron swinging.

The zombies clawed at her shield, their fingers scrabbling for purchase on the smooth surface. But she held firm, using the shield's weight to bash them back, to create a space for the others to work.

Zombies fell before them, their bodies piling up in a barricade of twisted limbs and shattered skulls.

Tommy could feel his strength flagging, could feel the burn of exhaustion settling into his muscles. Beside him, the others breathed hard, their faces slick with sweat and spattered with gore.

"We need to move," Zero said. "Head for the front doors, now!"

Roxy and Jimbo redoubled their efforts, carving a path through the press of bodies. Laila fell in behind them, using the shield to cover their retreat.

Tommy brought up the rear, his bat swinging to keep the zombies at bay.

Zero's rifle barked somewhere up ahead, it's muzzle flashes strobing the gloom.

Tommy reached the front door, bursting out into the fading daylight as they sprinted for the van.

Behind him, the zombies stumbled and lurched.

Tommy and the others reached the van well ahead of the shambling horde, piling inside with a frantic scramble of limbs.

Zero leapt behind the wheel, the engine roaring to life as he slammed it into gear.

The van leapt forward, tyres squealing as they tore out of the parking lot.

In the back, Tommy collapsed against the side wall, his chest heaving as he gulped down air. Roxy and Jimbo slumped down beside him.

Laila huddled in the passenger seat, the riot shield still clutched to her chest.

"We made it," Tommy said. "We're okay."

"We did good back there," Zero said. "Real good."

Roxy let out a shaky laugh. "Yeah, well, let's not make a habit of it, okay? I've had my fill of close calls."

Jimbo grunted, his head lolling against the window.

Laila said nothing, her gaze distant as she stared out at the darkening landscape.

They drove like that for a while, the others drifting in and out of restless sleep.

Tommy shifted his weight and kicked something at his feet. He picked up and turned Micky's half-emptied whiskey bottle in his hand.

He hesitated for a moment, a twinge of shame pricking at his conscience. But then, with a muttered curse, he unscrewed the cap and took a long, burning swallow.

The whiskey seared his throat, but he welcomed the pain, welcomed the numbing warmth that began to spread through his veins. He took another swig, then another, the world around him beginning to blur and soften at the edges.

"Looks like we're in business." Zero gestured to a building up ahead. "On the right."

Jimbo sat up. "Is that a sporting goods store?"

"Could be worth checking out.

"Let's do it." Tommy's words slurred slightly. "Let's take a look."

Zero guided the van into the store's parking lot, killing the engine as he scanned the darkened storefront. The others piled out, weapons at the ready, but Tommy lagged behind, his movements sluggish and uncoordinated.

He stumbled as he climbed from the van, the ground seeming to tilt and sway beneath his feet. He caught himself on the door frame, fingers gripping the metal as he fought to steady himself.

Roxy appeared at his side, her brow furrowed. "Tommy, are you okay? You seem a little off."

Tommy waved her off. "I'm fine, Rox. Just a tired is all. Nothing to worry about."

She leaned in closer, her nose wrinkling. "Have you been drinking?"

"I had a few sips earlier. Just to take the edge off, you know?"

"Hey! You two coming or what?"

Tommy's head snapped towards Zero's voice. He pushed off from the van, swaying slightly as he tried to find his balance. "Yeah, yeah. Keep your pants on."

Zero shot him a hard look. But he said nothing.

They approached the darkened building, Zero taking point with Tommy stumbling along in the rear. As they neared the front doors, Zero held up a hand.

After a tense moment, he gestured for them to follow as he slipped inside, rifle at the ready.

The store's interior was pitch black, the only illumination coming from their flashlights bobbing in the darkness.

Tommy squinted, trying to bring the shadowy shelves and displays into focus.

They moved deeper into the store, picking their way through the gloom.

The store was a mess, the shelves overturned and the floor littered with scattered merchandise. It was clear that the place had been picked over, either by other survivors or by the undead.

"Over here," Roxy said.

Tommy and the others drifted towards her.

"Sleeping bags, a portable stove, even some water purification tablets. This stuff could really come in handy out there."

Tommy nodded. "Good work, Rox."

As he turned to head back towards the front of the store, the room tilted and spun around him, his vision blurring and his balance deserting him. He stumbled, his foot catching on a fallen shelf and sending him sprawling to the ground.

Roxy rushed over and helped him to his feet. "Tommy, what the hell?"

He shook his head, trying to clear the fog from his mind. "I'm fine. Just tripped."

She led him outside, away from the others. "Tommy, this has to stop. You can't keep doing this, not out here. You're putting us all in at risk."

He bristled at her words. "I don't need a lecture, Rox. I know what I'm doing. The alcohol, it helps me cope. Helps me deal with what we've been through."

She shook her head, her lips pressing into a thin line. "That's a load of crap and you know it. You're not coping, Tommy. You're running away. And sooner or later, that's going to get someone killed."

Her words hit him like a slap. But still, he couldn't bring himself to admit it, couldn't bear to face the reality of his own weakness.

"I have it under control. I know my limits. I won't let it affect the group, I promise."

Roxy stared at him for a long moment, her eyes searching his face. "I hope you're right, Tommy. Because if you're not, if you can't get a handle on this..."

She turned and walked away, leaving him alone in the gathering darkness, the weight of his failure pressing down on him.

He watched her go, his heart heavy and his mind reeling. He knew she was right, knew that he was putting them all at risk. But the thought of facing the world sober, of confronting the raw, bleeding wounds of his own trauma and loss was too much to bear.

The others emerged from the store, their arms laden with camping gear.

Tommy lingered by the dumpsters, his head bowed and his shoulders slumped. He couldn't shake the feeling of shame that clung to him.

Laila approached him. "Hey. Are you okay?"

Tommy shrugged, his gaze fixed on the ground at his feet. "I don't know. You?"

Laila mirrored his shrug, a sad smile tugging at the corners of her mouth. "I heard what Roxy said."

Tommy stiffened, his jaw clenching. "She's got it all wrong. I don't have a problem, I just—"

"Tommy," Laila cut him off, her voice firm. "We've been down this road before, remember? The drinking, the self-destruction. It's not the answer. You need to keep your head clear, now more than ever." She reached out and grasped his wrists, pushing up his sleeves to reveal the bold black Xs tattooed on the backs of his hands. "You made a promise to yourself. A pledge to stay clean, to stay focused. Don't throw that away now, not when we need you most."

Tommy stared at the tattoos, his vision blurring with tears. He remembered the day he had gotten them, the fierce pride and determination he had felt as the needle etched the symbols of his commitment into his skin.

But now, looking at them in the harsh light of his own failure, they seemed like a mockery, a cruel reminder of all the ways he had let himself and the others down.

"I've failed, Lai. I've failed myself, failed Micky, failed all of you. I'm not strong enough to do this."

Laila shook her head, her grip on his wrists tightening. "That's not true. You've been through this before, and you came out the other side. You can do it again, I know you can. But you have to want it, have to be willing to fight for it."

"I'm so sick of fight...I'm tired, Lai. So damn tired."

She looked up at him. "Think of Niamh and Sean, waiting for you back in Philly."

"Don't."

"Do you want them to see you like this? Or do you want to be the man they know you can be, the father and partner they deserve?"

Tommy swallowed hard, his throat tight. Laila was right. He had to find a way to pull himself out of this downward spiral, to claw his way back to the surface. But it was hard, so hard. "I don't know if I can do it again. I'm not strong enough."

Laila's expression softened, her hands moving to cup his face. "You're one of the strongest people I know. And you're not alone in this. We're all here for you, every step of the way."

Tommy leaned into her touch, his eyes drifting shut as he let her words wash over him. He wanted to believe her, wanted to believe that he could find his way back, back to the man he used to be.

The sound of the van's engine sputtering to life pulled him from his thoughts. He looked up to see Zero leaning from the driver's window.

"Come on, Tommy boy. We need to get moving."

Tommy sighed. "I'm coming."

Laila grabbed his sleeve. "And you didn't fail Micky."

"I did."

"No. You tried...but there was nothing we could have done for him."

Tommy closed his eyes. "Then why do I feel so bad?"

Laila shrugged. "Because we wanted to help. Do you blame me for what happened?"

"Of course not."

"Then stop blaming yourself."

"But—"

"I'm serious." She gestured around her. "We've got enough crap to deal with without blaming ourselves for Micky. Do you think he'd blame us?"

"No."

"Well, that's settled then." She nodded towards the van. "But we really should get moving. Zero's giving us the stink-eye."

4. The Bridge

The van lurched over cracked asphalt as they rolled into the outskirts of St. Louis. Tommy stared out at the ruined cityscape, his gut churning. Skyscrapers jutted like broken teeth against the smoggy sky, their windows dark and lifeless. Abandoned cars clogged the roads, picked clean by scavengers.

Tommy's fingers twitched, aching for a bottle to ease the dread coiling in his chest. But he clenched his jaw, gripping his bat tighter instead. No more running. No more letting the others down. He had to face this head on.

Roxy white-knuckled the steering wheel. In the back, Zero and Jimbo rode in tense silence. Tommy could feel their eyes boring into him, the questions simmering under the surface.

Zero heaved a sigh. "We need to talk, Tommy boy."

"I know. I'm sorry."

Zero leaned forward. "Sorry? That's it? You're supposed to be leading us, watching our backs. But you're so caught up in drowning your demons you can barely stumble straight. We can't count on you like this. Can't trust you."

The words cut deep. But hadn't he said the exact same things to himself a thousand times? He was weak. Selfish. A piss-poor excuse for a so-called leader.

Jimbo clapped a heavy hand on Tommy's shoulder. "Dude...you're hurting. We all are. I get it. But pickling your liver won't fix it. That promise you made, the straight-edge code, those Xs on your hands. Remember why you chose that. You're better than this."

Tommy sucked a breath through his teeth. His throat burned. The tattooed Xs seared his skin, accusing. It would be so easy to dive back into that blissful oblivion, to tell them all to go to hell. But he couldn't run forever. Those blackout nights ended in blood more often than not—if not his, then someone else's.

"Alright." He met Jimbo's gaze, then Zero's. "No more bottles. No more excuses. I'm here, fully present. Won't let you down again."

"Guys..." Roxy brought the van to a stop and leaned over the dash to frown at something up the road. "I've got a bad feeling about this. Maybe we should try our luck somewhere on the fringes instead."

Zero shook his head. "No. We're running on fumes and prayers already. This is our best shot at supplies. We stick to the plan, but we play it smart."

The hangover still pulsed behind Tommy's eyes, but a sudden clarity cut through the fog. He turned to the others, crossing his arms. "Roxy's right. We're not doing this."

Zero's eyebrow arched. His fingers drummed against his rifle stock. "The city's our best shot at restocking ammo and supplies. We need this."

"No. It's too much of a gamble. Every time we hit a major metro, we're walking into a kill box. Too many zombies, too many angles for an ambush. The risk ain't worth it."

"Oh, so your grand plan is to just keep driving until the gas and food run dry?"

Tommy shook his head. "We've got enough rations and water to last a few days. That buys us time to find a safer spot to scavenge. Maybe hit some suburbs or small towns."

Zero's lips curled back from his teeth. "And what about firepower, huh? We try to fight off a horde with our current arsenal, we're screwed. I've got a few dozen rounds left. That's a spit in the ocean, Tommy boy."

Tommy couldn't shake the memories of Denver. Flashes of snapping jaws and grasping hands. Of Dee. Of Spike. Of Nix.

Roxy glowered at them. "Enough. Both of you. We vote." Her gaze cut to the others. "All in favour of taking the risk and scavenging the city, raise your hand."

Zero's arm shot up. He glared around the circle, daring anyone to defy him.

But he stood alone.

Laila hugged herself. Jimbo stared at his boots, shoulders hunched. Roxy just looked exhausted.

"Then it's decided." She sighed, rubbing her temple. "We keep driving, find somewhere off the beaten path to resupply."

Tommy let out a breath.

Zero's nostrils flared as he cursed under his breath. "When things go sideways, don't say I didn't warn you."

Roxy cranked the key. The engine coughed, sputtered, then growled to life.

As the city blurred by, Tommy's thoughts whirled.

Had he done the right thing, pushing them away from the city? Or had he just condemned them all to a slower, more brutal death?

His fingers itched for a bottle, for that liquid numbness.

But he clamped down on the craving, grinding his molars.

.

The van juddered to a halt at the foot of the Mississippi River bridge. Tommy leaned forward, squinting through the dusty windshield. At first glance, the bridge looked clear.

But as they crawled closer, the illusion shattered.

Cars choked the span. A twisted knot of steel and rubber. Doors gaped open. Shattered glass glittered on crumpled hoods.

Tommy's stomach clenched.

Roxy swore under her breath. "No way through that. We'll have to double back, find another crossing."

Zero shook his head. "We have to try."

Roxy sniffed. "Try what? We'd need a tank to punch through that scrapheap."

"So we make our own path. Inch by inch if we have to."

Roxy shot him a sidelong glance. "Alright. Whatever you say."

The van doors screeched open, hinges screaming in protest.

Tommy unfolded from the passenger seat, bat in hand.

Roxy, Laila, and Jimbo fanned out beside him.

Zero rolled his neck, his gaze sweeping over the bridge and the tangled mass of vehicles choking its lanes. "Alright, listen up. We're going to have to work together on this. Take it one vehicle at a time, clear what we can and shove what we can't." He turned to face them, his eyes hard. "Slow and steady wins this race. Watch your footing, and for God's sake, keep your eyes peeled for any corpses shambling around. Everyone clear?"

A chorus of nods and murmured assent rippled through the group.

"Okay then." Zero unslung his rifle and jerked his chin towards the bridge. "Let's do this."

They spread out, each taking a lane of the clogged bridge. Tommy approached the first vehicle blocking his path—a battered sedan crumpled against the guardrail.

He lined up with the others, planting his feet and bracing his hands against the car's twisted frame.

"On my count," Zero said. "Three, two, one - push!"

Tommy heaved, throwing his shoulder into the car with a grunt of effort. Beside him, Roxy and Jimbo did the same, their faces reddening with exertion.

Metal groaned, but the sedan remained stubbornly immobile.

"Again! Put your backs into it!"

Tommy repositioned and surged forward once more, straining against the unyielding mass of steel and rubber.

His muscles burned, his breath rasping in his lungs as he pushed with every ounce of strength he possessed.

But still it refused to budge, its frame wedged tight against the guardrail and the vehicles pressing in on either side.

"Damn it." Jimbo panted, sagging back, and wiping sweat from his brow. "This thing's not moving."

"We'll just have to try something else then." Zero scanned their surroundings, his gaze settling on a nearby lamppost, bent and twisted from some long-ago impact. "There. We'll use that as a lever, try to pry it loose."

Together, they wrestled the lamppost free of its moorings, the metal scraping against the asphalt.

They jammed one end under the sedan's bumper, Tommy and Roxy throwing their weight onto the opposite end.

"Okay, on three." Zero positioned himself beside them. "One, two, three—lift!"

Tommy strained as he fought to heave the car upward. For a heartbeat, he thought he felt it shift, just the barest fraction of an inch.

But, with a metallic shriek, the lamppost snapped clean in two, sending Tommy and the others sprawling to the ground.

"Son of a bitch." Zero snarled, tossing aside the broken lamppost. "Useless piece of scrap."

A strangled scream tore through the air.

Tommy whirled to see Laila sliding down the side of the van to land in a crumpled heap, her arms wrapped tight around her drawn-up knees.

"I can't." Her words were almost lost in the hitching gasps that shook her frame. "I can't do this anymore. We're trapped, don't you see? We're all going to die here."

Roxy ran to her side, dropping to her knees and gathering Laila into her arms. "Shh, hey now. None of that. We're going to get through this, you hear me? We'll find a way, just like we always do."

Laila shook her head, pressing her tear-streaked face into Roxy's shoulder. "Look around us! We'll never clear all this, not before the dead find us. It's hopeless."

"Enough!" Zero's shout cracked through the air, sharp and sudden enough to make them all flinch. He stormed over and glared at Laila. "Shut off the waterworks and get up. We don't have time for you to wallow in self-pity."

Roxy surged to her feet, her fists clenched at her sides. "Back off, Zero. Can't you see she's hurting? She needs comfort, not your macho hardass bullcrap."

Zero's lip curled in a sneer. "What she needs is to put on her big girl pants and help us find a way off this dam bridge. But by all means, keep coddling her. I'm sure the zombies will wait patiently for you to dry her tears and braid her hair before they chow down."

"Why, you insensitive prick." Roxy took a step forward.

"Whoa, whoa, time out!" Jimbo scrambled between them, thrusting his arms out. "Simmer down, both of you. I get that tensions are high, but this alpha dog crap is so not productive right now."

Zero rolled his eyes.

Roxy continued to glare at him, her jaw clenched tight.

Tommy moved to Laila's side, crouching down to lay a hand on her shaking shoulder. "He's right, Lai. I know you're scared. We all are. But giving in to despair now won't help us. We have to keep fighting, keep trying. For Micky's sake if nothing else."

Laila met his gaze, her eyes shimmering with unshed tears. After a long moment, she gave a jerky nod, allowing Tommy to help her to her feet.

Zero watched the exchange, something unreadable flickering across his face. He opened his mouth as if to speak, then seemed to think better of it, turning away with a shake of his head.

Tommy's fingers twitched on his bat.

But before he could take another step, cold steel kissed the nape of his neck.

"Drop the weapon, son. Nice and slow."

The voice was hard and clipped.

The others stared wild-eyed at the loaded muzzles—-a shotgun, two pistols, and an AK.

Slowly, he raised his free hand and let his bat clatter to the asphalt. Beside him, the others did the same.

A man stepped forward, his rifle never wavering from Tommy's forehead. Salt-and-pepper stubble cloaked a hard face. Cold hunter's eyes raked over them. "Gotta admit, you folks are a sight for sore eyes. Been slim pickings since the refugee trucks dried up."

Jimbo licked his lips. "Look, dude. We don't want any trouble. Y'all just ease off the hardware and let us mosey along, yeah?"

"You lot aiming to cross to the other side?"

"That's the notion," Zero said.

"It just so happens my associates and I operate a little water taxi service around here. Could punt you over, lickety-split."

Tommy blinked. "You could take us across?"

"Course, such a service don't come gratis. Not in times like this. It'll cost ya."

Tommy tore his gaze from the leader's face, and sought out the others. "What do you think?"

Laila shrugged.

Jimbo shook his head. "Dude, we've got nothing."

Zero nodded. "We're running on fumes."

Roxy took a single step forward. "The shield. It's the only bit of kit we can afford to lose."

Zero grunted and gave a tight nod.

The leader rubbed his beard. "What kinda shield we talking here?"

"Riot shield," Roxy said. "We'll even throw in a police baton too if that'll sweeten the deal."

Tommy turned back to the leader. "You heard her. The riot gear or nothing. What's it gonna be?"

The leader stared them down, unblinking. "The shield it is. Pile your asses and your jalopy on the ferry and don't tarry. But I'm warning you now—try anything squirrely and it'll be your hides drying in the sun. We clear?"

"As glass." He picked up his bat and jerked his chin at the others. "Back to the van. Slow and easy."

They moved as one, never turning their backs on the armed men.

Tommy's pulse thudded in his ears as the leader's gaze bored into him.

At the van, he reached for the rear door handle, the screech of metal on metal.

He rummaged through the detritus of their lives. There, wedged into the far corner, was the riot shield. Black and scuffed, the word POLICE emblazoned in chipped white letters.

He hefted it and advanced on the leader, steps measured, eyes trained on the man's trigger finger. "Here. Take it."

The leader snatched it, ran an appraising hand over the pitted surface. "Not bad. Could stop a few bullets at least."

Zero cleared his throat. "I'll keep hold of the baton. We'll hand it over once we're on the other side."

The leader's eyes narrowed, lips curling in the ghost of a sneer. But after a moment, he nodded. "Fine. But no more delays."

Roxy climbed into the driver's seat, her movements stiff and mechanical. Zero rode shotgun, his hand never straying far from his rifle. Laila, Jimbo, and Tommy clambered into the back.

The leader strode ahead, motioning for them to follow. His men fell in around the van, a loose cordon of guns and hostile stares.

The road sloped down, twisting between gutted buildings and burned-out cars.

Roxy stared straight ahead through the windshield, her jaw clenched tight.

The river stretched out ahead, a vast expanse of grey-brown water, choppy and frothing. And there, moored to a concrete jetty, was the ferry—little more than a rusted barge, a few car-lengths square, its metal siding was pocked with dents and choked with river weed. A single sagging rope served as a safety railing. The engine jutted from the rear, belching clouds of oily smoke.

Jimbo leaned forward. "Damn, you think that thing can hold us?"

Zero shrugged. "It had better."

"Yeah," Roxy said. "Not like we've got much choice."

The leader stopped at the ramp, one foot propped on the pitted metal. He turned, gesturing with the riot shield. "All aboard, folks. Next stop, the other side."

Tommy swallowed down the sudden taste of bile.

He caught Roxy's eye in the side mirror. Saw his own dread reflected back at him.

Wheels skidded on damp metal grating as the van lurched up the ferry's ramp. A squeal and clank as the gate crashed down behind them. Trapping them.

Tommy shoved the door open. The others clambered out after him, hands clutching weapons, eyes flickering in every direction. They fanned into a loose half-circle, backs to the van.

"Stay tight," Zero said, his gaze sweeping the deck.

The ferry chugged out into the seething chop of the river.

Tommy gripped the van's doorframe, knuckles white, stomach pitching with each wallowing lurch of the deck.

Around him, the others stood in a tight knot, weapons close to hand.

Zero glowered at the leader's back. Roxy kept Laila tucked under one arm. Jimbo bounced on the balls of his feet.

The leader stood at the prow, riot shield slung over one arm, the other draped over the rudder housing. He looked back at them, a smirk playing at the corners of his lips.

Tommy ground his teeth until his jaw ached. Every instinct screamed at him to make a move, to take the leader down. But he wrestled the impulse into submission.

Minutes crept by. Then the opposite shore drew near.

The ferry nosed up to the jetty with a screech of tortured metal. The leader cranked a lever and the gate clattered down to rest. He turned to face them, making no move to disembark. "End of the line, folks. Time to pay the piper."

"We gave you the shield," Zero said. "That was the deal."

"Ah ah ah." The leader waggled a finger. "The shield was for passage. The baton's for safe conduct off my boat. I ain't one to leave a job half finished."

Zero reached into the van, withdrew the police baton, and held it out at arm's length.

The leader took it and hefted it in his hand. "Much obliged." His tone was pleasant, almost friendly. "So, where you folks headed?"

"East coast."

The leader gave a low whistle. "Bad idea."

"Why? What do you know?"

"The big cities...New York, Boston, Newark...word is the dead took over. Those that survived went west."

"And...and Philly?"

"Can't say for sure. But if it's anything like its sisters...best hope your people got out while the getting was good."

Tommy jerked his head towards the ramp. "Let's go."

Jimbo frowned as the others piled into the van and turned to the leader. "Hey, boat dude. Quick question. You ever get dead-heads coming up out the river?"

The leader tapped his chin. "Now you come to mention it, no. Seems they ain't too keen on the water."

Jimbo nodded and climbed into the van. "Good to know."

"Y'all watch your asses out there," the leader grinned at Tommy. "And hey...thanks for the gear."

Roxy cranked the engine and the van trundled down the ramp, tyres crunching on weed-choked gravel.

As the rear wheels kissed the shore, Tommy twisted in his seat. "So, what now?"

Zero shrugged. "Now we find somewhere to sleep."

"We should look for somewhere like in Denver," Roxy said. "That warehouse was the best place we've found yet."

Zero nodded. "Good thinking. Let's keep an eye out."

"We should find a castle," Jimbo said. "One with a moat. Turns out the dead-heads don't like water."

Roxy cocked an eyebrow. "A castle? Here?"

Jimbo shrugged. "We should go to England. They've got castles all over the place there."

Tommy sniffed. "Yeah. One on every street corner."

"He's got a point," Zero said. "If they won't cross water, we can use that."

"Doesn't exactly help us now though, does it?" Roxy said.

Zero nodded. "I'll take what I can get at this point."

The road unwound before them, a dusty ribbon of asphalt winding through skeletal trees and fallow fields. They passed abandoned vehicles, their husks long since stripped of anything useful. Rotting corpses, human and animal, littered the verge, buzzing with flies.

An hour ground by, then two. The adrenaline ebbed, exhaustion rushing in to fill the void. Tommy's eyelids grew heavy, head lolling against the window.

Roxy steered them off the highway, following a rusted sign pointing towards an industrial district. Rows of squat, nondescript buildings hunkered under the leaden sky, their walls streaked with soot and graffiti.

She eased the van to a crawl, leaning forward to peer through the windshield. "There. That one looks promising."

Tommy followed her gaze to a sprawling warehouse, its corrugated metal walls pockmarked with rust. A faded logo, something with gears and cogs, adorned the facade.

Zero nodded. "Good a place as any. Pull around back, scope out the loading docks. I'll take point on foot."

Roxy guided the van into the alley behind the warehouse. She brought the vehicle to a stop beside a bank of loading bays, their roll-up doors daubed with crude gang tags.

Zero slid out, rifle held at the ready. He moved off towards the warehouse, hugging the wall.

Tommy and the others waited.

The seconds ticked by with glacial slowness.

Then Zero was back, his face grim. "We've got company. Couple dozen shamblers, at least."

Tommy sighed. "Can we punch through? Maybe lead some away, thin the herd?"

Zero shook his head. "Too many. Best to keep moving, find someplace else."

Laila shook her head. "But we've been driving for hours. If we don't stop soon..."

"We stop when it's safe."

The groans started.

Jimbo cried out. "They're pouring out of the alleys!"

Tommy whirled in his seat as a mass of zombies stumbled into view. "Gun it, Rox!"

Roxy floored the gas.

The van leapt forward with a roar, tyres squealing.

More zombies lurched out from the shadows ahead.

"Hold on!" Roxy cranked the wheel hard left, nearly putting the van up on two wheels as they careened down a narrow side street. Trash cans and cardboard boxes exploded in their wake, the impacts jarring bone and rattling teeth.

"There!" Tommy jabbed a finger at the windshield. "That parking garage. Head for the upper levels, buy us some breathing room."

Roxy glared at him. "After Dee? Are you insane?"

"Roxy's right," Zero said. "Head back to the highway."

Roxy wrenched the steering wheel right. The van fishtailed as they bounced over a kerb and back onto the main road.

In the side mirror, Tommy watched the horde of zombies boil out of the alleyways behind them, a seething mass of rotting flesh and grasping hands.

"They're closing in on us!" Jimbo's voice cracked, his knuckles white as he gripped the armrests.

"Just a little further." The van's engine roared as Roxy coaxed every last bit of speed from the van.

The highway loomed, the on-ramp just ahead.

"Come on, come on," Tommy muttered, his heart slamming against his ribs.

With a lurch, they were on the ramp.

Roxy didn't let off the gas, the van rocketing up the incline, the zombies falling away behind them.

They merged into traffic, such as it was, weaving between abandoned cars.

For a long moment, no one spoke.

Tommy slumped back in his seat, his muscles unclenching by slow degrees. "Everyone alright? Anyone hurt?"

A chorus of negatives and head shakes.

"Good driving, Rox." Jimbo wiped a hand over his sweaty face. "Seriously. You just saved our asses back there."

Roxy huffed a laugh, the sound thin and strained. "Let's not make a habit of it, yeah? I'm not looking to audition for NASCAR anytime soon."

"Too bad," Zero said. "You've got the nerves for it. Quick thinking, keeping us on the move like that."

Roxy shrugged. "Next time, let's just stick to the highway, yeah?"

Laila shuddered, curling into herself, her arms wrapped around her drawn-up knees. "I hate this. I hate not being able to stop, to rest. I feel like we're always running, always looking over our shoulders."

Tommy reached back to squeeze her ankle, wishing he had something more to offer. "I know, Lai. Believe me, I'm as tired of running as you are. But we'll find someplace safe. Someplace we can catch our breath."

"Will we?" Laila raised her head. "Sometimes...sometimes I wonder if there's anywhere left. If maybe the whole world is like this now. Just...just death and running. Forever."

"Hey." Roxy's voice was sharp, her eyes flashing to Laila. "We didn't make it this far to just lie down and die now."

"Roxy's right," Zero said. "Can't think like that. Just got to take it one day at a time. One mile at a time. Speaking of..." He leaned forward, looking at a passing road sign. "Says here Indy's about a hundred miles off. I say we keep on pushing, try and make the city limits by dark."

Tommy opened his mouth to argue, to say they should find a place to rest, to regroup. But the words died unspoken. "Indianapolis it is. Wake me when we get there."

He closed his eyes, trying to will his body to relax, to snatch what rest he could in the scant hours they had before reaching the city. Despite the weariness, sleep was slow to come.

He shifted in his seat, his skin crawling with a restless energy. His fingers tapped a staccato rhythm on his thigh, his jaw clenching and unclenching as he stared out at the passing landscape without really seeing it.

What he wouldn't give for a drink right now. Something to take the edge off, to quiet the screaming in his head. His eyes flicked to the back of the van, to the jumble of bags and gear piled on the floorboards

He began picking through bags, his hand groping around food cans and dirty clothes.

His fingers closed around the neck of a bottle, the glass warm and slightly tacky against his skin.

He breathed when he dragged out the whiskey bottle.

"Hey, whoa, what do you think you're doing?" Jimbo's hand closed around his wrist, his grip firm but gentle.

Tommy blinked, startled out of his reverie. He looked down at the bottle in his hand, then back up at Jimbo's concerned face. "I just...I need a little something to help me sleep, that's all."

Jimbo shook his head. "Nah, dude. You promised."

Tommy's fingers tightened on the bottle. "It's just a sip, Jimbo. It's not a big deal."

"It is a big deal, T. You know it is." Jimbo's voice was soft, but there was an undercurrent of steel beneath the words. "We need you clear-headed and sharp."

Tommy stared at the bottle, at the way the light refracted through the cloudy liquid within. Jimbo was right. He knew he was right. But the thirst was like a physical thing, tearing at his insides.

"I can't sleep, Jimbo," he said, hating the whine in his voice. "I just...I need something to quiet my head, you know?"

Jimbo squeezed his wrist, then gently pried the bottle from his fingers. "I know, dude. Believe me, I know. But this ain't the answer. You'll sleep. You just need to give yourself a chance to rest, to let go for a little while."

Tommy watched as Jimbo tucked the bottle back into the depths of the gear, out of sight and out of reach. He felt a pang of loss, of longing. "You win." He slumped back into his seat. "I'll try."

Jimbo clapped him on the shoulder. "That's all any of us can do. Just keep trying."

Tommy let his eyes drift shut, the rumble of the road and the purr of the engine a familiar lullaby. He felt the pull of sleep.

And he didn't fight it.

5. The Storm

The rhythmic drumming of heavy rain brought Tommy from his sleep. He blinked and rubbed his eyes as he peered out at the water-streaked world.

Roxy leaned forward, squinting into the downpour. The wipers slashed back and forth, struggling to keep up with the deluge.

"Damn, it's really coming down out there," Tommy said. "Can hardly see a thing."

"Just keep your eyes peeled," Zero said, his gaze never leaving the road ahead. "Weather like this, it's the perfect cover for an ambush."

Tommy shifted in his seat, his muscles stiff. He glanced over at Laila, huddled against the window. "Hey. You okay?"

Laila startled at his words, blinking as if coming out of a daze. "Yeah, I'm just...I'm tired, Tommy. So damn tired."

Tommy's chest tightened at the weariness in her voice. He opened his mouth to respond, to offer some words of comfort or encouragement. But before he could speak, Roxy let out a sharp curse, slamming on the brakes.

The van lurched and skidded, hydroplaning before coming to a juddering halt.

"What the hell, Rox?" Zero braced himself against the dashboard.

"Look!" Roxy pointed through the windshield, her finger trembling.

Tommy leaned forward, squinting through the rain-streaked glass.

At first, he couldn't make out anything beyond the grey curtain of water. But then, just visible through the downpour, was a seething mass of bodies.

Hundreds of them, maybe more, milling and shambling in the road ahead.

"Holy crap, dude," Jimbo said. "That's gotta be the biggest herd we've seen."

Tommy swallowed hard. "We can't go through that. We'll never make it."

"We'll have to backtrack," Zero said. "Find another way around."

Roxy nodded, already throwing the van into reverse. But as she hit the gas, the engine revved and whined, the wheels spinning uselessly in the mud.

"Come on, come on."

But it was no use. The van was stuck fast, mired in the soft, waterlogged earth.

"Damn it." Zero slammed a fist against the dashboard. "We're trapped."

Tommy twisted in his seat, peering back the way they'd come.

The road behind them was gone, swallowed up by the rising waters.

The rain turned the highway into a churning river.

"We can't go back. The road's washed out."

A heavy silence fell over the van, broken only by the drumming of the rain and the distant moans of the herd.

"So what do we do?" Laila asked. "We can't just sit here and wait for them to find us."

Tommy rubbed a hand over his face, his mind racing. "We need to draw them away. Create a distraction, lure them off the road so we can get through."

Zero frowned. "And how exactly do you propose we do that, Tommy boy?"

Tommy held up a hand. "We use the storm to our advantage."

Roxy cocked an eyebrow. "How do you figure?"

"Think about it. The rain, the wind, the thunder...it's the perfect cover. We can draw them away from the road, and then use the storm to mask our escape."

"That's actually not a terrible idea," Roxy said. "Dangerous as hell, but it might work."

Laila shook her head. "I don't like it. Too many things could go wrong."

"You got a better plan?" Zero asked. "Because I'm all ears."

Laila closed her eyes and shrugged.

"Alright then," Tommy said. "Let's do this before we lose the light completely."

They gathered what they could from the van—flashlights, a few precious road flares. Anything that could cut through the rain.

Then, with a last shared look, they stepped out into the deluge.

Wind whipped at Tommy's face, cold and sharp. In seconds, he was soaked through, his clothes plastered to his skin.

He squinted through the stinging rain, barely able to see more than a few feet ahead.

They fanned out along the highway's edge, scavenging the derelict vehicles for anything that gleamed. Side mirrors, chrome fittings, CDs—they took it all, stuffing their pockets until they bulged.

As they worked, Tommy caught glimpses of Roxy and Zero binding rags and branches into makeshift human shapes.

He darted from car to car as the zombies' moans carried on the wind.

"Tommy!" Roxy appeared at his side, rain streaming down her face. "We're ready. Let's move."

He nodded, and together they crept forward, placing their assembled lures in a wide arc before the stalled van. The highway's shoulder dropped away into a steep, wooded embankment, choked with underbrush. They worked their way down the slope, stabbing branches into the sodden earth to hold the decoys upright.

The zombies shuffled closer.

Tommy hardly dared to breathe as he adjusted a final dummy.

A hand clamped down on his shoulder and he nearly cried out. He spun to see Zero, crouched low, his finger to his lips.

Zero pointed back towards the road. Towards the idling van.

Tommy followed his gaze and his stomach dropped.

Another pack of zombies weaved between the abandoned cars.

And they were headed straight for the van.

A piercing scream tore through the rain.

Laila.

Tommy charged up the embankment, slipping and clawing at the mud.

Zero and Roxy pounded at his heels.

They crested the rise to find Jimbo on the van's roof, his golf club whirling as he battered at the grasping hands clawing at him from all sides.

Laila fought next to him, delivering clubbing blows with her tyre iron..

The zombies swarmed the van, their fingernails screeching against the metal as they fought to reach their prey.

Tommy leapt forward with a hoarse shout, his bat connecting with the nearest zombie's skull. He drove his foot into a knee joint, feeling it crumple.

All around him, the air sang with the wet smack of metal on flesh as the others laid into the monsters.

Roxy hacked in a frenzy of silver. Zero fired shots, taking zombies down..

"Get in the van!" Tommy swung his bat. "Move!"

Jimbo clambered down, using his golf club to clear a path. He wrenched the passenger door open and all but flung Laila inside. "Go, go!"

Tommy and the others fell back, forming a tight half-circle around the van.

The zombies pressed in, heedless of the blows that rained down.

A gnarled hand caught Tommy's sleeve and he lashed out blindly, feeling his bat sink into something soft.

Behind him, the van's engine coughed and sputtered. Then it roared to life.

"Tommy, come on!" Roxy reached back to seize his collar.

She hauled him backwards and he stumbled.

A zombie lunged, its jaws snapping inches from his face. He shoved it away, gagging on the stench of rot.

Another stooped to grasp at his legs and he drove the bat's handle into its eye socket.

Roxy yanked him again and he fell backwards, sprawling onto the van's rain-slicked floor.

"Drive!" Zero slammed the rear doors shut, twisting to brace his shoulders against them as the zombies threw themselves against the other side.

The wheel spun in the mud and the tyres screamed as Jimbo stamped on the gas.

They rocketed forward, ploughing through the zombies that tried to block their path.

Bodies crunched under their wheels, bones snapping and skulls popping.

Gore sprayed up to coat the windows in blurred crimson streaks.

"Is...is everyone okay?" Laila asked.

"Still here," Roxy said. "Zero?"

He made a grunt of affirmation.

Tommy just closed his eyes and let his head thunk back against the wall. His whole body ached, a bone-deep throb that spoke of new bruises layered over old.

Jimbo slammed on the brakes. "That wasn't the main herd, dudes."

Tommy's eyes snapped open at Jimbo's words. "What do you mean, that wasn't the main herd?"

Jimbo pointed through the windshield, his hand shaking. "Look."

Tommy leaned forward, following Jimbo's gaze. At first, all he could see was the grey curtain of rain. But then, movement caught his eye. A shimmer, a ripple in the downpour.

And then the zombies came into view. Dozens, scores, hundreds—a seething, writhing mass of decaying flesh and grasping hands. They shambled up the highway towards them.

"Oh God," Laila said. "There's so many."

Roxy's hand found Tommy's, her fingers icy and trembling. "What do we do?"

Tommy swallowed hard, his mind racing. They couldn't stay in the van—it was a death trap, an easy target for the horde. But to abandon it, to flee into the storm...

"We run. We lead them away from the highway. It's our only chance."

Zero nodded. "Tommy's right. We stay here, we're dead."

They gathered what weapons they could, Roxy's machete. Zero's rifle was empty, the last precious bullets spent in the melee. He slung it over his shoulder anyway, a grim set to his jaw.

Then, with a last shared look of desperate resolve, they threw open the van's doors and spilled out into the rain.

The zombies were close now, close enough that Tommy could hear the wet rattle of their breath, could smell the sweet, sickly stench of decay. He hefted his bat, the wood slippery in his grip.

"This way!" He plunged into the wooded embankment, the others close on his heels.

Branches whipped at his face, snagging in his hair and clothes. Underbrush clutched at his ankles, almost dragging him down, the ground a slick morass of mud and rotting leaves.

Behind them, the zombies crashed through the woods. The storm seemed to spur them on, the howling wind and driving rain drowning out all other sound.

Tommy ran, slipping and staggering, half-blind in the deepening gloom, his lungs burning, his muscles screaming in protest.

But he couldn't stop, couldn't slow.

To falter now was to die.

Lightning speared the sky, throwing the forest into stark relief.

Thunder cracked a second later, so close it made his teeth ache.

A root caught Tommy's foot and he went sprawling, the breath whooshing from his lungs as he hit the ground hard. His bat flew from his hand, vanishing into the undergrowth.

"Tommy!" Roxy's scream cut through the storm. She skidded to a halt, whirling to face the oncoming horde.

Zero and Jimbo stopped too, forming a ragged line.

Tommy scrambled to his knees, his hands scrabbling in the muck for his lost weapon.

His fingers closed around a branch, rotten wood crumbling in his grip. He cast about desperately, panic clawing at his throat.

The zombies lurched closer, their moans rising.

Roxy slashed out with her machete, the blade hissing through the rain. It struck meat and bone, black blood spraying.

Zero wielded his empty rifle like a club, the butt cracking against skulls.

Jimbo shoved Laila behind him, then stepped forward with a wordless snarl.

And then the zombies were on them, a wave of clutching hands and snapping teeth.

Tommy rose to meet them empty-handed, his heart a jackhammer in his chest.

He lashed out with fists and feet, feeling skin split and bones shatter.

A zombie's hand snagged his shirt and he twisted, using its own momentum to fling it into a tree.

Another's jaws gaped inches from his throat and he rammed his knee into its chest, sending it staggering.

All around him, the others fought with desperate strength.

Zero swung his rifle in great, crushing sweeps, the stock smeared with gore.

Laila fought with a wild abandon, her tyre iron making pulp of rotting flesh.

Jimbo's scream pierced the tumult, high and terrified. A zombie had broken through their line, its gnarled hands locked around his throat.

He thrashed and bucked, but its grip was iron.

Tommy charged forward, a roar tearing from his throat.

He crashed into the zombie, bearing it to the ground in a tangle of limbs. They rolled, a confusion of mud and snapping teeth.

Tommy ended up on top, his hands locked around its throat. He squeezed with all his strength, feeling cartilage crunch beneath his fingers.

The zombie thrashed, its jaws gaping, its breath a fetid wave. Tommy's arms trembled with the effort of holding it down, his vision narrowing to a tunnel.

With a sickening crunch, its head lolled back, neck shattered.

Tommy released his grip, panting, his chest heaving. He looked up, blinking the rain from his eyes.

The others had formed a tight knot around him, a ring of battered bodies and dripping weapons. But the zombies pressed in from all sides, an inexorable tide of flesh.

"We can't keep this up," Zero said. "There's too many of them."

"We've got to make a break for it," Roxy said. "Get back to the van."

Tommy shook his head, struggling to his feet. "No. We have to lead them away." He spotted his bat half-submerged in the mud, and hefted it.. "We keep moving. Draw them deeper into the woods."

Jimbo let out a strained laugh. "Deeper? Dude, I can't even see my own feet."

Tommy gripped his bat tighter, rain streaming down his face.

Trees stood all around. The only light came from the fitful flashes of lightning.

But what choice did they have?

"Stay close. And if we get separated, head for high ground. Don't stop moving."

He plunged into the seething dark, the others crashing after him, their laboured breathing mingling with the rasp of the zombies and the pounding of the rain.

Mud sucked at his feet, threatening to drag him down with each step.

Branches whipped his face, drawing blood.

His world narrowed to the burn of his muscles, the fire in his lungs.

Behind him, the zombies came. An endless, relentless tide, their snarls and moans rising.

Time lost all meaning. There was only the next step, the next desperate gulp of air. The next flash of lightning, the next clap of thunder.

At some point, Tommy realised he could no longer hear the others. He was alone, running through shadows and rain. But still he didn't slow, didn't falter.

He ran through exhaustion, through pain. He ran until his vision blurred and his legs turned to rubber, until each breath was a serrated knife in his lungs.

He broke through the treeline and staggered to a halt, his hands braced on his knees as he gulped great lungfuls of air.

He was on a hilltop, the land falling away in a steep drop before him.

The storm still raged, the wind lashing the treetops below into a frenzy. But the rain had slackened, the lightning fading to distant flickers on the horizon.

He sank to his knees, his legs giving way.

Tommy closed his eyes, the rain mingling with the tears on his cheeks. "Please let them be okay.

But only the wind answered him.

Tommy stumbled to his feet, his legs trembling. He cupped his hands around his mouth and shouted into the wind. "Roxy! Zero! Jimbo! Laila! Can anyone hear me?"

His voice was swallowed by the storm, the words ripped away by the howling gale. He strained his ears, desperate for any sign of a response. But there was only the drumming of the rain, the creak of the trees, and the groans of the undead.

He tried again, louder this time. "Roxy! Zero! Jimbo! Laila! Where are you?"

Still nothing.

He couldn't have lost them.

He refused to believe it.

They had to be out there somewhere, fighting their way through the storm, searching for him just as he searched for them.

He dug into his pockets, his numb fingers scrabbling for anything that might help. They closed around the smooth surface of a wing-mirror, the edge of a flashlight.

He dragged them from his pocket and flicked on the torch.

He tilted the mirror, angling it to catch the light.

Tommy waved it back and forth, sweeping the beam through the trees.

He kept at it, his arm aching with the effort. The rain pounded against his back, soaking through his already drenched clothes. His teeth chattered, his body shaking.

Out of the corner of his eye came a flicker of light. He whirled, the beam of his flashlight wavering.

Another flash, a glint of reflected light, winking at him from the depths of the forest.

"Tommy!" The shout was faint, almost lost beneath the wind.

"Roxy!" He screamed her name, his voice raw and desperate. "Roxy, I'm here!"

He raced down the hillside, slipping and skidding on the wet grass.

"Tommy! Where are you?"

"Here! I'm here!" He crashed through the underbrush. The beam of his flashlight danced wildly, illuminating brief snatches of rain-lashed foliage, glistening bark.

He saw them. Roxy, Zero, Jimbo, and Laila huddled together in a small clearing, their weapons clutched tight, their faces turned towards him.

He burst into the clearing. "I thought I'd lost you. I thought..."

"We're here," Laila said. "We're okay."

Zero clapped him on the shoulder. "We need to move."

A moan drifted through the trees, low and guttural.

Tommy froze.

"Run." Zero yanked Tommy's sleeve. "Back to the highway. Move!"

They fled, crashing through the underbrush.

The moans grew louder, the wet snap of branches, the crunch of shambling feet.

Tommy pushed himself harder, faster, skidding onto the rain-slick asphalt of the highway, mere feet from the van.

"Get in!" Zero flung himself into the driver's seat.

Tommy and the others piled into the back.

The doors slammed shut, muffling the moans of the oncoming horde.

The engine roared to life, the van lurching forward.

Zero stepped on the gas, tyres squealing.

They ploughed through the first rank of zombies, bodies crunching beneath the wheels.

But there were more, always more.

They surged around the van, an endless tide of grasping hands and gnashing teeth.

Zero swerved, the van fishtailing, metal screeching as rotting fists pounded against the sides.

"Watch out," Roxy said. "You're going too close to the shoulder."

Zero growled through gritted teeth, wrestling with the wheel.

The van shuddered, the tyres spinning uselessly.

Zero slammed his fist on the steering wheel. "We're stuck!"

Zombies pressed in from all sides, their hands clawing at the windows. The glass spiderwebbed under the onslaught.

"Gun it!" Roxy shouted. "Get us out of here!"

Zero snarled, pumping the gas. "I'm trying."

The engine screamed, the whole van shaking with the force of it.

Tommy braced himself against the door.

The van surged back onto the road.

Zero fought for control, wrenching the wheel hard to the left.

They careened around an overturned truck, the bumper screeching against the rusted metal.

Tommy risked a glance behind them. The herd receded into the distance. But they were still coming, their moans carrying over the rain.

"Faster!" Tommy shouted. "We've got to get some distance between us and them!"

Zero rocketed down the abandoned highway. The wipers struggled to keep up with the pounding rain, the world beyond a blur of black and grey.

He wove between the abandoned cars, scraping past on sheer momentum.

Jimbo cursed as they sideswiped a hatchback, the impact jostling them in their seats.

The van hurtled down the highway, the storm raging around them. Tommy stared out the window, watching the landscape blur past, his mind numb, his body aching.

Roxy clambered into the passenger seat. "That was too close. Way too damn close."

Jimbo nodded, his face drawn. "That was intense, dude."

"We got lucky," Zero said. "If Tommy hadn't come up with that plan, if we hadn't been able to distract them..."

Laila shivered, hugging herself. "I thought we were done for. I really did."

Tommy swallowed. "We made it. That's what counts."

"This time," Roxy said. "But what about the next? Or the one after that?"

"Rox has a point," Zero said. "Who knows what else is waiting for us out there."

"Indianapolis isn't too far from here," Jimbo said. "We need to find somewhere to stop."

"We will," Tommy said. "We've come this far, haven't we?"

Zero nodded. "We need to be adaptable. That's the key. We can't afford to get caught flat-footed again."

"Easier said than done," Roxy said.

"Maybe. But it's our only choice."

Silence descended on the van. Tommy let his head fall back against the seat, his eyelids heavy.

"You did good back there, Tommy boy." Zero said. "Kept your head on straight, came up with a plan. We need that."

Tommy felt a flush of shame. "I almost didn't."

Jimbo leaned forward, his hand falling on Tommy's shoulder. "Almost, dude. You stayed strong. That's what counts."

Tommy shook his head. "It's hard, man. Harder than last time."

"I know. Believe me, I know. But you've got to keep fighting. For Niamh, for Sean, for all of us."

"Jimbo's right," Roxy said. "We need you, Tommy. We need you clear-headed and sharp."

Tommy squeezed his eyes shut, fighting against the sudden sting of tears.

"I'll help you," Jimbo said. "I'll keep an eye on you, make sure you stay on the straight and narrow. We'll get you through this, dude. All the way to Philly."

Tommy opened his eyes, meeting Jimbo's gaze. "You'd do that?"

"Of course. It's either that or having you getting drunk and rowdy." He opened his hands. "Trust me, dude. This is purely selfish. I wanna get through this—we all do—and you being crap isn't going to help anyone."

Tommy nodded. "Okay. Okay, I'll try."

"You need to do more than try," Zero said. "There's too much at stake."

Tommy looked down. "I know."

"We should find a place to stop for the night. Somewhere defensible, where we can catch our breath."

Tommy thought of Niamh and Sean, out there somewhere. Were they safe? Were they even still alive? The questions gnawed at him, a constant ache in his chest.

But he couldn't afford to dwell on them, couldn't let himself be consumed by the fear and the uncertainty. He had to stay focused, had to keep putting one foot in front of the other.

What else could he do?

6. The Barn

The van trundled down the muddy track, headlights stabbing through the sheets of rain. Tommy leaned forward, peering out into the storm-lashed night. Dark shapes loomed on either side, trees thrashing in the wind.

A flash of lightning illuminated a weathered sign: "Harris Farm." The letters were faded, the wood rotting at the edges.

The track opened up into a gravel yard, a farmhouse hunched at its centre. To the left, a large barn sagged beneath the weight of years, its paint peeling in long, curling strips.

Zero brought the van to a halt, the engine idling. He turned to face the others, his expression grim. "This place looks deserted, but we can't afford to take chances. Tommy and I will do a perimeter check, make sure it's clear. The rest of you, stay put and keep your eyes peeled."

Tommy grabbed his bat and slid out into the rain, the water cold against his skin. He hunched his shoulders against the downpour, squinting into the darkness as he fumbled with his flashlight.

Zero appeared at his side, rifle at the ready. He jerked his chin towards the barn. "That's our best bet for shelter. Sturdy walls, defensible entrance. We should check there first."

Tommy nodded, his eyes scanning the shadows. Wind howled around them, driving the rain in stinging sheets.

Every rustle, every creak set his nerves jangling. It would be all too easy for a shambling figure to slip from the darkness, to catch them unawares.

They approached the barn, Tommy's bat raised, Zero's rifle held low and ready. Tommy tried the door, the wood groaning on rusted hinges. It swung open to reveal a cavernous interior, the air thick with the scent of old hay and engine oil.

Zero flicked on his flashlight, the beam cutting through the gloom. Hulking shapes resolved into farm equipment—a tractor, a thresher, coils of chain. The floor was packed dirt, scattered with straw. "Looks clear. Big enough to park the van, too."

They completed a circuit of the interior, checking the loft and the stalls. No sign of the dead, or anything living.

Satisfied, they returned to the van. Tommy rapped on the passenger window, and Roxy cranked it down a crack. "Barn's secure. And it's dry. We can hole up there for the night."

Roxy nodded. "What about the house? There could be supplies in there, maybe even beds."

From the back, Jimbo snorted. "Yeah, or a pack of cannibal hicks just waiting to turn us into jerky."

Roxy shot him a glare. "We're in the middle of nowhere, Jimbo. Who exactly do you think is out here?"

"I don't know, Rox. That's kinda the point. Better safe than turned into people-burgers, is all I'm saying."

Tommy chewed his lip. His body ached for a real bed, for a chance to be warm and dry. But Jimbo had a point. "I don't like it. Too many unknowns. We stick to the barn, at least for tonight."

Zero nodded his agreement. "Tommy's right. We're exposed enough as it is. No sense taking extra risks."

Roxy sighed. "Fine. Let's just get inside before we all drown."

Zero hopped back into the driver's seat and eased the van into the barn.

Tommy and Jimbo wrestled the doors shut behind them, securing the rusty latch with a loop of chain.

The others piled out of the van, grabbing their packs and supplies. Tommy helped Jimbo and Roxy unload the sleeping bags and mats from the back.

"I'll take some of those up to the loft," Roxy said, gathering an armful of bedrolls. She headed for the wooden ladder leaning against the loft opening and began climbing up.

Tommy climbed the rickety ladder to the hayloft, his bat slung across his back. The rough wood creaked under his weight. At the top, he paused, breathing in the musty scent of old hay and dust.

The loft was a large, open space, the floor covered in a thick layer of straw. Bales were stacked along the walls, forming makeshift barriers. The roof sloped down on either side, the rafters hung with cobwebs.

Tommy unslung his pack, setting it down in a corner. The others followed suit, arranging their belongings in a rough circle.

Rain hammered on the roof, the barn shuddering under the onslaught.

Tommy moved to one of the windows, peering out into the night. The glass was filthy, streaked with grime, but he could just make out the dark shapes of the trees, thrashing in the gale.

He shuddered, turning away. His skin prickled, every nerve thrumming with tension.

Behind him, the others were busy hanging their wet clothes on a length of chain Zero had strung between two posts. Shirts and jeans dripped, the fabric heavy with rain.

Laila sat apart from the rest, huddled against a bale, her knees drawn up to her chest, her eyes distant, unfocused.

Tommy crossed over to her, crouching down at her side. "Hey. You okay?"

She blinked, seeming to come back to herself. "Yeah. I'm fine."

He reached out, laying a hand on her arm. "Talk to me, Lai. What's going on in that head of yours?"

She shrugged, not meeting his eyes. "Nothing. I'm just tired."

"We're all tired. But this is more than that. You've been pulling away, isolating yourself. That's not like you."

"What's the point? Of any of this? We're just delaying the inevitable."

"Don't say that. We're going to make it through this."

"How? How are we going to make it? Every day is just a fight to stay alive, and for what? So we can do it all again to-morrow?"

He swallowed hard, his throat tight. "I know it seems hopeless. Believe me, I feel it too. But we can't give up. We have to keep fighting"

She held his gaze, searching his face. At last, she sighed, her shoulders slumping. "I'm trying, Tommy. I really am. But it's hard. It's so hard."

He pulled her into a hug, feeling the way she trembled against him. "I know. But you're not alone, Lai. Remember that."

She clung to him, her face pressed into his shoulder as the barn groaned and shuddered.

"This place isn't going to hold forever," Zero said. "We need to shore it up, make it as secure as we can."

Tommy pulled back from Laila, meeting Zero's grim gaze. "What do you suggest?"

Zero jerked his chin towards the stacked bales. "We use those to block the windows, the doors. Create a barrier between us and whatever's out there."

Tommy nodded. "The loft, too. We can pull up the ladder, make it a last line of defence."

Roxy stirred from where she sat, her shoulder pressed against Jimbo's. "What about escape routes? If they breach the barn, we need a way out."

Zero considered, his eyes scanning the loft. "There's a window at the back, leads out onto the roof. We secure a rope, we can use it to rappel down if needed."

"And then what?" Jimbo asked. "Where do we go? We're miles from anywhere."

"We cross that bridge when we come to it, Jimbo," Roxy said. "Right now, we focus on getting through the night."

Jimbo sighed. "One night at a time. Guess that's all we can do, huh?"

Tommy got to his feet, squaring his shoulders. "Alright. Let's get to work. Zero, you and Jimbo start on the windows. Roxy, you, and Laila see what you can do about that ladder. I'll take the door."

They split up, each to their appointed task. Tommy crossed to the loft door, studying the heavy planks, the rusted hinges. It was sturdy enough, but he didn't like the way it shuddered in the wind, the way the gaps around the edges whistled with each gust.

He set his shoulder to a nearby hay bale, grunting with effort as he shoved it into place. The straw scratched at his skin, the dust tickling his nose, but he ignored it. He worked methodically, building a wall around the door, a barricade against the night.

It might not hold back an attack, but it would buy them some time.

As he worked, his mind wandered, spinning out scenarios, contingencies.

If the dead breached the barn, if they were overwhelmed...what then?

Where would they go?

How would they survive?

There were no easy answers. No safe havens, no refuges from the nightmare that had engulfed the world.

The others worked quickly, piling bales and debris in front of the windows until only narrow slits remained to allow glimpses of the storm raging outside.

As the final barricades went up, a sense of relief washed over the group. For tonight at least, they would have a relatively secure shelter from the elements and any threats.

Zero rummaged through their supplies, producing some cans of beans and a packed of potato chips. "Feast fit for a king."

They gathered around, opening the cans and passing them around to share the cold contents.

No one complained.

After eating, they sorted out their sleeping arrangements in the loft. The thin bedrolls and musty hay bales didn't make for the most comfortable beds, but at least it was dry.

"I'll take first watch," Tommy said. "I managed to grab a couple hours sleep in the van."

The others nodded, too exhausted to object. One by one they bedded down amid the hay, pulling jackets and blankets up tightly against the drafts.

Tommy settled back against the wall, his bat within easy reach, and prepared to keep vigil.

The sounds of the others' breathing soon joined the patter of rain as Roxy, Jimbo, Laila and Zero drifted off to sleep.

Tommy sat in the hayloft, his back against a bale. The others slept around him, their breathing slow and even, punctuated by the occasional snore from Jimbo.

His mind raced. And beneath it all, a constant, gnawing craving. An itch beneath his skin, a dryness in his throat.

He needed a drink. Just one to quiet the screaming in his head, the images that flashed through his mind every time he closed his eyes.

He pushed to his feet, pacing the length of the loft. The boards creaked under his weight, the sound loud in the stillness. He froze, glancing at the others, but none of them stirred.

He crept to the ladder, peering down into the darkness below.

The van sat where they'd left it.

He knew what was in there, tucked away in the back. A bottle of whiskey.

Just one sip.

Just enough to keep the shakes at bay, to dull the constant, aching fear.

He climbed down the ladder, his heart pounding.

He reached the van, trying the handle.

Locked.

Of course it was.

Zero was too cautious, too paranoid to leave it unsecured.

Tommy cursed under his breath, his hands shaking as he patted his pockets, searching for the keys.

Nothing.

Zero must have them.

Tommy's gaze fell on the cracked window, the glass spiderwebbed with fractures.

It would be so easy to break it, to reach inside and grab the bottle.

Just a quick smash, a moment of pain, and then relief.

He raised his fist, his breath coming hard and fast.

"Tommy?"

He spun to find Jimbo at the foot of the ladder, his face shadowed, his expression unreadable.

"What are you doing?"

Tommy swallowed. "I was just...I needed some air."

Jimbo cocked his head, his eyes flickering to the van, the raised fist. "And that involves breaking into the van because?"

Tommy flushed. "It's none of your business, Jimbo. Just go back to sleep."

Jimbo sighed, scrubbing a hand over his face. "Tommy, Tommy, Tommy. We've talked about this, dude. I'm not going to let you do this to yourself."

"Do what? I'm not doing anything."

"Then why are you creeping around in the middle of the night, trying to score a drink?"

Tommy's shoulders slumped. "I need it, man. I can't...I can't handle this. The constant fear, the not knowing. It's eating me alive."

Jimbo nodded. "I get it. But this?" He gestured to the van, the broken window. "This isn't the answer. It's never the answer."

Tommy laughed. "Then what is? What's going to make this better? Because from where I'm standing, there's no end to this. No way out."

Jimbo stepped towards Tommy, laying a hand on his shoulder. "Come on. Let's go back up. We can talk about this."

Tommy hesitated, the urge still thrumming through his veins. But he nodded, allowing Jimbo to steer him back to the ladder.

They climbed in silence, the only sound the creaking of the rungs, the distant moan of the wind.

At the top, Jimbo settled against a bale, patting the straw beside him. "Take a seat, dude."

Tommy sank down, his legs folding underneath him. He picked at a loose thread on his jeans, not meeting Jimbo's eyes. "I'm sorry. I don't...I don't know what's wrong with me."

"There's nothing wrong with you, T. You're hurting. We all are. This thing, this...apocalypse...it's messing with everyone's head. I'd be more worried if it didn't bother you."

Tommy shook his head. "It's more than that. I can't stop thinking about Micky. About the others. Dee, Spike, Nix, Kim...they're all gone, Jimbo. And for what? What was the point of it all?"

Jimbo sighed, leaning back against the bale. "I don't know, dude. I wish I did. I wish I had some grand answer, some profound truth to lay on you. But the fact is, there is no point. No reason. It's just chaos. Random, meaningless chaos."

"That's...bleak, man. Talk about taking the black pill."

Jimbo chuckled. "Yeah, well. Welcome to the apocalypse, my friend. Bleak is the new normal."

"I miss them. Micky, especially. We went through so much together. Learned to play, learned what punk was all about. He was my best friend, Jimbo. My brother." He looked down at his hands. "I can't help blaming myself. I keep going over it. I should have been there. I should have kept an eye on him. But instead..."

Jimbo nodded, his eyes distant. "I know. And I know it hurts like hell. But Micky's demons, his addiction...that wasn't on you. You tried, man. You tried so hard to help him. But in the end, it was his choice. His battle to fight."

Tommy's throat tightened, tears pricking at the corners of his eyes. "I should have done more."

"You were there. You were always there. But you can't save someone who doesn't want to be saved. Believe me, I know."

Tommy looked at him, frowning. "What do you mean?"

Jimbo sighed. "I had my own issues, back in the day. Speed, mostly. It got bad for a while. Real bad."

"I never knew that."

Jimbo shrugged, a small smile playing at the corners of his mouth. "Not exactly something I advertise, you know? But yeah. I was a mess. Thought I had it under control, thought I could handle it. But it was handling me."

"What changed?"

"Zero, believe it or not. He was there for me, in his own Zero way. Never judged, never preached. Just made sure I didn't fall too far down the rabbit hole."

Tommy nodded. "That's why he was so hard on Micky. Why he's always on my case about the drinking."

"He sees himself in you, T. Or at least, who he used to be. He doesn't want you to make the same mistakes he did."

Tommy was silent for a long moment, digesting that. Then he laughed. "I used to think I had it all figured out, you know? Thought I knew what punk was, what it meant. Raging against the machine, sticking it to the man. All that cliched crap."

Jimbo grinned. "Hey, we were all young and stupid once."

"But now? With all this?" Tommy gestured around them. "None of that matters anymore. It all seems so petty. So meaningless."

Jimbo nodded. "That's because it is, dude. All that stuff, the politics, the posturing...it was always just noise. Just a distraction from what really matters."

"And what's that?"

"This. Us. The people we love, the bonds we forge. That's what punk is, dude. Not the clothes, or the music, or the attitude. It's the spirit. The fire inside. The thing that keeps us going, even when the world's gone to hell."

Tommy felt something loosen in his chest, a knot of tension unravelling. Jimbo was right.

He'd been so focused on the trappings, on the surface level crap, that he'd lost sight of what truly mattered.

His friends. His family. The people who stood by him, no matter what. That was what he was fighting for. What he'd always been fighting for.

He leaned back against the bale, his eyes growing heavy.

The craving was still there, a dull ache in the back of his mind. But it seemed more distant now, less urgent.

He glanced at Jimbo, a small smile playing at the corners of his mouth. "Thanks, man. For...for everything. For being here."

"Anytime, dude. That's what family's for."

Tommy hesitated, a question forming on his lips. He wanted to ask about Roxy, about the new closeness between her and Jimbo. But something held him back. It wasn't his business, wasn't his place to pry.

And besides, he was tired. So damn tired. The events of the day were catching up to him, leaving only the heavy drag of exhaustion.

He yawned. "Think I'm going to hit the hay. You good to keep watch?"

"I got this, dude. You get some shut-eye. I'll wake you if anything happens."

Tommy nodded, his eyes already slipping closed.

Tommy stood at the window of the hayloft, watching as the first rays of dawn crept over the horizon. The air was still, almost serene.

For a brief moment, he could almost forget the reality of their situation and lose himself in the gentle play of light and shadow across the fields stretching out before him.

A rustle of movement behind him broke the spell. Tommy turned to see the others starting to stir, emerging from their sleeping bags and blankets.

Roxy sat up, running a hand through her tangled hair, and wincing as her fingers caught on knots.

Jimbo stretched with a series of pops from his joints.

Zero was already on his feet, rifle slung over his shoulder as he surveyed the barn.

Laila remained seated on her bedroll, her eyes fixed on some unseen point in the middle distance.

Tommy cleared his throat, drawing their attention. "So, what's our play?"

Zero shifted, his hand falling to the stock of his rifle. "Indianapolis. We need supplies."

Tommy frowned. "I don't know, man. We've seen what happens when we go into the big metros. Too many variables, too many ways for things to go sideways."

Roxy pushed herself to her feet. "We can't keep running on beans, Tommy. Sooner or later, we're going to have to take a risk."

"A calculated risk." Tommy shook his head. "Not a suicide mission."

She crossed her arms. "So what do you suggest? We just keep wandering, hoping we stumble across a fully stocked Wal-Mart in the middle of nowhere?"

"No. But I think we need to be smart. Scout the outskirts first, get a feel for what we're walking into. If it looks bad, we keep moving."

Jimbo nodded. "Dude's got a point, Rox. We go in guns blazing, we're liable to bring every zombie and creep in the city down on our heads."

Zero grunted, his fingers tapping against his thigh. "Fine. We do it your way. But we need to move fast. I'm out of ammo, and I don't fancy taking on a herd with just my winning personality."

"What about a melee weapon? Something that won't run out of ammo."

Zero shot him a look, eyebrow arched. "You might be happy wading into the thick of it with just a baseball bat, but I'm not."

Tommy shrugged. "Better than ending up zombie chow because you ran out of bullets."

Roxy stepped forward. "Nobody's ending up zombie chow. We stick to the plan, play it smart, and we'll be fine." She turned to the others, her expression softening. "But first, we need to eat. Can't save the world on an empty stomach, right?"

Jimbo grinned. "Now you're talking, Rox. But no more beans."

Zero shook his head. "Alright, alright. We break out the gourmet rations, then we head out. But let's make it quick."

As the others began to rummage through their packs, pulling out cans and packets of food, Zero turned to Tommy "Before we go, we should check the farmhouse. See if there's anything we can use."

Tommy hesitated, glancing out the window "I don't know, man. It looked pretty abandoned last night."

Zero snorted. "In that storm, a pack of cannibals could have been having a barbecue on the front porch and we wouldn't have seen them. Better safe than sorry."

Tommy sighed. "Alright. But we're careful. No unnecessary risks."

"Careful's my middle name, Tommy boy."

Tommy turned to the others. "Anyone else coming to check out that farmhouse?"

Jimbo and Roxy exchanged a look.

Laila shrugged.

"We'll get the van ready to go," Jimbo said. "In case we need to make a quick exit."

Tommy nodded. "Sound good, man." He hefted his bat and nodded at Zero. "You ready?"

"Always."

Tommy stepped out into the morning light, the air fresh and crisp after the storm.

Zero took a deep breath. "Glad that rain's stopped. Nothing worse than wet socks."

"I hear that."

They approached the farmhouse, taking care to stay quiet.

The structure loomed before them, its paint peeling, its windows dark.

They circled the perimeter, checking for any signs of danger—zombies, people, traps. But the place seemed deserted, still, and silent in the early morning light.

Tommy peered through the windows, trying to get a sense of what lay inside. But the rooms were shadowed. No signs of movement, no hint of life.

Zero found the back door unlocked and eased it open, wincing as the hinges creaked.

They stepped into a kitchen, the floor littered with pots and pans, the counters strewn with shattered plates.

Zero held up a hand, his head cocked.

Tommy froze, straining his ears.

Had he heard something?

A footstep, a breath?

But there was only silence.

They moved further into the kitchen, checking the cupboards as they went. They found a few things they could use—tins of soup, crackers, even a box of pop tarts.

Zero grinned as he stuffed a package of Twinkies into his pack. "Woody Harrelson would be proud."

Tommy frowned. "What?"

"Zombieland."

Tommy nodded. "Oh, yeah."

A strange buzz filled the air, low and insistent. Tommy looked around, trying to pinpoint the source. "You hear that?"

Zero nodded, his brow furrowed. "Probably the electricity acting up. Best not to touch any outlets."

Tommy moved into the living room and froze.

Three bodies lay on the floor, their flesh torn, their bones showing through the ragged wounds.

A man, a woman, a child.

A family, no doubt, left to the mercies of the undead.

Flies buzzed around the corpses, their wings glinting in the half-light. Tommy retched, his stomach heaving.

Zero stepped over the bodies, his face set in a grim mask. He picked up a shotgun that lay near the man's outstretched hand, checking the chamber. "Empty."

He looked around, his eyes scanning the room. "No ammo. But we should take it anyway. Never know when it might come in handy."

Tommy nodded, not trusting himself to speak.

The sight of the child, its tiny body broken and torn, shook him to his core. He tried not to think about Sean.

Zero moved towards the stairs, his rifle at the ready.

Tommy hesitated, his skin crawling. "I don't know, man. Maybe we should just go."

Zero shook his head. "We need to be thorough. There could be more supplies upstairs."

Tommy sighed, but followed, his bat clenched tight in his fist.

They checked the bedrooms, the bathroom, even the attic. They found a few more useful items—shampoo, soap, a bottle of bleach. Zero grabbed a couple of pillows, stuffing them into his pack.

As they made their way back downstairs, Tommy paused, looking back at the bodies on the living room floor. "What should we do about them?"

Zero shrugged. "Nothing we can do. We don't have time for a proper burial, and a fire would just attract attention."

Tommy nodded, his throat tight. It felt wrong to just leave them there. But Zero was right. They had to think of the living, not the dead.

He stepped out into the sunlight, blinking in the sudden brightness.

The others were waiting by the van, their faces tense.

"Any luck?" Roxy asked.

"We found some supplies, but no trouble."

"Good. Let's load up and get out of here."

They piled into the van, Roxy taking the wheel.

As the engine rumbled to life, Tommy looked back at the farmhouse, silent against the brightening sky. He thought of the family inside, their lives cut short, their bodies left to rot.

It was a harsh reminder of the world they lived in now. A world where the dead walked, and the living fought for survival.

7. Fuel Pump Relay

The van cruised down the deserted highway, the engine rumbling as they approached the outskirts of Indianapolis.

Tommy leaned back in the passenger seat, his brow furrowed. "We still looking at going into Indy for a supply run?"

Roxy shook her head, her eyes fixed on the road ahead. "No way. Columbus is only three hours away if the roads are clear. We should just keep moving."

"She's right," Zero said. "We need to keep pushing forward."

Tommy frowned at him. "You were the one pushing for this."

"Yeah? Well, maybe Roxy has a point. We can last a few more hours on what we have, Tommy boy."

Tommy sighed. Roxy and Zero had a point, but they couldn't keep running on empty forever.

Jimbo leaned forward, his head popping up between the front seats, a grin splitting his face. "Dudes, I've got an idea. Why don't we swing by the Indy Speedway? Take a few laps, blow off some steam. It'd be a blast."

Zero fixed Jimbo with a stare. "Are you serious? We're in the middle of a zombie apocalypse and you want to play racecar driver?"

Jimbo held up his hands, his grin widening. "Hey, I'm just trying to keep things interesting. We could all use a little fun, right? Maybe we could Mad Max this thing."

Tommy shook his head, a small smile tugging at the corners of his mouth. He glanced over his shoulder at Laila, who sat hunched against the window, her arms wrapped around herself, her gaze distant. She'd hardly said a word since they'd left the farm.

"What do you think, Lai? Indy or Columbus?"

She blinked, seeming to come back to herself. "I don't care. Just...I don't care."

Tommy's chest tightened at the flatness in her voice. But he didn't know how to help her, how to ease the burden she carried.

He turned his attention back to the road stretching out ahead of them. "Okay, let's put it to a vote. All in favour of pushing on to Columbus?"

Roxy raised one hand from the wheel. Zero's hand shot up too. After a moment's hesitation, Laila lifted her hand.

Tommy glanced over at Jimbo, who shrugged. "Majority rules, dude."

Tommy nodded. "Alright then. Columbus it is. Let's just hope the roads are clear."

Roxy pressed down on the gas, the van surging forward, her jaw set in concentration as she navigated the empty highway.

"You okay?"

She flicked her gaze to him before turning back to the road. "I don't know. I just...I just want to get home."

He reached over, giving her shoulder a quick squeeze. "We'll be fine."

She nodded, but the tightness around her mouth didn't ease. "I hope you're right."

Tommy swallowed hard, his own longing for home, for Niamh and Sean, rising up to choke him. "We'll make it back, no matter what it takes."

She held his gaze for a long moment, searching his face for something. Then she sighed, focusing back on the road.

The van sputtered and rolled to a stop, the engine dying with a final, wheezing cough.

Roxy frowned, twisting the key in the ignition.

The engine cranked, the sound harsh and grating, but it refused to turn over. "Damn it!" She slammed her palm against the steering wheel. "Not now. Not here."

Jimbo leaned forward from the backseat. "What's going on? Why'd we stop?"

"Van's dead." She tried the key again, but got only a sickly clicking in response. "Won't start."

Zero unfolded himself from the backseat, reaching for the door handle. "Pop the hood. Let me take a look."

Roxy complied and Zero made his way around to the front of the van and lifted the hood. He disappeared from view, obscured by the raised metal.

Jimbo scratched at his beard, his eyes flickering from the open hood to the empty road stretching out ahead of them. "This is bad, dudes. Like, really bad. We're sitting ducks out here."

Roxy shot him a glare. "You think? Tell us something we don't know."

Tommy sighed, pinching the bridge of his nose. His head throbbed, a dull ache pulsing behind his eyes. He needed a drink.

But he pushed the thought away, forcing himself to focus on the problem at hand. "Okay, let's not panic. Zero knows his way around an engine. If anyone can get us moving again, it's him."

Laila shifted in her seat, her arms wrapped around herself. "And if he can't? What then?"

Tommy met her gaze, seeing the fear and exhaustion etched into her face. "Then we'll figure something out. We always do."

Roxy snorted, shaking her head. "Sure, because that's worked out so well for us so far. Face it, Tommy. We're screwed."

Before Tommy could respond, Zero reappeared at the driver's side window, his face grim. "It's the fuel pump relay. Damn thing's fried."

Tommy blinked, the words washing over him without really sinking in. "The what now?"

Zero sighed. "The fuel pump relay. It's what sends power to the fuel pump. Without it, the engine won't get any gas."

"Okay, so how do we fix it?"

"We don't. Not without a replacement."

Tommy threw up his hands. "Great. That's just great. And where exactly are we supposed to find one of those?"

Zero shrugged, his eyes hard. "We could try to scavenge one from another car. But that's assuming we can find one that's compatible."

Roxy leaned back in her seat, her arms crossed over her chest.

Tommy rubbed at his temples, the ache behind his eyes intensifying. He glanced over at Laila, hoping for some support, some guidance. But she remained silent, her gaze distant and unfocused.

"Okay, look. We need to make a decision. We can't just sit here waiting for something to happen. Let's head into the city, find one of these fuel cap thingies."

Zero rolled his eyes. "Fuel pump relay."

"Whatever, man. Let's get moving."

Tommy crept along the abandoned street, his bat held at the ready, his senses straining for any sign of danger. Behind him, the others fanned out in a loose formation, their weapons clutched tight.

The suburb was deathly still, the only sound the occasional creak of a settling house or the distant moan of the wind. Cars sat abandoned in driveways, their doors hanging open, their interiors picked clean by desperate survivors.

Tommy's eyes darted from vehicle to vehicle, searching for anything that might serve as a replacement for their dead fuel pump relay. But so far, they'd come up empty. "This is a waste of time. We can't just keep poking around in every wreck we come across, hoping we'll find the right part."

Roxy shot him a glare, her machete glinting in the fading light. "So, what's the alternative? In case you hadn't noticed, our ride is currently DOA. Unless you've got a spare van hidden up your ass, this is our only option."

Tommy opened his mouth to retort, but Zero silenced him with a sharp look. "Enough. Both of you. Sniping at each other isn't going to help."

They moved deeper into the suburb, the houses looming dark and silent on either side.

A pack of zombies burst from a side street, their rasping moans filling the air as they charged towards the group.

Tommy had a split second to register the sight of rotting flesh before they were on them.

He swung his bat in a vicious arc, the wood connecting with the nearest zombie's skull.

Roxy's machete whistled through the air, cleaving a zombie's head from its shoulders.

Jimbo's golf club caved in another's face, sending teeth and chunks of bone flying.

Laila's tyre iron rose and fell, each blow accompanied by a grunt of effort.

Zero had his rifle up, but he didn't fire. Instead, he used the butt of the weapon like a club, smashing it into the zombies' faces and driving them back.

Tommy lost himself in the rhythm of the fight, his world narrowing to the swing of his bat and the stench of death.

He moved on instinct, his muscles burning, his breath coming in ragged gasps.

A zombie lunged at him, its fingers clawing at his face.

He ducked under its grasp and brought his bat up in a vicious uppercut, the impact snapping its head back with a sickening crack.

Another came at him from the side, its teeth bared in a feral snarl.

He spun to meet it, but before he could strike, a machete blade burst through its skull, spraying him with gore.

Roxy grinned at him, her face splattered with blood. "Watch your six, T. These bastards are sneaky."

He flashed her a grateful smile. "Thanks for the save."

She shrugged, already turning to meet the next attack.

The zombies kept coming, a seemingly endless tide of grasping hands and gnashing teeth.

Tommy could feel his strength flagging, his arms growing heavy with each swing of his bat.

"Hey, uglies! Bet you can't catch me!"

Tommy turned to see Jimbo standing atop the roof of a nearby car, his club held high.

The zombies turned towards him, drawn by the sound of his voice.

Jimbo grinned, beckoning them forward. "That's right, come and get me, you rotting sacks of meat!"

The zombies surged towards him, their hands scrabbling at the vehicle's sides.

Jimbo danced back across the roof. "Olé! Toro, toro!"

Taking advantage of the distraction, Tommy and the others fell upon the remaining zombies with renewed ferocity.

Laila was a whirlwind of violence, her tyre iron rising and falling in a relentless rhythm as Roxy and Zero fought back-to-back.

Tommy let the rage take him. Every swing of his bat was a scream of defiance, a refusal to lay down and die.

They fought until the last zombie fell, until the only sound was the rasp of their own laboured breathing.

Tommy stood amidst the carnage, his chest heaving, his bat slick with gore.

Jimbo hopped down from the car, his club resting jauntily on his shoulder. "Well, that was fun. Who's up for round two?"

Roxy shot him a look, her machete still held at the ready. "Speak for yourself. I feel like I just ran a damn marathon."

Laila leaned heavily against the nearest car, her face drawn. "I don't know how much more of this I can take."

Tommy's heart ached for her. For all of them. They were all running on fumes, their nerves stretched to the breaking point.

But what choice did they have? To give up now would be to surrender to the inevitable.

He forced himself to straighten, to meet their eyes with a steady gaze. "I know you're all tired. I am too. But we can't stop now. Not when we're on the final stretch."

Zero snorted, his rifle slung over his shoulder. "But we're no closer to finding a replacement for the van."

Tommy's jaw clenched, his fingers tightening on the grip of his bat. "So we keep looking. We didn't come this far just to give up at the first sign of trouble."

Roxy stepped forward, her eyes hard. "Tommy's right. We've been through worse than this. We just need to keep our heads on straight and watch each other's backs."

The street was quiet once more, the only sound the soft rustling of the wind through the abandoned houses.

They moved from vehicle to vehicle, popping hoods and rummaging through engine compartments.

"Come on, come on." Tommy's fingers scrabbled at rusted bolts and frayed wires. "It's got to be here somewhere."

Roxy wrenched open another hood. She dug through the exposed engine, tossing aside useless bits of plastic and metal.

"Anything?" Tommy called out.

She shook her head, slamming the hood back down with a curse. "Nothing. Just like the last five."

Jimbo leaned against a nearby lamppost, his chest heaving as he gulped down air. "We're running out of time, dudes. Those dead-heads could be back any minute."

"You think I don't know that?" Tommy snapped, immediately regretting his tone. He took a deep breath, trying to calm his racing heart. "Just...just keep looking. We'll find it."

Zero stood nearby, his eyes narrowing as he surveyed the street. "We should leave."

Tommy rounded on him, his teeth bared. "And go where, huh? You want to just walk to the next town, hope we get lucky? The van is our only chance."

Zero met his gaze, his eyes hard. "The van's dead, Tommy boy. And we will be too if we don't get the hell out of here."

Tommy opened his mouth to argue, but Laila cut him off. "Over here! I think I found something!"

They rushed over to join her, crowding around the rusted sedan she was leaning over. She held up a small plastic rectangle, her face splitting into a triumphant grin. "Fuel pump relay. Looks like ours."

Zero took it from her hand, turning it over in his fingers, holding it next to the old one. "Nice work."

She flinched when he clapped her on the shoulder. "Let's get back to the van and get the hell out of here."

Tommy and the others set off back the way they had come, retracing their footsteps through the silent suburb.

He took the lead, his bat held at the ready..

Behind him, the others followed, their footsteps echoing off the asphalt. They moved quickly, urgently, driven by the knowledge that every second counted.

They were halfway back to the van when the first zombie appeared, shambling out from behind a burnt-out car, its skin mottled and grey, its eyes milky and lifeless.

Tommy dispatched it with a single swing of his bat, the wood crunching through its skull with ease. But more groans came..

"Form up! Tight circle, watch each other's backs!"

They came together in a loose formation, their weapons held at the ready.

Roxy and Jimbo took the flanks, while Zero and Laila covered the rear.

The zombies came at them from all sides, their rasping moans filling the air.

Tommy struck hard, his bat swinging back and forth.

Beside him, the others fought with a savage grace. Roxy's machete flashed in the sun, severing limbs and heads with each blow. Jimbo's golf club whistled through the air, caving in skulls and shattering bones.

But for every one they put down, two more seemed to take its place. They were being overwhelmed, the sheer numbers of the undead pressing in on them from all sides.

Tommy's arms burned with fatigue. He could feel the others flagging too, their movements growing sluggish and uncoordinated.

And then, just when he thought they might be overrun, he caught sight of the van, sitting just a few hundred yards away..

"Move! Push through, get to the van!"

They surged forward as one, their weapons flashing in the sun.

Zombies fell before them, their bodies crumpling.

But more kept coming. Tommy could feel his strength flagging, his vision narrowing to a tunnel.

When they reached the van, Zero scrambled for the driver's side door, fumbling with the handle.

The door swung open and he practically dove inside and opened the hood.

Tommy and the others formed a tight circle around the van as Zero slipped back out, their weapons held at the ready.

The zombies pressed in from all sides, their hands clawing at the windows, their faces contorted with mindless hunger.

"Hurry, Zero!" Tommy shouted over the din of moans and the clash of metal on bone. He swung his bat in a wide arc, smashing through the skull of a particularly persistent zombie.

Roxy was a whirl of flashing silver at his side, her machete slicing through rotten flesh like it was nothing. Jimbo wielded his golf club like a medieval mace, the heavy head pulping brains with every swing.

Laila had her back pressed against the van.

Tommy risked a glance over his shoulder. "Zero! Talk to me, man!"

"Almost there. Just need to connect the damn wires."

A zombie lunged for Tommy's face and he barely got his bat up in time. It caught the creature under the chin, snapping its head back with a crunch. He kicked out, his boot connecting with its chest and sending it staggering back into the pressing horde.

"We can't hold them much longer!" Roxy's voice was ragged with exertion, her machete a blur of motion.

"Just a few more seconds!" Zero's shout was almost lost beneath the snarling.

Tommy gritted his teeth, his arms screaming with every swing of the bat. He could feel his strength ebbing, his reactions slowing.

A zombie slipped past Jimbo's guard, its teeth snapping inches from his throat.

Laila screamed, lashing out with her tyre iron and caving in the side of its head.

Jimbo stumbled back, his features pale.

"Got it!" Zero leapt inside, slamming the door behind him. The engine roared to life. "Everyone in, now!"

They raced towards the van doors, Tommy and Roxy clearing the way.

Jimbo dove into the passenger seat,

Laila scrambling into the back.

Tommy and Roxy piled in after her, slamming the doors shut on grasping fingers and snapping teeth.

Zero floored the gas and the van shot forward, tyres squealing.

They ploughed through the mass of zombies, bodies crunching beneath the wheels.

Gore splattered the windshield, obscuring Zero's view, but he didn't slow down.

Tommy twisted in his seat, watching through the window as the horde receded behind them.

Stragglers still stumbled after the van, their arms outstretched, but they were losing ground with every second.

He slumped back in his seat, his chest heaving as he gulped down air. His arms felt like lead, his hands aching from gripping the bat. He looked around at the others, taking in their shell-shocked expressions, the way they trembled with exhaustion and spent adrenaline. "Everyone okay?"

Roxy nodded, her machete still clenched to her chest.

Jimbo managed a shaky thumbs-up.

Laila stared straight ahead, her face blank.

Zero guided the van along the highway. "That was too damn close, We can't keep cutting it this fine."

Tommy scrubbed a hand over his face, smearing blood and sweat. "I know. But we made it. That's what counts."

Roxy let out a shuddering breath. "This time. What about the next? Or the one after that? Our luck's going to run out eventually."

Tommy took in a breath. "We'll make it, Rox."

She held his gaze for a long moment, then nodded, some of the tension draining from her frame. "Okay. Okay. So what's our next move?"

Tommy looked out the window, at the ruined landscape rolling by. "We keep going until we hit Columbus. Catch our breath at your place. And then we push on to Philly."

Roxy nodded. "Sounds good."

Tommy turned to Zero. "Hey, man. Thanks for getting the van running again. I don't know what we would have done without you."

Zero shrugged, his eyes still fixed on the road ahead. "It was nothing. Just basic mechanics."

Tommy shook his head, a rueful chuckle escaping his lips. "Basic for you, maybe. I wouldn't have known where to start. I mean, that fuel cap thing? I wouldn't have even known what to look for."

Zero glanced over at him, one eyebrow raised. "Fuel pump relay. Seriously, though. How the hell did you guys survive touring without knowing anything about engines?"

Tommy felt his cheeks heat up. "We, erm...we just called a tow truck if something went wrong. Pulled into the nearest repair shop and let them handle it."

Zero snorted, shaking his head. "Unbelievable. You're telling me you just cruised around the country in a van, no clue how to fix it if something went wrong? That's just asking for trouble."

Tommy opened his mouth to defend himself, but Roxy cut him off. "It doesn't matter. What matters is that we made it. We're all in one piece, and home is in sight. That's what counts."

Zero grunted, but didn't argue. He turned his attention back to the road, his jaw set.

8. The Gas Station

The sun hung low on the horizon as the van navigated the cluttered highway leading into Columbus.

Zero wrestled the steering wheel, his eyes darting between the abandoned vehicles littering the road.

Roxy leaned forward from the backseat, her brow furrowed. "We're not going to make it back to my place before dark at this rate."

Zero grunted, swerving to avoid a stalled pickup truck. "We need to find a place to set up camp for the night. I don't want to be driving in the dark, not with the headlights drawing every dead-head and scavenger for miles."

Roxy frowned. "I don't know. We're so close. If we push through, we could be sleeping in real beds tonight."

Tommy shook his head. "Zero's got a point, Rox. It's not worth the risk. We're all exhausted. We need to rest, regroup."

Jimbo leaned forward, his elbows resting on his knees. "I'm with T on this one. I don't fancy getting stranded in the middle of the night with a busted axle or worse."

Laila remained silent, her gaze distant as she stared out the window.

Roxy sighed, running a hand through her hair. "Alright, let's put it to a vote. All in favour of finding a place to camp for the night?"

Tommy and Zero's hands shot up, followed by Jimbo's. After a moment, Laila raised her hand.

Roxy scowled, her arms crossed tightly over her chest. "Fine. But I still think we should keep moving."

Jimbo reached over, placing a hand on her knee. "I know you want to get home, Rox. We all do. But we've got to play it smart, you know? Better to lose a few hours now than risk losing everything."

Roxy held his gaze for a long moment before sighing, the fight draining out of her. "Yeah, I know. I just...I hate this. Feeling like we're so close, but still so far away."

Tommy nodded, his chest tight. "We'll get there. But Jimbo's right. We've got to be smart about it."

Zero slowed the van as they approached an abandoned gas station, its windows dark, its pumps standing silent. "This could work. Decent visibility, solid walls. We could fortify the inside, set up watch rotations."

Tommy peered through the windshield, his eyes scanning the darkened interior of the station. "Looks quiet. But we should do a sweep, just to be sure."

Zero brought the van to a stop, killing the engine. "Agreed. Tommy, you're with me. Roxy, Jimbo, watch the perimeter. Laila, stay with the van, keep the engine running in case we need to make a quick getaway."

They piled out of the van, weapons at the ready.

Tommy fell into step beside Zero as they approached the gas station, his bat held loosely at his side.

The door was unlocked, swinging open with a soft creak as Zero shouldered it aside. They moved through the interior, flashlight beams cutting through the gloom.

The shelves were mostly bare, no doubt picked clean by scavengers. A few scattered wrappers and empty cans littered the floor, crunching beneath their feet as they swept the aisles.

The back room was empty save for a few scattered papers and a metal desk. Zero checked the corners, his rifle held at the ready, but there was no sign of life, living or undead.

"We're clear."

"What do you think?"

"It's secure enough." Zero lowered his rifle. "Let's get the others."

They emerged back into the main room, giving the all-clear signal to the others waiting outside.

Roxy and Jimbo helped Laila inside, while Tommy and Zero set about barricading the doors and windows with whatever furniture they could find.

Once the station was as secure as they could make it, they set about making camp.

Jimbo rummaged through their supplies, coming up with a few cans of beans and some crackers.

Roxy laid out the bedrolls in a tight circle, while Laila sorted through their medical supplies, taking inventory of what they had left.

They ate in silence, huddled around a small camping lantern.

The beans were cold and the crackers were like sawdust in Tommy's mouth, but he forced himself to eat, knowing he needed the energy.

As the last of the light faded outside, Tommy stood, stretching his arms above his head. "I'll take first watch. The rest of you should try to get some sleep. We've got a long day ahead of us tomorrow."

The others murmured their agreement, settling down onto their bedrolls.

Tommy grabbed his bat and made his way over to the window, peering out into the darkness.

Behind him, he could hear the soft rustling of fabric as the others shifted and settled.

Jimbo and Roxy were whispering to each other, their voices too low for Tommy to make out the words. But he could see the way they gravitated towards each other, the casual intimacy of their touches confirming his suspicions about their relationship.

He felt a pang of something like jealousy, or maybe just longing.

It had been so long since he'd had that kind of connection with someone, that easy comfort and affection.

He thought of Niamh, of the way she would curl into his side as they lay in bed together, her head resting on his chest. The way she would smile at him in the mornings, her hair tousled from sleep.

God, he missed her. Missed Sean. He missed them with an ache that went soul-deep, a constant throb in his gut.

He forced himself to look away from Roxy and Jimbo, to focus on the task at hand. He couldn't afford to get lost in memories, in might-have-beens.

The night wore on, the silence broken only by the soft sounds of sleep and the occasional distant moan of a deadhead.

Tommy paced the length of the gas station, his bat tapping a restless rhythm against his leg.

Every shadow seemed to hold a threat, every creak of settling wood a potential warning of danger. His nerves stretched to breaking.

The shelves loomed over him in the darkness.

On a whim, he ducked behind the counter, his fingers skimming over the detritus. Old papers, empty cans, a handful of tarnished coins. And tucked into the far corner, a glint of glass caught his eye.

He reached for it, his hand closing around the neck of a bottle.

He pulled it out, squinting at the label in the dim light. Vodka, the cheap stuff that burned going down and left a sour taste in your mouth.

Tommy's heart kicked into a higher gear, his mouth suddenly dry.

It had been so long since he'd had a drink, since he'd felt that familiar warmth spreading through his veins, the blessed numbness that came with it.

He should put it back.

But God, he was so tired. Tired of fighting, tired of being strong, tired of the constant, gnawing fear.

Just one drink, he told himself. Just one, to take the edge off, to quiet the screaming in his head.

He could control it, keep it from spiralling out of hand.

Everyone else was asleep.

No one else needed to know.

Before he could talk himself out of it, he unscrewed the cap, the sharp scent of alcohol wafting up to fill his nostrils.

He raised the bottle to his lips, hesitating for a fraction of a second.

Then he tipped it back, the vodka searing his throat as it went down.

He welcomed the burn, the way it chased away the chill that seemed to have settled into his bones.

One drink became two, then three.

The world started to soften at the edges, the constant hum of anxiety in his chest easing, replaced by a warm, floating sensation.

He wandered the aisles of the store, his steps unsteady, his bat dragging along the floor.

He hummed tunelessly under his breath, snippets of Clash songs, half-remembered.

He was so lost in his own head, in the comforting haze of the alcohol, that he didn't hear the footsteps behind him until it was too late.

"Tommy?" Jimbo's voice was rough with sleep. "What are you doing?"

Tommy whirled, the room spinning around him. He blinked, trying to focus on Jimbo's face, but it kept slipping away from him. "Jimbo, hey." His words came out slurred. "I was just...I needed a little something..."

Jimbo's eyes fell to the bottle dangling from Tommy's hand, his brow furrowing. "Oh, dude. Where did you even find that?"

Tommy shrugged. "Under the counter. Hidden treasure, right?"

Jimbo shook his head, stepping forward and plucking the bottle from Tommy's fingers. "This isn't treasure, dude. This is poison, and you damn well know it."

Tommy's face fell. "Don't...don't tell me what I know. You don't get to judge me, Jimbo. You haven't been through what I've been through."

"No, I haven't. But I know pain, Tommy. I know what it's like to want to drown it out. But trust me, that road doesn't lead anywhere good."

Tommy slumped back against the shelves. "I'm just so tired. Tired of being scared all the time, tired of not knowing what's coming next."

Jimbo set the bottle aside, moving to stand beside Tommy. He rested a hand on his shoulder, the warmth of his touch seeping through the fabric of Tommy's shirt. "I get it, T. But this? This isn't the answer. You're stronger than this. You're better than this."

Tommy shook his head, tears pricking at the corners of his eyes. "Am I? Because from where I'm standing, I'm a pretty piss-poor excuse for a leader. For a father. I mean, what kind of man abandons his family in the middle of the goddamn apocalypse?"

"You didn't abandon them."

"I did. I left them to play a stupid, stupid tour. I should have been with them. I should have been there, and I wasn't? What kind of man does that make me, huh? Abandoning his family for some stupid dream?"

"The kind that's trying his best to get back to them. The kind that's willing to do whatever it takes to keep them safe. That's who you are, Tommy. That's the man I know."

Tommy sniffed, wiping at his eyes with the back of his hand. "I just...I don't know if I can do this anymore. I don't know if I'm strong enough."

Jimbo squeezed his shoulder. "You are. You're one of the strongest people I know. And you're not alone in this. You've got us. We're all in this together, dude."

Tommy let out a shaky breath, some of the tightness in his chest easing. "I'm sorry. I shouldn't have...I shouldn't have let myself slip like that. It won't happen again."

Jimbo gave him a small smile. "It's okay, dude. We all have our moments. The important thing is that you don't let them define you, that you keep pushing forward." He glanced around the store. "Why don't you try to get some rest? I can take over watch for a bit, let you sleep off the booze."

Tommy hesitated, the thought of closing his eyes, of letting his guard down, sending a flicker of unease through him. But his limbs felt heavy, his head fuzzy. "Yeah, okay." He pushed himself off the shelves, swaying slightly as the room tilted around him. "Thanks, Jimbo. For...for everything."

Jimbo clapped him on the back, steering him towards the bedrolls. "Anytime, dude." He helped Tommy settle down onto his bedroll, pressing a bottle of water and a handful of crackers into his hands. "Here, try to get some of this down you. It'll help with the hangover."

Tommy took a sip of the water, the coolness soothing his raw throat. He nibbled at a cracker, his stomach churning.

Jimbo stood, grabbed his golf club, and headed for the window. "Get some rest, T. Things will look better in the morning, you'll see."

Tommy let his eyes drift shut, the exhaustion of the day, the alcohol in his system, dragging him down into a dreamless sleep.

The first pale fingers of dawn crept through the cracks in the barricaded windows, casting a watery light over the interior of the gas station.

Tommy groaned, his head pounding in time with his pulse as he struggled to sit up.

His mouth tasted like a rat had crawled inside and died, his tongue thick and furry against his teeth.

He squinted against the light, the events of the previous night coming back to him in hazy flashes.

The vodka. Jimbo's intervention. The crushing weight of his own guilt and fear.

He pushed himself to his feet, swaying slightly.

The others were already up and moving, packing up their meagre supplies and checking their weapons.

Laila glanced over at him, her brow furrowing. "You okay, Tommy? You look like hell."

He winced, rubbing at his temples. "Yeah, I'm fine. Just a bit of a headache, that's all."

She frowned, stepping closer. Her nostrils flared, her eyes widening. "Is that...is that alcohol I smell?"

"Lai, it's not what you think..."

"Not what I think?" Her voice rose, sharp and accusing. "What, you expect me to believe you just happened to find a bottle of mouthwash lying around?"

Zero looked up from where he was checking the scope on his rifle, his eyes narrowing. "What's going on?"

Laila gestured to Tommy. "Our fearless leader here decided to down a few last night while the rest of us were sleeping, while he was supposed to be on watch. Real responsible, Tommy. Real smart."

Tommy flinched, his cheeks burning. "I'm sorry. I made a mistake, okay? It won't happen again."

Zero's jaw clenched, his knuckles whitening on the stock of his rifle. "Damn right it won't. We can't afford to have you compromised, Tommy boy. Not now, not ever."

Jimbo stepped forward, his hands raised. "Hey, let's all just take a breath, okay? Tommy screwed up, he knows that. But we've got bigger things to worry about right now."

Roxy nodded, her gaze darting to the windows. "Jimbo's right. We need to focus on getting to Columbus, on getting off this damn road. I just want to get home."

Laila opened her mouth to argue, but before she could get a word out, a low moan drifted through the air.

They froze, their heads whipping towards the sound.

"Damn it." Zero raised his rifle, his eyes scanning the parking lot outside. "We've got company."

Tommy grabbed his bat and joined Zero at the window, peering out into the grey dawn light.

The gas station was surrounded, a shambling horde of zombies closing in from all sides.

"How the hell did they sneak up on us like that?" Roxy said, her machete gripped tight.

"Doesn't matter now." Tommy's mind raced, calculating distances, angles of approach. "We need to get to the van, and fast."

Zero nodded. "Tommy's right. We punch through, make a run for it. Laila, Jimbo, you're with me. We'll clear a path. Rox." He tossed her the keys. "You get the van started and be ready to gun it as soon as we're in."

Everyone moved to the door, their weapons at the ready.

"On three," Zero said, his hand on the door handle. "One, two, three!"

He wrenched the door open and they surged out into the morning light, a battle cry tearing from their throats.

The zombies turned as one.

Tommy charged forward, his bat whooshing through the air as he brought it down on the nearest zombie's head. The skull caved in, gore splattering his face and chest.

He spun, already seeking his next target, his muscles burning with the strain.

The zombies pressed in from all sides, all grasping hands and snapping teeth.

Beside him, Zero wielded his rifle like a club, the stock smashing through rotten flesh.

Laila was a whirlwind of flashing metal, her tyre iron caving in skulls with sickening crunches.

Jimbo's golf club rose and fell, each blow accompanied by a grunt of effort. He shattered kneecaps and spines, sending the zombies sprawling to the blood-slicked asphalt.

Zombies came from all sides, shambling out from behind cars and lurching up from behind the gas station.

A zombie lunged at Tommy, its teeth bared in a snarl.

He tried to dodge, but his foot slipped in a puddle of gore and he went down hard, his bat flying from his hand.

The zombie was on him, its fingers clawing at his face, its jaws snapping inches from his throat.

Tommy screamed, thrashing wildly as he tried to throw the creature off.

But it was strong, far stronger than its wasted frame would suggest.

It bore down on him, its putrid breath hot on his face, its eyes alight with a terrible hunger.

His vision began to tunnel, his lungs burning as he struggled for air.

This was it. This was how he was going to die, torn apart by a monster wearing a human face.

The weight lifted from his chest.

He blinked, gasping for breath as he tried to make sense of what had happened.

Jimbo stood over him, his golf club dripping with gore, his face splattered with blood.

The zombie lay twitching at his feet, its head caved in.

"Come on, dude!" Jimbo reached down to haul him to his feet. "No time for naps, we've got to move!"

Tommy staggered upright, his ankle screaming in protest. He must have twisted it in the fall, but there was no time to worry about that now.

He scooped up his bat, forcing himself to put weight on his injured foot. He gritted his teeth and pushed through the pain. "We need to get to the van! Cut a path, now!"

He swung his bat in a wide arc, the wood crunching through the skull of a zombie. Thick, dark blood sprayed across his fac.

The others fought shoulder to shoulder, each protecting the other's back as they inched towards the van.

But the horde was relentless, the press of bodies threatening to overwhelm them at any moment.

Tommy's arms burned with fatigue, his breath coming in ragged gasps. His ankle throbbed with each step, the pain mounting until it was almost blinding.

But he couldn't stop. Couldn't falter.

The van was so close, just a few more yards.

If they could just break through...

A zombie lunged at him from the side, its fingers snagging in his shirt.

He spun, bringing his bat around in a vicious backhand.

The blow caught the creature in the temple, snapping its head to the side with a crack.

But the momentum of the swing threw him off balance, his injured ankle giving way beneath him. He crashed to the ground, his vision swimming as the pain threatened to drag him under.

Dimly, he was aware of the others closing ranks around him, their weapons flashing in the sun as they fought to keep the zombies at bay.

Laila shouted his name, her voice high and desperate.

He tried to push himself up, but his arms wouldn't cooperate.

The world was spinning, the edges of his vision darkening.

And then Jimbo was there, his face looming over him. "Tommy, come on. You've got to get up. We're almost there, just a little further!" He reached down, his hand closing around Tommy's wrist.

With a grunt, he dragged Tommy to his feet, slinging an arm over his shoulders.

Together, they staggered forward, Jimbo half-carrying, half-dragging Tommy towards the van.

Roxy reached it first, wrenching the driver's side door open and scrambling inside.

The engine roared to life, the sound galvanizing the zombies to new heights of frenzy.

"Come on!" She leaned out the window. "Hurry the hell up!"

Tommy put on a burst of speed, his lungs burning.. He could hear the others behind him, their laboured breathing, the wet smack of their weapons against rotting flesh.

They reached the van, piling in through the side door.

Roxy stomped on the gas, tyres squealing as they fought for purchase on the blood-slick lot.

Zombies swarmed the van, their hands clawing at the windows, their moans rising.

The van lurched forward, ploughing through the horde.

Broken bodies crunched beneath the wheels, gore splattering the windshield.

Tommy twisted in his seat, watching as the gas station receded behind them, the zombies still coming, still reaching for them with their decaying hands.

He looked around at the others, taking in their shell-shocked expressions, the way they trembled with exhaustion and spent adrenaline.

Roxy's knuckles were white on the steering wheel, her jaw clenched tight as she navigated the carnage.

In the back, Laila sat hunched over her tyre iron, her face hidden behind a curtain of sweat-soaked hair.

Zero leaned against the door, his rifle cradled in his arms, his eyes distant.

Jimbo grinned as he clapped Tommy on the shoulder. "That was a close one, eh?" His voice shook with barely suppressed laughter. "Thought we were goners for sure."

Tommy shook his head. "Yeah, well...let's not make a habit of it, okay? I don't think my heart can take much more of this."

Jimbo's grin widened. "Aww, where's the fun in that? Nothing like a little brush with death to make you feel alive, right?"

Tommy groaned, letting his head fall back against the seat. His ankle throbbed in time with his heartbeat, the pain a dull, insistent ache.

But it was a good pain, in a way. A reminder that he was still here, still breathing.

Still fighting.

The road stretched out before them, the sun climbing higher in the sky with every passing mile.

Columbus was close now, so close he could almost taste it.

And beyond that, Philly. Niamh. Sean.

He would make it back to them. He would be the man they needed him to be, the partner and father they deserved.

9. The Squat

The van rolled through the outskirts of Columbus. Abandoned vehicles sat rusting on the kerbs, their windows shattered, their doors hanging open.

Storefronts gaped dark and empty, their shelves stripped bare by looters and survivors.

Tommy sat in the back of the van, his injured ankle propped up on the seat beside him. Every bump and jostle sent fresh waves of pain shooting up his leg, but he gritted his teeth and tried to ignore it.

Roxy drove, her eyes scanning the road ahead.

Zero rode shotgun, his rifle in his lap, his jaw clenched tight.

In the back, Jimbo and Laila sat in tense silence, their weapons close at hand.

"Roadblock ahead," Zero said. "Looks like someone tried to barricade the street."

Roxy slowed the van, edging forward.

The roadblock stood before them, a haphazard pile of cars and furniture and scavenged junk. It stretched from one side of the street to the other, leaving only a narrow gap in the centre.

Tommy leaned forward to peer out the windshield. "Can we get through?"

Zero shook his head. "Not without moving some of that crap out of the way." He turned to the others, his eyes hard. "Tommy, Jimbo, Laila—you're with me. Roxy, stay with the van. Keep the engine running and be ready to move as soon as we're through."

They piled out of the van, weapons at the ready. Tommy winced as he put weight on his injured ankle, but he forced himself to move, to follow Zero as he picked his way through the debris.

They worked quickly, shoving aside chairs and tables, rolling tyres and hunks of twisted metal out of the way. The sound of their efforts seemed to echo in the stillness, each scrape and clatter making Tommy start.

His hands trembled for a drink.

The low, guttural moan of the undead filtered through the streets.

Jimbo pointed his golf club towards the noise. "Looks like we've got company."

Zero's head snapped up, his eyes scanning the shadows. "Keep working. Laila, watch our backs. Jimbo, Tommy—double time it."

Jimbo gave a mock salute. "Sir. Yes, Sir!"

They redoubled their efforts, sweat pouring down their faces as they heaved and hauled.

The moans grew louder, closer, shuffling feet nearing with every passing second.

"Almost there." Tommy grunted, shoving aside a final piece of debris. "Just a little more..."

Zombies shambled out from a side street in a wave of rotting flesh and snapping teeth.

Tommy swung his bat, the wood connecting with the nearest zombie's throat, its head snapping back.

Beside him, Jimbo and Laila fought with a desperate ferocity.

Zero stood at the barricade, his rifle butt smashing down on skulls. "Fall back! Back to the van, now!"

Tommy retreated, fighting every step of the way, each step sending a jolt of pain through his ankle.

The zombies pressed in from all sides, their hands clawing at clothes and hair, their jaws snapping inches from exposed skin.

But then they were through, diving into the back of the van as Roxy gunned the engine.

The tyres screamed as they fought for purchase, the van lurching forward with a bone-jarring jolt.

The van smashed through the remaining barricade, broken bodies crunching beneath the wheels. But she didn't slow down, didn't hesitate.

Roxy tore through the streets of Columbus, leaving the zombies and the barricade behind.

Beside her, Zero pored over a map, his brow furrowed. "Take a left up ahead," he said, tracing a finger along the crinkled paper. "There's a side street that should get us around."

Roxy shook her head, her eyes never leaving the road. "No way. That street's a dead end. We'll get trapped for sure."

Zero looked up, his jaw clenched. "The map says—"

"I don't care what the map says," Roxy snapped, her voice tight. "This is my city, Zero. I grew up here. I know these streets. You don't."

Tommy leaned forward from the backseat. "Maybe we should listen to Zero, Rox. He's gotten us this far."

Roxy shot him a glare. "And I'm telling you, that street is a deathtrap. We need to go around, take the main road."

Zero shook his head. "The main road's probably crawling with dead-heads. We'll be overrun in minutes."

"So we'll deal with them. We've handled worse before."

Tommy watched the exchange with growing unease.

Laila let out a sharp gasp. "Look out!"

Roxy slammed on the brakes, the van skidding to a halt mere inches from an overturned delivery truck. The street ahead was completely blocked, the asphalt choked with abandoned vehicles and debris.

"Damn it." Roxy threw the van into reverse. "Hold on." She executed a sharp U-turn.

Tommy braced himself against the door, his heart pounding in his chest.

They raced back the way they had come, but their path was blocked by a shambling horde of zombies.

Roxy swerved to avoid them, the van careening wildly as she fought to maintain control.

"I told you we should have taken the side street," Zero said.

Roxy ignored him, her focus on the road ahead.

She wove between abandoned cars, the van's bumper scraping against twisted metal and shattered glass.

A lone zombie lurched out from behind a burnt-out pickup truck.

Roxy tried to swerve, but the van clipped the creature, sending it flying into the windshield with a sickening crunch.

Roxy screamed.

She stamped on the brakes, the van fishtailing wildly as it skidded to a halt.

For a moment, no one moved, no one breathed.

Tommy stared at the zombie's face, its milky eyes boring into his own through the cracked glass.

And then Zero was moving, his rifle already in his hands. "Out. Everyone out, now."

They scrambled from the van, Tommy gritting his teeth against the pain in his ankle.

He scanned the street, his bat held at the ready, but the horde was already closing in, their rasping moans filling the air.

"We need to move," Zero said. "Lead the dead-heads away. Stick close, watch each other's backs."

He took point, his rifle smashing down on the zombie's neck, before tossing the creature from the van.

Tommy fell in behind him, Jimbo and Laila bringing up the rear.

Roxy stood frozen, staring at the crumpled body of the zombie.

Jimbo grabbed her arm, giving her a rough shake.

"Rox, come on, dude. We have to go."

She blinked, seeming to come back to herself. With a shaky nod, she fell into step beside him, her machete gripped tight in trembling hands.

Zero led the way, swinging his rifle like a club, its heavy butt smashing into the heads and necks of the advancing zombies.

Tommy's bat connected with the side of a zombie's head, the impact sending a jolt of pain up his arms.

He grunted, swinging again and again, each strike a battle against both the undead and the searing pain in his ankle.

Jimbo's golf club slicing through the air with precision. He aimed for the knees and heads, toppling zombies with each calculated blow.

Laila's tyre iron swung in wide arcs, the solid metal crunching through bone and sinew. She moved with a fierce determination, her eyes scanning constantly for any zombies that slipped past Zero and Jimbo.

Roxy stayed close to Jimbo, her machete slicing through the air, its blade arcing down, severing a zombie's arm before slashing across its throat.

Zero kept them moving. "Keep pushing forward! We need to lead them away from the van."

They wound through the streets, the horde shambling after them, the air thick with the stench of decay.

Tommy's breath came in ragged gasps, but he forced himself to keep up, to stay in the fight.

He rounded a corner, the narrow alleyway forcing the zombies into a bottleneck.

"Here!" Zero shouted. "Hold them here!"

The group formed a line as the zombies pressed forward, their bodies piling up in the confined space.

The mass of zombies thinned, their numbers reduced by the onslaught.

Zero stepped back. "We've done enough. Get back to the van."

The group broke away, retreating down the alley and back towards the main street.

The van came into view, still running, its engine a reassuring hum in the chaos.

Roxy threw open the door, scrambling inside. "Move it!"

Zero was next, followed by Jimbo and Laila. Tommy brought up the rear, his injured ankle screaming in protest with each step.

With a final burst of speed, he reached the van, diving inside just as Roxy slammed her foot on the gas.

The horde receded behind them, the last of the zombies left far behind as they sped away.

Tommy slumped back in his seat, his breath coming in heavy gasps.

Roxy's hands trembled on the wheel, but she kept her eyes on the road, her jaw set.

Zero sat beside her, his rifle across his lap, a rare smile tugging at his lips. "Good work, everyone."

Jimbo let out a whoop, his golf club resting across his knees. "That was close, dude."

Laila gave a tired nod, her eyes meeting Tommy's.

He nodded, leaning back in his seat. He closed his eyes, trying to block out the throbbing pain in his ankle, the gnawing hunger in his belly.

They drove on in silence, the ruined streets of Columbus passing by in a blur of shattered glass and crumbling brick.

And with every mile, every turn, Tommy felt the weight of their situation pressing down on him.

He kept his mouth shut and his eyes open, scanning the streets for any sign of danger. They passed burnt-out storefronts and looted homes, the evidence of violence and desperation written in every shattered window and blood-stained wall.

Fresh barricades blocked off side streets and alleyways. Bullet casings glinted on the sidewalk.

The city seemed to stretch on forever, the streets twisting and turning in an endless maze of destruction.

With every block, every turn, Tommy felt his hope dwindling, his faith in their ability to make it out alive growing thin.

A grim smile spread across Roxy's features. "Not too far now."

She guided the van through the obstacles.

In the back, Tommy, Jimbo, and Laila sat in tense silence, their weapons close at hand.

As they approached an intersection, Roxy slowed the van.

A barricade loomed ahead, a wall of cars and debris, manned by a group of survivors.

They were armed, their weapons trained on the approaching vehicle.

"Damn it," Roxy said. "I'm going to turn us around."

Before she could act, more survivors emerged from the side streets, surrounding the van.

They were trapped, outnumbered, and outgunned.

Roxy brought the van to a stop, her breath hitching in her throat.

For a long moment, no one moved, no one spoke.

One of the survivors, a tall man with a shaved head and a patchwork of scars across his face, stepped forward. He raised a hand, a pistol dangling loosely from his fingers. "That's far enough," he called out. "This is our territory now. Turn around and go back the way you came."

Tommy leaned out the window, his hands raised. "We don't want any trouble. We're just trying to get through, to get to our friend's place. We've got some supplies we could trade, if you're willing."

The man's eyes narrowed. "We've got plenty of our own. What we need is for you to get the hell off our turf."

"Please," Roxy said. "I just want to get home. Surely you can understand that."

For a moment, something flickered in the man's eyes, a hint of empathy, of understanding. But then it was gone, his face hardening. "I said, turn around. We won't ask again."

Suddenly, Zero was moving, his rifle snapping up to his shoulder. He sighted down the barrel, his finger hovering over the trigger.

"Zero, don't!" Tommy called.

The man's eyes widened, his own gun coming up to point at Zero's head. "Put it down. Put it down now, or I swear to God I'll blow your damn head off."

Zero didn't move, didn't blink.

The others in the van shifted, their hands tightening on their weapons.

Jimbo leaned from the window. "Come on, dude. This isn't the way. We can still talk this out."

But Zero wasn't listening. His finger tightened on the trigger, the muscles in his jaw clenching.

And then, in a flash of movement, the man was diving to the side, his gun barking as he rolled.

The bullet whizzed past Zero's ear, shattering the windshield in a spray of glass.

Zero fired back, his own shot going wide.

The survivors scattered, taking cover behind cars and dumpsters.

"Go!" Zero leapt inside. "Go now!"

Roxy slammed on the gas.

Bullets pinged off the metal, the sound deafening in the enclosed space.

Tommy and the others flattened themselves against the floor.

Zero continued to fire out the window.

They careened through the streets, the van weaving and dodging as Roxy tried to evade their pursuers taking potshots at the fleeing vehicle.

Zero cursed, his eyes scanning the streets. "There!" He pointed to a narrow alleyway. "Try to lose them in the side streets!"

Roxy wrenched the wheel, the van skidding as it turned. They bounced over the kerb, trash cans and debris flying as they ploughed through the narrow gap.

The alleyway was tight, barely wide enough for the van.

Roxy gritted her teeth, her knuckles white on the wheel as she manoeuvred through the narrow passage.

Gunfire echoed behind them.

"Keep your heads down!" Zero shouted, his rifle still in hand. He squeezed off a few more shots, but the click of an empty chamber rang out. "Damn it!"

"We need to keep moving," Tommy said. "Roxy, can you get us out of here?"

"I'm trying!"

The alley opened up into a deserted street. Roxy didn't slow down, veering left and then right.

The van rattled and groaned, but it held together, carrying them further away from the danger.

"Is everyone alright?" Tommy turned to Jimbo and Laila.

"We're fine," Laila said, her voice barely a whisper. "Just keep going."

Roxy's eyes flicked to the side mirror. "I think we lost them. But we can't stop now. We need to get to my place. It's not far."

Zero nodded. "Alright, but keep your eyes open. They might not give up so easily."

They drove in silence for a few more blocks.

Tommy tried to ignore the throbbing pain in his ankle, focusing instead on their surroundings.

Roxy gestured along the street. "My place. Just up ahead."

The building came into view, a derelict apartment complex.

Roxy's hands shook as she guided the van towards the entrance, her eyes welling up with tears. "This is it. Home."

Still a block away, she pulled the van to a stop, wiping her eyes.

"Rox, let me take over," Zero said.

She nodded and slid over to the passenger seat. Zero took the wheel, navigating the van the last few yards to the front of the building.

Tommy looked around as they came to a stop. The building was a mess, the windows boarded up, graffiti covering the walls.

Jimbo whistled. "Looks like the place has been wrecked."

Roxy took a deep breath. "This is it. It's our squat."

Tommy climbed out of the van, baseball bat still in hand, and surveyed the area. The street was empty, but the sense of unease lingered. They were safe for the moment.

Zero turned to Roxy. "It's better than nothing."

Roxy nodded, a small smile breaking through her tears. "Yeah. It's home."

Tommy limped towards the entrance, his bat resting on his shoulder. "Let's get inside. We can figure out what to do next from here."

Tommy and the others followed Roxy through the apartment complex. Her boots crunched on shards of glass and splintered wood, each step echoing through the empty halls, its walls covered in faded graffiti.

Roxy led them past what had once been a communal area, now littered with broken furniture and scattered belongings.

She gestured to a door on their right. "That was Dee's room. We used to hang out there, make plans for taking on the underground."

Tommy peered inside the room, the mattress upturned and the walls adorned with old band posters.

The building was silent.

They moved on, Roxy pointing to a metal door leading to the basement. "We played our first gig down there. It's where we formed the Minks."

She called out a few names, her voice echoing down the corridors, but there was no response.

The place was clearly abandoned, the signs of recent struggle evident in the overturned furniture and the occasional bloodstain on the walls.

They climbed the stairs to the third floor, the wooden steps groaning and creaking beneath their weight.

Every sound seemed amplified in the silence.

As they reached the third floor, the hallway stretched out before them in semi-darkness.

The signs of violence were more pronounced here—doors ajar, frames splintered, personal belongings scattered as if abandoned in haste.

Roxy's pace slowed, her hand trailing along the wall as she moved forward.

She came to a stop outside her apartment, the door hanging off its hinges, the frame broken.

Roxy hesitated, her hand trembling as she reached for the door.

Zero and Jimbo flanked her. "We've got your back, Rox," Zero said.

Roxy nodded, taking a deep breath. "Thanks. This was home...it still is, I guess."

She pushed the door open, stepping inside with a soft, wounded sound.

The apartment lay in ruin, its furniture overturned and smashed, the cushions torn and scattered. The walls were pockmarked with bullet holes, the floor sticky with dried blood.

Roxy moved through the space like a ghost, her fingers trailing over the remnants of her past life. She paused at a shattered picture frame, the photo inside torn and faded. It was a snapshot of her and the Minks. "They're gone." The flung the frame across the room. "They're all gone."

Tommy stepped forward, but then stopped himself when Jimbo placed an arm around her.

"Rox, I'm so sorry. I can't even imagine..."

She shook her head, her eyes brimming with tears. "I knew it was a long shot. But I just...I needed to see it for myself, you know? I needed to know for sure."

"What you going to do now?"

She looked up at him, her eyes shimmering. "I don't know. I hadn't really thought about it, you know? I was so focused on getting here, on finding something...anything." She shook her head, a bitter laugh escaping her lips. "But there's nothing here for me now. My band, my friends...they're all gone. And this place..." She gestured at the ruined apartment. "It's not home anymore. It's just a shell."

Zero moved to her other side, his face soft. "You're not alone. You've got us."

She leaned into him, her head coming to rest on his shoulder. She kissed the top of her head and stroked her hair.

Tommy watched, a flicker of confusion washing through him. He had thought that Roxy and Jimbo were...but now this?

He shook his head, trying to clear the cobwebs from his mind. It didn't matter. All that mattered was that Roxy had someone to lean on, someone to help her through this.

They stayed like that for a long moment, the silence broken only by the soft sounds of Roxy's tears.

And then, slowly, she pulled away, wiping at her eyes with the back of her hand. She took a deep, shuddering breath, and marched across the room. She yanked open a closet and pulled out a guitar case.

She flipped the lid and ran a finger across a gleaming acoustic guitar.

"Nice," Tommy said. "Looks old."

Roxy nodded and closed the lid. "Learned to play on this thing." She gave a half smile. "Classically trained."

"Wait. You can play classical?"

"Grade Eight. But then I discovered power chords and never looked back."

Tommy chuckled. "Damn. I skipped that first step."

Roxy's fingers tightening on the guitar case. "I want to keep going with you guys. I want to see this through, to find some kind of purpose in all this madness." She looked up at Tommy, her eyes searching his face. "Is that okay with you? I don't want to be a burden, or—"

"Of course it's okay," he said cutting her off. "You're one of us now, Rox. We're family."

Laila nodded. "He's right. We're in this together, for better or for worse."

Zero clapped his hands together. "Alright then. Let's grab whatever supplies we can and get the hell out of here. We've got a long road ahead of us."

They made their way back down the stairs, picking their way through the debris.

As they emerged into the street, Tommy felt a sudden, overwhelming sense of loss wash over him.

Was this what awaited him in Philly?

Is this what he would find when he finally made it back to Niamh and Sean?

A ruined home, a shattered life, nothing but ghosts and memories.

He shook his head, trying to push the thought away.

He couldn't think like that, couldn't let himself give in to despair.

He had to believe that they were still out there, that they were waiting for him.

But as he looked around at the others, at the haunted expressions on their faces, he couldn't help but wonder if he was just fooling himself. If he was chasing a dream that had long since turned to ashes.

"So what now?" Jimbo asked. "Where do we go from here?"

Zero sighed, running a hand over his hair. "We're less than four hours from Pittsburgh. But after this, I'm not holding out hope there's much left to go back to."

"Might be the same for Philly," Laila said.

"No," Tommy snapped.

Laila shook her head. "We've driven more than halfway across the country—this thing is everywhere. I don't think anywhere's safe."

"We'll deal with that if we have to. I'm focused on getting back to Philly. That's it."

"I know you don't want to hear this, but you have to face the possibility that Niamh and Sean might be..."

"Don't. They're alive. They have to be."

She sighed, her shoulders slumping. "I hope you're right. I really do. But we have to be realistic. We have to accept that the world we knew is gone, that the people we loved might be gone too."

"I can't accept that. I won't. They're out there, Lai. They're waiting for me. And I'm going to find them, no matter what it takes."

She held his gaze for a long moment, her eyes searching his face. And then, slowly, she nodded. "Okay, Tommy. Okay. We'll keep going. But you have to promise me something."

He frowned, his brow furrowing. "What?"

"You have to promise me that you'll be careful. That you won't let this search consume you, that you won't lose yourself in it. Because if you do, if you let it take over...then you'll be no good to anyone, least of all Niamh and Sean."

He swallowed hard, his throat tight. "I'll try."

"Promise."

"I promise. I'll be careful."

"That goes for the drink too."

Tommy's nostrils flared, but he kept himself in check. "I know. I'm getting through it."

She squeezed his hand. "Good."

They stood there for a moment, the weight of their shared grief and uncertainty pressing down on them.

Zero cleared his throat. "We should get moving. We've got a long way to go, and we don't want to be caught out in the open after dark."

They made their way back downstairs, grabbing anything of use along the way.

Back outside, Roxy tucked the guitar case into the back of the van, along with a few other small mementos—a battered old leather jacket, a handful of faded photographs. They made their way back to the van.

Tommy watched as Zero helped Roxy into the passenger seat, his hand lingering on the small of her back just a moment too long.

Tommy fell into step beside Laila as they made their way back to the van. "Is Roxy...are she and Zero...?"

Laila shrugged, her eyes fixed on the ground. "I don't know. I thought maybe she and Jimbo had a thing going, but..." She shook her head. "Honestly, it's not really any of our business."

Tommy frowned. "It might be, if it causes problems within the group. We can't afford any distractions."

Laila sighed. "I know. But what can we do? We can't control how people feel, Tommy. All we can do is try to keep it from tearing us apart."

He nodded. She was right, of course. They had enough to worry about without adding interpersonal drama to the mix.

But as he climbed into the back of the van, as he watched Roxy and Zero exchange a loaded glance, he couldn't shake the feeling that this was only the beginning.

The van rumbled to life, the engine coughing and sputtering as Zero guided them back out onto the ruined streets.

Tommy leaned his head against the window, watching the shattered city roll by in a blur of broken glass and crumbling concrete.

He closed his eyes, letting the rumble of the engine and the soft murmur of conversation wash over him.

He thought of Niamh and Sean, of the promise he had made to find them.

He clung to it still, clung to the hope that somewhere out there, they were still alive and waiting for him.

10. Conspiracies

Tommy jerked awake, the remnants of a nightmare still clinging to the edges of his mind. He blinked, rubbing the sleep from his eyes, and looked out the window.

They were on a highway cluttered with abandoned cars and the occasional rotting corpse. Zero was behind the wheel, his eyes fixed on the obstacles ahead.

"Where are we?"

Laila shrugged. "Still headed to Pittsburgh. It's been slow-going."

Tommy shifted in his seat, his muscles stiff, his ankle aching. His head throbbed, a dull pain pulsing behind his eyes.

He needed a drink.

Laila placed a hand on his arm. "You okay?"

He managed a nod, not trusting himself to speak.

Zero swerved to avoid an overturned semi, the motion jostling them in their seats. "You know, I've been thinking," he said. "This whole thing, this zombie outbreak? It's not natural. It's not some freak accident or random mutation."

Tommy sighed. "Don't start, Zero. Not now."

"It's all connected, Tommy boy. That's what you need to realise. That's what you're not seeing. It's all about the bigger picture. It's all about connecting the dots."

"Dude, we've been through this," Jimbo said. "It was the lizard people, remember? It leaked from their base in Antarctica."

Laila snorted out a laugh.

"The globalists, the New World Order, the Great Reset. They've been planning this for years, decades even."

Roxy leaned forward, her brow furrowed. "What are you talking about?"

"Think about it," Zero said. "A pandemic that just happens to wipe out most of the population, leaving only scattered pockets of survivors? A virus that turns people into mindless, violent drones? It's the perfect setup for a totalitarian takeover."

Tommy shook his head, a bitter laugh escaping his lips. "You're crazy. You really think some shadowy cabal engineered a zombie apocalypse just to, what, implement a one-world government?"

Zero shot him a glare, his lip curling. "Open your eyes, Tommy boy. It's all right there, hidden in plain sight. The Georgia Guidestones, Agenda 2030, the World Economic Forum. They've been telling us their plans for years, but we were too blind to see it."

Laila shifted in her seat, her gaze darting between them. "Guys, maybe we should just focus on the road, yeah? This isn't helping."

"No," Tommy said. "Let him speak. I want to hear this. I want to hear how he thinks Bill Gates or George Soros or whoever the hell is behind all of this."

Zero slammed on the brakes, sending them lurching forward in their seats. He twisted around to face Tommy, his eyes blazing. "You think this is a joke? You think I'm just some paranoid nutjob, is that it?"

Tommy met his gaze. "I think you're giving them too much credit. I think you're seeing patterns where there are none, because it's easier than facing the truth."

"And what truth is that, huh?"

"That the world is random and chaotic and cruel. That sometimes, bad things just happen, and there's no grand conspiracy behind it. That we're all just trying to survive in a universe that doesn't give a damn about us."

Zero laughed, a harsh, humourless sound. "That's where you're wrong, Tommy boy. There's always a bigger picture, always someone pulling the strings. And if you can't see that, then maybe you're the one who's blind."

Jimbo cleared his throat, his hands held up. "Whoa, okay dudes, let's all just take a breath, yeah?"

Roxy shook her head, her gaze fixed on Zero. "Who knows? Maybe he's onto something. If what you're saying's true, where do we fit into all this?"

Zero carried on driving. "We don't fit into it, that's the point. We're the outliers, the ones who slipped through the cracks. We're the ones who are going to expose the truth and bring the whole damn system crashing down."

Tommy snorted, crossing his arms over his chest. "Right. Because a band of punks is going to take on the New World Order and win."

"You got a better idea, Tommy boy? You want to just keep running, keep hiding, keep pretending like everything's going to go back to normal someday? Newsflash, asshole—this is the new normal. This is the world we live in now, and we'd better start getting used to it."

"Enough," Laila snapped. "Both of you, just...enough. We can't do this, not now. We have to stick together, have to focus on surviving. Because if we don't..." She trailed off.

Tommy felt a pang of guilt. She was right. They couldn't afford to be at each other's throats, not when every day was a fight for survival.

But he couldn't just let it go, couldn't just sit back, and let Zero fill their heads with his paranoid fantasies. "You're wrong, Zero. You're wrong about all of it. And I'm not going to just sit here and let you spout your conspiracy theories like they're gospel truth."

Zero's face hardened. "You want to walk, Tommy boy? You want to strike out on your own, see how far you get without me watching your back?"

Tommy's eyes widened. He looked around at the others, at Roxy and Jimbo and Laila, trying to gauge their reactions. But they just stared back at him. "This is my van. I'm the one who got us this far, and I'm the one who's going to get us the rest of the way."

Zero laughed. "Your van? And who's the one who got it running again when it broke down, huh? Who's the one who's been keeping us on the road? Face it, Tommy boy—without me, you'd be dead in a ditch somewhere, another rotting corpse for the zombies to chew on."

Tommy's hands clenched into fists, his nails biting into his palms. He wanted to argue, wanted to tell Zero exactly where he could shove his arrogance. But the truth was, he had a point.

Without Zero's mechanical skills, without his grim determination and ruthless pragmatism, they might not have made it this far.

"And as for your leadership," Zero continued, his lip curling in a sneer, "what leadership? You're a sheep, Tommy boy. You've been following my lead since day one, letting me make the hard decisions, the necessary choices. And now you want to pretend like you're the one in charge?"

Tommy opened his mouth to retort, but Roxy beat him to it. "Maybe he has a point, Tommy. Maybe we should hear Zero out, at least consider the possibility that there's more going on here than meets the eye. I mean, think about it—what are the odds of something like this just happening by chance? Of a virus that just happens to turn people into zombies, that just happens to spread across the entire country, maybe even the world in a matter of weeks? It doesn't add up."

Tommy stared at her. "You can't be serious, Rox. You can't honestly believe—"

"I'm not saying I believe anything," Roxy said, holding up her hands. "I'm just saying we should keep an open mind, that's all. Because if there is some kind of conspiracy at work here, some kind of larger plan, then maybe knowing about it could give us an edge. Maybe it could help us survive."

Jimbo shifted in his seat. "Roxy's got a point, dude. I mean, I'm not saying I buy into all this New World Order crap, but you've got to admit, it's a little...convenient. The way everything just fell apart so quickly, the way society just...collapsed?"

Tommy looked around at them, at these people he'd come to think of as his family, his heart sinking. "Fine. You want to follow Zero down the rabbit hole, be my guest. But I'm telling you, it's a mistake. It's a distraction, a waste of time and energy that we can't afford. We need to focus on surviving, on getting to the east coast, on finding our families and—"

"And then what?" Zero cut in. "What happens when we get there, Tommy boy? What happens when we find out that there's nothing left, that everything we've been fighting for is gone? What then, huh?"

Tommy swallowed, his throat tight. "Then we keep going. We find someplace safe, someplace we can start over. We build something new, something better."

"You want to 'build back better,' huh?" Zero shook his head, a rueful smile playing at the corners of his mouth. "You really are a sheep, aren't you? Still clinging to your fairy tales, your happy endings. Well, I've got news for you, Tommy boy—there are no happy endings, not anymore. There's only survival, only the fight to stay alive. And if you can't see that, if you can't accept it...then maybe you're the one who doesn't belong with us."

The words hit Tommy like a punch to the gut, leaving him breathless. He looked to the others for support, for some sign that they didn't agree, that they still believed in him. But they wouldn't meet his gaze.

"Screw you, Zero. Screw you and your nihilistic red pill crap. You want to give up, to just accept that this is the way things are now? Fine. But I'm not going to stop fighting. I'm not going to stop hoping. Because if we lose that, if we lose the belief that there's something better out there, then we might as well just lay down and die."

Zero stared at him for a long moment. Then he shrugged, turning back to the wheel. "Suit yourself, Tommy boy. But don't come crying to me when reality comes knocking."

After a long moment, Tommy sighed. "Look, I can't be doing with all this conspiracy crap, alright? It's not helping anyone."

Zero shook his head, his fingers tightening on the wheel. "You need to wake up, Tommy boy. You need to open your eyes and see what's really going on."

"Oh, yeah? And what's that, exactly?"

"The truth. The truth about the world we live in, about the people who run it. You think this is the first time something like this has happened?"

Tommy snorted. "Right. And I suppose you've got proof of that, do you?"

"Proof?" Zero laughed. "You want proof? How about Operation Northwoods, huh? The CIA's plan to stage false flag attacks on American soil and blame it on Cuba, just to justify an invasion. Or COINTELPRO, the FBI's campaign to infiltrate and disrupt activist groups in the 60s and 70s. Iran-Contra, Watergate, Tuskegee, MK-Ultra, WMDs in Iraq, Operation Mockingbird, Operation Paperclip...the list goes on and on. Conspiracies are everywhere,"

"And wat am I supposed to do with a barrage of names like that? How is any of that supposed to help us survive?"

"It's not about survival. It's about understanding the world we live in, about seeing through the lies and the propaganda. You want to know what you should do? You should do your own research. You should question everything you've been told, everything you think you know. Because I guarantee you, most of it is a lie."

Tommy shook his head, a bitter laugh escaping his lips. "Right. So I should just, what, spend my days reading conspiracy blogs and watching YouTube videos? I should just ignore the fact that we're in the middle of a zombie apocalypse and focus on, on what, exactly? On proving that the moon landing was faked, that the earth is hollow, that lizard people are secretly running the world?"

Zero's jaw clenched. "You're just like everyone else, blindly following along, never questioning the official narrative. You think you're some kind of rebel, some kind of punk rock hero, but you're just another NPC."

Tommy's eyes narrowed. "And what does that make you, huh? Some kind of enlightened truth-seeker? Hate to break it to you, Zero, but you're just another sheep, following whatever conspiracy theory you read on the internet. Right-wing gun-nut conspiracy crap."

"Right-wing?" Zero laughed. "Oh that's rich. You think you have me all figured out, don't you Tommy boy? Think I fit into your neat little boxes. But that's where you're wrong. I'm not right-wing. I'm not left-wing. I'm above that whole paradigm. I'm a true punk, a true anarchist. Not like you weekend warrior types."

Tommy bristled. "You calling me a part-time punk? A poseur? I've lived this life. I've bled for this scene. And you have the nerve to—"

"To what? Call it like I see it? You think because you play in a band, because you've got some tattoos and piercings, that makes you a punk?" Zero sniffed. "Nah. Being a punk is a mindset, a way of life. It's about rejecting all systems of control and oppression, tearing them down brick by brick."

Tommy shook his head. "You want to talk punk? Punk's about building something better, not just smashing everything to bits. It's about unity, equality, supporting each other. Not whatever pseudo-intellectual 'wake up sheeple' crap you're spouting."

Zero opened his mouth to retort, but Roxy cut him off. "Enough! I swear, if I have to listen to one more second of you two arguing over who the 'real' punks are, I'm going to scream. This isn't helping anyone!"

Tommy and Zero glared at each other. After a long, tense moment, Tommy looked away. "Fine. Agree to disagree, I guess."

Zero snorted. "Whatever helps you sleep at night, Tommy boy."

The van lapsed into an uneasy quiet, broken only by the rumble of the engine and the occasional squeak of the wipers against the windshield.

Jimbo leaned forward. "Dude, you ever think about how the earth might be flat? And like, the moon is really just a spotlight or something?"

Tommy stared at him. "What?"

"No, think about it. It makes sense, right? I mean, have you ever seen the curve of the earth? Have you ever been to space?"

Tommy pinched the bridge of his nose. "Jimbo, I swear to God..."

Zero waved a hand. "Flat-Earthers are there to distract you from the real issues."

"I said, enough!" Roxy snapped.

The van lapsed into an uncomfortable silence, the air thick with tension.

Tommy sat back in his seat, his mind racing. He knew he should say something, should try to smooth things over, to bring them back together. But the words wouldn't come.

Jimbo shifted in his seat, clearing his throat. "Anyone know any good jokes?"

No one answered.

"Alright, alright." He raised a finger. "Here's one. Why don't zombies eat comedians?" He looked around. "Anyone?"

No response.

"Because they taste funny." Jimbo sucked his teeth. "Ooh, tough crowd."

He tapped his chin. "Okay. How about this one? What's a zombie's least favourite food? Rox?"

Roxy shrugged.

"Fast food—they can never catch it!"

Laila groaned.

Jimbo clapped. "See? You are listening!"

"Can someone stop him," Laila said.

"I've got loads more of these." Jimbo grinned at her. "What's a zombie's favourite street?"

Laila rolled her eyes. "Go on."

"A dead end!"

Roxy sighed. "Zero, can you pull over?"

"Sure, what is it?"

"We should let Jimbo out here. He can walk the rest of the way."

Zero chuckled. "She's got a point, Jimbo. Any more dad jokes and we're cutting you loose."

Jimbo nodded. "Understood, dude. Just one more—"

"No!" the others said as one.

The sun hung low on the horizon as the van rolled to a stop in a clearing off the highway, just outside Wheeling's city limits.

Tommy climbed out, his muscles stiff and aching from the long hours on the road. He stretched, wincing as his joints popped.

Around him, the others piled out of the van, their faces drawn and weary.

Zero set about securing the perimeter, his rifle held at the ready.

Roxy and Jimbo unloaded their supplies, stacking boxes of canned goods and bottled water near the centre of the clearing.

Laila hung back, her arms wrapped around herself, her gaze distant.

Tommy frowned. Laila had been withdrawing more and more with each passing day, retreating into herself. He knew she was still grappling with Micky's death, with the guilt and the grief of it all. He wished he knew how to help her, how to ease the burden she carried. But the words always seemed to catch in his throat.

He shook his head, forcing himself to focus on the task at hand. They needed to set up camp, to get a fire going and some food in their bellies. There would be time to talk later.

As the last of the light faded from the sky, they gathered around the flickering flames of the campfire, huddled in their jackets against the chill of the night air.

They ate in silence, the only sound the scrape of spoons against tin cans and the occasional pop and crackle of the fire.

Tommy's gaze drifted to Zero, sitting apart from the others, his back against a tree and his rifle across his lap. He sighed, setting down his empty can and pushing himself to his feet.

He crossed the clearing, stopping a few feet away from Zero. "Hey, man. Can we talk?"

Zero looked up at him. "What about?"

Tommy rubbed the back of his neck. "Look, I just wanted to say I appreciate everything you've done for us. Keeping the van running, scavenging for supplies, watching our backs. We wouldn't have made it this far without you."

Zero grunted, his gaze sliding away. "Yeah, well. Someone's got to do it."

"I mean it, Zero. You've been there for us, even when things got tough. Even when I wasn't...when I wasn't at my best."

Zero's eyes snapped back to his, his brow furrowing. "This about what happened in the van?"

Tommy nodded, his throat tight. "Yeah. I just wanted to apologise. For snapping at you like that. I was out of line."

Zero was silent for a long moment. Then, slowly, he shook his head. "Nah, man. You weren't out of line. You were right. I was being an asshole."

Tommy blinked. "Oh. Uh...thanks?"

Zero snorted. "Don't get used to it, Tommy boy. I'm not in the habit of admitting when I'm wrong."

Tommy felt a laugh bubble up in his throat, the tension draining out of him. "Yeah, well. Maybe we can both work on that, huh?"

Zero chuckled, shaking his head. "Maybe so." He sobered, his gaze turning serious. "Look, Tommy...I know I can be a lot to deal with sometimes. But I want you to know, I've got your back."

Tommy swallowed, his chest tightening. "And I've got yours. We're in this together, right?"

Zero nodded, holding out his hand. Tommy clasped it, feeling the calluses on Zero's palm, the strength in his grip.

Then Zero pulled away, clearing his throat. "Alright, enough of this. You should get some rest, Tommy boy. I'll take first watch."

Tommy hesitated, but the exhaustion was already tugging at his eyelids, the ache in his muscles growing more insistent. "You sure? I can stay up a bit longer, if you need me to."

Zero waved him off, already settling back against the tree. "I got this. Go on, get some shut-eye. I'll wake you in a few hours."

Tommy nodded and made his way back to the campfire, settling down on his bedroll. The others were already asleep, their breathing slow and even. He let his eyes drift shut, letting the warmth of the flames and the soft sounds of the night lull him into a doze.

But sleep wouldn't come. His mind raced, replaying the events of the day, the argument with Zero, the tension that had settled over the group. He tossed and turned, trying to get comfortable on the hard ground.

A soft giggle pulled him from his thoughts. He sat up, blinking, his gaze searching the darkness beyond the circle of firelight.

At the edge of the treeline, he saw two figures, their silhouettes illuminated by the moonlight filtering through the branches.

Roxy and Jimbo, locked in a passionate embrace.

He watched, his heart pounding, as Roxy wrapped her arms around Jimbo's neck, pulling him closer. Jimbo's hands slid down her back, coming to rest on her hips. Their lips met in a slow, deep kiss.

Tommy looked away, his face burning. He felt like an intruder, like he was witnessing something private, something not meant for his eyes.

But he couldn't deny the pang of jealousy that twisted in his gut, the longing for that kind of connection, that kind of intimacy.

The crunch of footsteps brought his attention back to the present. He looked up to see Laila settling down beside him, her knees drawn up to her chest. She stared into the flames, her expression unreadable.

"Can't sleep either, huh?"

Laila breathed a sigh. "I'm fine. Just thinking."

He followed her gaze, watching the embers dance and swirl. "What about?"

"About Micky. About everything."

He nodded. "It's okay to miss him, you know. To grieve. We all are."

She drew in a shuddering breath, her shoulders hunching. "I know. But I can't keep looking back. I have to keep moving forward, keep fighting."

Tommy reached out, laying a hand on her arm. "I'm here for you, whenever you need me."

She looked at him and gave a slight nod. "I know, Tommy. And I'm grateful, I really am. But right now...right now I think I just need to be alone for a bit. To process everything."

He squeezed her arm, then let go, giving her space. "Okay. But if you change your mind, if you need to talk, you know I'm here."

She managed a small smile. "Thanks, Tommy."

He watched as she rose, making her way to her own bedroll on the other side of the fire. She lay down, turning her back to him, her body curled in on itself.

Tommy sighed, running a hand through his hair. His gaze drifted back to the treeline, but Roxy and Jimbo were gone, vanished into the shadows.

He shook his head, trying to push down the uneasiness that coiled in his gut. It was none of his business, what they did. They were all adults, all capable of making their own choices.

But still, he couldn't help but worry. Couldn't help but wonder what it would mean for the group, for their chances of survival, if things went sour between them.

He lay back down, staring up at the star-strewn sky. They were so close now, so close to the east coast, to Philly, to Niamh and Sean.

Just a few more days, a few more miles, and he'd be home.

The first hints of dawn were just beginning to paint the sky a pale grey when Tommy jolted awake. For a moment, he lay still, trying to place what had woken him.

The snap of a twig.

The rustle of leaves.

Something was moving in the woods.

He sat up, his hand reaching for his bat.

Around him, the others slept on, oblivious.

Roxy and Jimbo were curled together on the other side of the dying fire, their heads close.

Zero still sat propped against a tree, his rifle cradled in his arms, his head nodding.

Tommy scanned the treeline, searching for any sign of movement.

The forest was dark and still, the only sound the distant call of a bird, the gentle sigh of the wind through the branches.

A harsh crack split the air, followed by the thud of running feet.

Tommy scrambled to stand, "Get up! We're under attack!"

Figures burst from the trees, their faces smeared with dirt and paint. They carried an assortment of weapons—clubs, knives, guns.

Zero shot forward, tackling the nearest attacker to the ground.

They rolled in the dirt, grappling, trading blows.

Zero's fists slammed into the raider's face, once, twice, three times, until the man went limp beneath him.

Laila bolted to her feet, her tyre iron in hand.

Tommy grabbed her arm, pulling her close. "Stay with me," he said, positioning them back-to-back. "We'll take them together."

The raiders grabbed at the group's supplies, hauling away boxes of food and bottles of water.

Shots rang out, muzzle flashes strobing in the dim light.

Jimbo charged at a raider who was attempting to make off with their medical kit.

He swung his golf club in a wide arc, catching the man across the back of the head.

The raider stumbled, dropping the kit, and Jimbo pressed his advantage, raining down blows.

They crashed into a tree, sending supplies scattering.

The raider lashed out with a knife, the blade catching Jimbo's arm.

Jimbo hissed in pain, but didn't let up, driving his knee into the raider's gut.

Roxy was a blur of motion, her machete flashing in the firelight. She caught one of the raiders across the thigh, sending him stumbling.

Zero was on him in an instant, slamming the butt of his rifle into the man's face.

The raider crumpled, his nose a shattered ruin.

Tommy swung his bat, feeling it connect with flesh and bone.

A raider staggered back, clutching at his ribs.

Tommy kicked out, catching him in the knee, and the man went down hard.

The raiders melted back into the trees, their pounding footsteps fading into the distance.

Tommy stood, his chest heaving, his bat slick with blood. He looked around, taking stock.

Jimbo was pressing a hand to his bleeding arm, his face pale.

Roxy was winded, a bruise already forming on her cheek.

Zero paced the perimeter of the camp, his rifle at the ready. "They'll be back. This was just a probing attack, testing our defences. We need to move before they regroup."

Laila sank to the ground, her arms wrapped around herself. She was shaking, her breath coming in short, sharp gasps. Tommy went to her, crouching down beside her.

"Hey. It's okay. We're okay. We made it through."

She looked up at him, her eyes brimming with tears. "I thought they were going to kill us."

He pulled her into a hug, feeling the way she trembled against him. "I know. I'm so sorry, Lai. I should have been more alert, should have seen them coming."

She shook her head, pulling back to look at him. "No, Tommy. This isn't your fault. We were all caught off guard."

"We need to move," Zero said. "Now. We're too exposed here, too vulnerable."

Tommy nodded, pushing himself to his feet. He held out a hand to Laila, helping her up. "Zero's right. We can't stay here. Let's pack up what's left, see how bad the damage is."

They moved quickly, gathering what supplies remained. The raiders had made off with a significant portion of their food and water, as well as some of their medical supplies. But they still had the van, still had their weapons.

"Alright," Zero said. "Let's roll out.""

They climbed into the van, Roxy taking the wheel, Zero riding shotgun. Tommy slid into the back with Laila and Jimbo, his bat close at hand.

They would make it. They had to. There was simply no other choice.

11. Mom's Basement

The fog hung low over the outskirts of Pittsburgh, a thick, cloying mist that seemed to swallow sound and light.

Tommy sat in the back of the van, his bat gripped tight in his hands. He stared out the blood-splattered window, his eyes scanning the ruined landscape, searching for any sign of movement, any hint of danger.

Beside him, Laila huddled in on herself. She hadn't spoken in hours, not since the attack at the campsite. Tommy's gut twisted with worry for her, for all of them.

They'd fought so hard to make it this far. Pittsburgh was the last big hurdle, the final stretch of highway between them and Philly. Between them and home.

But looking out at the desolate streets, the abandoned cars and debris-strewn sidewalks, Tommy couldn't shake the feeling that the worst was yet to come.

Roxy guided the van down a narrow side street, the buildings pressing in close on either side.

"Take a left up here," Zero said. "There's an old service road that should get us around the worst of the congestion."

Roxy nodded, spinning the wheel. The van lurched and bounced over the uneven pavement, jostling them in their seats.

"We've got dead-heads!" Zero said.

Tommy turned to the windshield. Zombies, dozens of them, maybe hundreds, shambled out from between the cars, crawling over hoods and roofs, their faces slack and hungry, their eyes milky white.

Roxy slammed on the brakes, the van skidding to a halt mere inches from the horde. "Where the hell did they come from?"

"Doesn't matter," Zero said. "We have to go through them."

Tommy nodded, adrenaline surging through his veins. He knew this drill. But it never got any easier, never got any less terrifying.

Roxy hit the gas, the van surging forward. They ploughed into the horde, bodies crunching beneath the wheels, gore splattering the windshield.

Tommy and Laila leaned out the windows, their weapons swinging, smashing through skulls and limbs.

But there were too many of them, an endless sea of grasping hands and snapping teeth. They pressed in from all sides, their fingers scrabbling at the doors, at the windows.

"We're going to get stuck!" Roxy said, her knuckles white on the wheel. "I can't push through!"

"There!" Zero pointed to a narrow alley, barely wide enough for the van. "Take it, now!"

Roxy wrenched the wheel, the van careening into the alley. They scraped past dumpsters and fire escapes, sparks flying, metal screeching.

Zombies stumbled after them, but the tight confines slowed them down, bought them a few precious seconds.

They burst out onto another street, this one clearer.

Roxy floored it, the engine roaring as they sped away from the horde.

Tommy slumped back in his seat, his heart slamming against his ribs.

He glanced over at Laila, saw the way her hands shook, the way she stared straight ahead, her eyes unseeing. He reached out, laid a hand on her arm. "You okay?"

She flinched at his touch, pulling away. "I'm fine."

Tommy swallowed, a bitter taste in his mouth. He wanted to push, to make her talk to him, to break through the walls she'd thrown up. But he knew it would only make things worse, only drive her further away.

So he let it go, turning his attention back to the road, back to the city unfolding around them.

They drove in silence, the only sound the hum of the engine, the crunch of debris beneath the tyres.

The streets grew narrower, the buildings taller.

Tommy had been to Pittsburgh before, back when the band first started touring. He remembered the bustling sidewalks, the gleaming storefronts, the noise and the energy and the life.

Now, it was a hollow shell of its former self. The windows were dark and empty. Cars sat abandoned in the middle of the road.

And everywhere, the dead. They wandered the streets in packs, their clothes hanging in tatters, their flesh grey and rotten. They stumbled and lurched, their movements jerky and uncoordinated.

Zero barked out directions to Roxy, guiding her down side streets and back alleys, always staying one step ahead of the hordes.

They took a hard right, the van skidding on the slick pavement.

They approached an old arcade, its neon sign dark and lifeless, its windows boarded over.

Zero made a half-smile. "I used to practically live in this place."

Roxy slowed the van, glancing over at him. "Yeah?"

Zero nodded. "Every weekend. Before I discovered punk. I'd be in there from open to close, blowing my allowance on tokens."

Tommy leaned forward. "What games did you play?"

"Everything. But Street Fighter IV was my jam. I got so good with Blanka, nobody could touch me."

Jimbo chuckled from the back. "Street Fighter was cool, but Dance Dance Revolution was where it was at. I was a beast on those pads."

"I was more into the classic stuff," Roxy said. "Pac-Man, Galaga. But I did love me some Time Crisis. Something satisfying about that light gun."

Tommy nodded. "Guitar Hero for me. Guess that's not surprising, huh?"

A zombie lurched out from behind a parked car, its arms outstretched, its jaw hanging slack.

Roxy jerked the wheel hard to the left.

The van clipped the zombie, sending it spinning. It hit the ground hard, its skull shattering on the pavement. Black blood sprayed across the asphalt.

Roxy fought for control. She stomped on the brakes, the tyres screaming as they skidded to a stop.

For a moment, no one moved, no one breathed.

Zero shook his head, his eyes hard. "We can't afford any more distractions. We need to stay focused, stay sharp. One mistake out here, and we're all dead."

Roxy eased the van back into gear, steering them down another narrow street, the city stretching on and on.

She guided the van into an underpass, the concrete walls closing in around them. The headlights cut through the gloom, illuminating the road ahead.

As they neared the far end of the tunnel, a mass of zombies blocked the exit.

"Turn us around," Zero said. "Quick!"

Roxy threw the van into reverse, but as she spun the wheel, Tommy's stomach dropped. More zombies were flooding in from the entrance they'd just passed through.

"We're trapped." Roxy killed the engine, plunging them into silence.

The group exchanged worried glances in the dim light.

"What now?" Jimbo asked.

Zero ran a hand through his hair. "We could try to ram our way through. The van's tough, it might make it."

"And if it doesn't?" Tommy said. "We'd be stranded in the middle of that horde with no escape."

Roxy shook her head. "We can't risk damaging the van. It's our only reliable transportation."

They all fell silent for a moment.

"We have to clear a path," Tommy said, his grip tightening on his bat. "It's the only way forward."

"There are so many of them..." Roxy said.

"We don't have a choice," Zero said. "We fight our way out or we die in here."

Roxy nodded. "Alright, let's do this. We'll take the exit ahead—it's a shorter distance to cover."

Tommy burst from the van, falling into a fighting stance.

Roxy raised her machete, her teeth bared in a feral snarl.

Laila remained frozen, her tyre iron at her side.

"Laila!" Tommy shouted. "Laila, stay with me!"

But she remained rooted, her stare blank.

The zombies closed the gap, all grasping hands, and gnashing teeth.

Tommy's bat collided with rotting flesh, bone splintering beneath the impact. He kicked another aside, pivoted, smashed the skull of a third.

A hand seized Tommy's shoulder, dragging him backwards. He buckled, twisting to ram his elbow into the zombie's chest. The grip slackened and he caved in the creature's head.

He turned just in time to see a zombie lunge for Laila. She stood immobile, paralysed.

"No!" Tommy threw himself forward, his bat whooshing through the air. It struck the zombie's temple. Blood splattered across Tommy's face, hot and sticky.

Laila stared up at him, her eyes wide, brimming with tears.

Behind them, Jimbo cried out. Tommy spun to see him grappling with a zombie, its teeth snapping inches from his throat.

Roxy was there, her machete severing the creature's spine. It flopped to the ground, twitching.

And then, silence.

The fight was over as abruptly as it had begun.

Tommy stood amidst the carnage, his chest heaving, his skin crawling.

He turned to Laila, crouching down beside her. "Hey, you alright?"

She looked up at him, blinking slowly.

She opened her mouth, closed it again.

Finally, she gave a small, jerky nod.

Zero stalked the perimeter, his rifle up, his eyes scanning the shadows.

Jimbo approached, laying a hand on his shoulder. "We should get moving, dude. We don't want to get trapped down here."

Zero whirled on him, his face contorted. "You think I don't know that? I know this city better than anyone. I'll decide when it's time to move."

Jimbo held up his hands, taking a step back. "Whoa, easy. I was just trying to help."

"I don't need your help. I don't need anyone's help."

Tommy stepped between them, his hands up. "Alright, let's all just take a breath. We're all on edge, all running on fumes. But we can't turn on each other, not now."

Zero glared at him for a long moment, then looked away. His hands were trembling, his knuckles white around the grip of his rifle. "Whatever, Tommy boy."

Roxy climbed back in the van. "Come on. We don't have time for macho posturing. Let's get moving."

The van rolled to a stop. Tommy leaned forward, peering out the windshield.

Overturned trash cans and abandoned cars littered the street, the houses in various states of disrepair. Some had broken windows, their curtains fluttering in the breeze. Others had doors hanging off their hinges, or holes punched through their walls.

Zero stared at a burned down house. The roof had collapsed inward, the walls stained with smoke.

The engine ticked as it cooled.

No one moved, no one spoke.

They just sat there, staring at the burnt-out husk of Zero's home.

Zero opened the passenger door, his movements slow, almost reluctant. "Let's take a look."

Tommy exchanged a glance with Jimbo, but followed suit, stepping out of the van.

They stood in a loose semicircle, their weapons held at the ready, their eyes scanning the surrounding houses for any signs of movement.

But the street was deserted, the only sound the whisper of the wind through the trees.

Tommy watched as Zero walked forward, his boots crunching on gravel. The grass was overgrown, the flowerbeds choked with weeds.

Zero paused at the edge of the yard, his gaze distant.

Tommy wondered what he was seeing, what memories were playing out behind his eyes.

He couldn't imagine what it must be like, to come back home and find it like this.

Zero strode forward, approaching the ruined shell of the house. The others followed, picking their way through the debris.

Inside, the floorboards had been reduced to charcoal, the walls blackened and crumbling. Ash swirled in the air, catching in Tommy's throat, and stinging his eyes.

In the corner of what had once been the living room, Tommy spotted a charred lump that might have been a couch, or an armchair. A few twisted pieces of metal poked up from the rubble, the remains of a lamp or an end table.

But there was no sign of any bodies, no indication of what had happened to Zero's mother. Tommy didn't know if that was a good thing or a bad thing.

Zero stood in the middle of the room, his head bowed, his shoulders slumped.

Tommy exchanged a glance with Roxy. What could they say? What words of comfort could they offer that wouldn't sound hollow?

Jimbo stepped forward, placing a hand on Zero's shoulder. "I'm sorry, dude. I can't imagine how hard this must be."

Zero shook his head. "It's just a house..." His voice cracked. "It doesn't matter."

Laila reached out, her fingers brushing against a half-melted trophy. "Is this yours?"

Zero glanced over, his brow furrowing. For a moment, Tommy thought he might snap at her, might lash out.

"Yeah. My mom was so proud. She kept that damn thing on the mantel, polished it every week."

Laila picked up the trophy, turning it over in her hands. "First Place, Pittsburgh Junior Marksman Competition."

She handed it to Zero, a small smile tugging at the corner of her mouth.

Zero took the trophy, his fingers tracing over the words. For a moment, his face crumpled.

Then he shook his head, setting the trophy back down on the shelf.

Roxy cleared her throat, looking around at the ruined room. "We should keep moving. Get anything you need and we'll head to Jimbo's."

"Yeah. Yeah, you're right." Zero turned and strode towards a door under the stairs. A sign hung on it, the words 'Ezra's Room' printed on white paper, with a 'No Entry' sign underneath.

Tommy nudged Laila, pointing to the sign. "Ezra? You think that's Zero's real name?"

Laila shrugged, her eyes fixed on Zero as he fiddled with the lock.

After a moment, the door swung open, revealing a set of stairs leading down into darkness.

Zero clicked on his flashlight, the beam cutting through the gloom. "My room's down here. Come on."

Tommy followed him down the stairs, his own flashlight bobbing in the shadows. The air grew cooler as they descended, the smell of burnt wood making way for damp earth and mildew.

At the bottom, Zero's flashlight swept across the room, illuminating a cluttered space. A bed sat in one corner. A desk stood against the opposite wall, a computer monitor perched on top, surrounded by a tangle of wires, and recording equipment. Tommy spotted a microphone, a guitar leaning against an amp.

Posters plastered the walls—punk bands, cult movies, WWE wrestlers. Tommy recognised a few of the names—C. M. Punk, The Undertaker—but most were unfamiliar.

Zero crossed to the bed and knelt down, reaching underneath. He dragged out a large duffel bag and hefted it onto the bed.

Tommy caught a glimpse of the contents as Zero unzipped it—the glint of a rifle barrel, the dull gleam of bullets, the neatly packed coils of rope and other survival gear.

He leaned over to Laila, lowering his voice. "Damn. All he's missing is the tinfoil hat."

Laila snorted, a smile tugging at her lips.

Their laughter died as Zero straightened up, his face cast in sharp angles by the flashlight's glare. He glowered at them, his eyes hard. "You got something to say, Tommy boy?"

Tommy held up his hands, the grin fading from his face. "No, man. Just...admiring your setup here. That's quite the collection."

"No. That's just my bug-out bag." He crossed to a metal locker in the corner and turned a combination lock. He opened the door, revealing a rack of firearms.

Roxy let out a low whistle. "What the hell, Zero? You planning on starting your own militia or something?"

Zero didn't answer. He reached inside and pulled out a shotgun, tossing it to Tommy.

Tommy caught it, the weight of it heavy and solid in his hands.

Next came a pair of hunting rifles, which Zero handed to Jimbo and Roxy. Finally, he pulled out a handgun and offered it to Laila.

"Why so many guns?" Roxy asked.

Zero met her gaze. "For this exact scenario."

"You were preparing for the zombie apocalypse?"

"Zombies, no. Apocalypse, yes." He reached back into the locker and pulled out several boxes of ammunition, tossing them to the others.

Tommy caught one, the cardboard rough against his palms.

"Take as much as you can carry. We don't know when we'll be able to resupply."

Tommy nodded, stuffing the box into his backpack. He grabbed a handful of loose shotgun shells, shoving them into his pockets.

Zero finished packing and zipped up the bag, slinging it over his shoulder. "Alright, let's move. I don't want to stay here any longer than we have to."

They filed back up the stairs, Tommy bringing up the rear, his arms laden with weapons and ammunition.

As they emerged back into the living room, Tommy couldn't help but take one last look around. The burned-out shell of a family home, the charred remains of a life that no longer existed.

Tommy adjusted his grip on the shotgun and followed the others out into the waiting sunlight.

Outside, the group began loading up the van with their newly acquired weapons and supplies.

Roxy and Laila organised the gear in the back.

Jimbo approached the driver's side door. "I'll take the wheel from here. I know the best route to my place from here."

Roxy nodded, tossing him the keys. "All yours, big guy."

While the others busied themselves with preparations, Zero remained on the kerb, his gaze fixed on the burnt-out shell of his home.

Tommy walked over to join him. "Hey, man. You alright?"

Zero remained silent for several seconds before nodding. "I will be. I just need to come to terms with the fact that my mom's probably dead."

Tommy placed a hand on Zero's shoulder. "I'm sorry, man. Really."

"Part of me hopes she got out somehow. But I doubt it. And worse, she could be in one of those FEMA camps."

Tommy shook his head. "If she's alive, isn't that enough?"

Zero's face hardened. "I'd rather be dead than in one of those places. At least that way, I die on my own terms."

Before Tommy could respond, Zero turned abruptly and strode back to the van.

As Zero climbed into the passenger seat, Tommy took one last look at the ruined house.

The weight of all they'd lost, all they continued to lose, settled heavy on his shoulders.

With a deep breath, he pushed the feeling aside and joined the others in the van.

Jimbo started the engine and pulled away.

Tommy caught Zero staring out the window, watching his old life fade into the distance.

Tommy let his eyes drift shut. He pictured Niamh's face, Sean's smile. He imagined the way their arms would feel around him, the way their laughter would sound in his ears.

It was a fantasy. A dream of a future that might never come to pass. But it was all he had to keep him from giving up.

Jimbo sat behind the wheel, his eyes focused on the road ahead as he maneuvered around the streets of Pittsburgh.

As they drove on, Jimbo started pointing out landmarks. "See that building over there?" He nodded towards a dilapidated structure on the corner. "That's where Anarchy's Child played our first gig. Man, we were so nervous. No one knew what to make of a punk band with the drummer doing lead vocals."

"We sucked so hard back then," Zero said.

"I remember this one show," Jimbo said. "We were opening for this big-name band, and the crowd was just not feeling us. I mean, they were straight-up booing. But Zero, he just stepped up to the mic and started ripping into them, telling them they were a bunch of posers who wouldn't know real punk if it bit them on the ass. And somehow, it worked. By the end of our set, they were cheering for us."

Jimbo brought the van to a stop outside an apartment building, the engine's rumble fading to silence. The group sat for a moment, scanning the area for any signs of immediate danger.

"Alright," Jimbo said. "This is it. My place is on the third floor."

Zero nodded. "Let's do a quick perimeter check before we head in."

Tommy exited the van. He gripped his newly acquired shotgun, his eyes darting between shadows and potential hiding spots.

"Roxy, you and Laila take the left side," Zero said. "Tommy and I will go right. Jimbo, keep watch on the van. Any sign of trouble, give the signal."

As Tommy and Zero rounded the corner of the building, Zero held up a hand, stopping them in their tracks.

He pointed to a partially open door at the back of the building.

They approached, Zero taking point with his rifle raised.

Tommy covered him, shotgun at the ready.

Zero nudged the door with his foot, revealing an empty hallway beyond. He lowered his weapon. "Looks clear, but stay alert."

They rejoined the others at the van, each reporting no immediate threats.

"Alright, dudes," Jimbo said. "Let's grab what we need and head up. I don't want to be out in the open any longer than necessary."

Tommy and the others unloaded essential supplies and weapons from the van, distributing the weight among them.

Loaded down with gear, Tommy moved towards the apartment block.

Jimbo paused at the entrance, his hand on the door handle. He took a deep breath. "Ready?"

Tommy nodded.

Jimbo pushed open the door, and entered.

Inside, the building stood quiet, the only sound the echo of their footsteps on the concrete floor.

Jimbo led them up the stairs to his apartment.

"Home sweet home," he said, ushering them inside.

The apartment was dusty but untouched. Posters of punk bands covered the walls, interspersed with shelves of CDs and vinyl records.

Jimbo made a beeline for the kitchen, rummaging through the cabinets. "I knew I had some good stuff stashed away." He emerged with an armful of canned goods and boxed meals. "Feast your eyes on this, my friends. We're eating like kings tonight!"

The group gathered around the small dining table. As Jimbo heated up a can of soup on his gas stove, he turned to Zero with a grin. "Hey man, I know you're probably itching to hop on the internet and do some research, but I'm afraid the Wi-Fi's been out for a while."

Zero folded his arms. "Hilarious."

As they ate, the mood in the room lightened, laughter and conversation filling the space.

"Listen," Tommy said. "I know we're all exhausted, and this place feels like a godsend after everything we've been through. But we can't stay here long. We need to keep moving, need to get to Philadelphia."

Roxy frowned, leaning forward. "We're safe, we have food and shelter. Why can't you take a day or two to rest, to regroup?"

Jimbo nodded. "We've been running non-stop since Berkley."

Tommy shook his head. "Every day I waste here is another day Niamh and Sean are out there. I can't...I won't let them down."

Zero met his gaze. "Don't be a fool, Tommy boy. At least rest tonight."

Laila pursed her lips. "He's right."

"Fine. One night."

The living room of Jimbo's apartment glowed with the warm light of a dozen candles.

Tommy and the others had gathered there, settling in with an assortment of blankets and pillows scavenged from around the apartment.

Roxy jumped to her feet. "I have an idea." She raced for the door. "Be right back!"

The others exchanged curious glances, but before anyone could ask what she was up to, Roxy had disappeared into the hallway.

Zero raced after her, his rifle in hand.

A few minutes later, they returned, Roxy's battered guitar case slung over her shoulder.

Jimbo's face lit up. "Dude!"

Roxy grinned, setting the case down and flipping it open. "Thought we could use a little music."

Jimbo leapt to his feet, disappearing into his bedroom. He emerged a moment later, a set of bongos tucked under his arm. "I'm so in." He sat down cross-legged on the floor.

The others arranged themselves around the room, Roxy setting up on the worn couch, Zero sprawling on the carpet. Tommy found himself sandwiched between Zero and Laila, a pillow propped behind his back.

Roxy strummed a few chords, tuning the strings until they rang true. Then, with a grin, she began to strum the chords of 'New Rose' by *The Damned*.

Jimbo joined in on the bongos, his hands flying over the drumheads in a complex rhythm. The others began to clap along, grins spreading across their faces.

Jimbo and Roxy began to sing, belting out the lyrics.

Tommy found himself singing along, the words coming back to him like a long-lost friend.

For a moment, the world outside fell away, the horrors and the heartache forgotten in the sheer joy of the music.

As the song ended, Roxy segued into a slowed-down version of 'Prayer of the Refugee' by *Rise Against*.

Jimbo switched to a softer beat, his fingers caressing the drumheads.

Tommy closed his eyes, letting the music wash over him. In his mind's eye, he saw a different living room, a different group of friends. Niamh, her feet propped up on the coffee table, her head bobbing along to the beat. Sean, his face split in a wide grin, air-guitaring with wild abandon.

A lump rose in his throat, and he swallowed hard, forcing the memories back. He couldn't afford to get lost in them, not now. Not when there was still so much to do, so far to go.

As if sensing his thoughts, Roxy's voice softened, the lyrics taking on a wistful tone.

Beside him, Laila let out a shuddering breath, her hand finding his in the darkness. He squeezed it gently, offering what comfort he could.

The song ended. And, then, the room was silent.

"You know, when all this started," Jimbo said. "I thought it was the end of the world. I mean, it kinda was, I guess. But I never thought I'd find something like this, you know? Something like...family."

Roxy nodded, her fingers still resting on the fretboard. "I know what you mean. Before, it was just about surviving, about getting through each day. But now it feels like we're actually fighting for something."

They traded stories back and forth, remembering the highs and lows of their journey.

As the laughter and reminiscing wound down, Tommy found himself thinking about the future. "What do you think it'll be like, when this is all over? I mean, assuming we make it through."

Roxy shrugged, her fingers plucking idle notes on the guitar. "I don't know. I try not to think about it too much. It's hard to imagine anything beyond just surviving."

Jimbo leaned back on his hands. "I'd like to think we could rebuild, you know? Start over, make something better than what we had before. A world where people look out for each other, where we don't take things for granted."

"A world without zombies would be a good start," Zero said.

Laila shifted, drawing her knees up to her chest. "I just want to feel safe again. To not be afraid all the time, to not worry that every noise, every shadow is something trying to kill us."

Tommy nodded. "We'll get there. We've made it this far. We just have to keep going, keep fighting."

"What about you guys?" Laila said. "What's next?"

Jimbo shrugged. "I'm staying here. The rest of you are welcome to crash for as long as you want. And I mean that."

Tommy nodded. "I appreciate that, man. But I'm itching to get home."

"I get it, dude."

"I'm staying," Zero said. "But you two can keep the weapons. Just promise me you'll keep them clean like I showed you."

"Thanks, Ezra. Bit of a step up from living in your mom's basement, huh?"

Zero smirked. "Watch it, Tommy boy."

Roxy sighed. "I'm done with running."

"Looks like it's just you and me," Laila said

"You and me." He gave a slow nod. "We'll head out at first light then. If we're lucky, we can make it to Philly by nightfall."

Jimbo reached out, clasping Tommy's shoulder. "I just wanted to say thanks. For everything. I know it hasn't been easy, leading us through all this. But we couldn't have made it this far without you."

"I couldn't have done it without all of you. We're family now. And I promise, I'll do everything I can to get us back together when this thing's over."

"I'm gonna hold you to that, dude."

The morning sun cast long shadows across the street as Tommy and Laila loaded the last of their supplies into the van.

Tommy hauled a backpack filled with canned goods, his muscles straining with the effort. Beside him, Laila sorted through a box of medical supplies.

"Do you think we have enough gas? I don't want to run out halfway to Philly."

Tommy nodded, his gaze sweeping over the piles of gear. "We've got plenty. And if we need more, we can always find some along the way."

Zero emerged from the back of the van, wiping his hands on a rag. "Tyres are good. Engine's running smooth. You should be good to go."

"Thanks, man." Tommy clapped him on the shoulder. "Don't know how we'd have got through this without you."

Zero grinned. "You wouldn't, Tommy boy."

"Yeah. You're probably right." He turned to face the others, gathered on the sidewalk to see them off. Jimbo stood with his arms crossed, his expression sombre. Roxy leaned against the building, her eyes shadowed and distant.

"Well," Tommy said. "I guess this is it."

Jimbo stepped forward, pulling him into a tight hug. "You take care of yourself out there, you hear me? Don't go doing anything stupid."

Tommy chuckled, returning the embrace. "I'll do my best."

Roxy pushed off the wall, her gaze meeting Tommy's. "You sure about this? Leaving, I mean. We could all stay here. Make a go of it."

"I can't, Rox. I have to find them."

She nodded. "I get it. Just be careful, okay?"

"I will. I promise."

They said their final goodbyes, exchanging hugs and handshakes. Tommy tried to memorise their faces, the sound of their voices. He didn't know when, or if, he would see them again.

As they climbed into the van, Tommy paused, his hand on the door. "You know, you could come with us. There's room."

Jimbo shook his head, a sad smile on his face. "Nah, dude. This is your journey. Your fight. We've got our own battles to face here."

Zero nodded, his jaw tight. "Stay safe, both of you. If you ever need anything, you know where to find us."

With that, Tommy swung into the driver's seat, slamming the door behind him. Laila slid into the passenger side.

As the engine roared to life, Tommy felt a pang of guilt, of regret. He was leaving his friends behind, abandoning them to an uncertain fate. But he knew he had no choice. He had to keep going, had to find his family.

Beside him, Laila sat in silence, her gaze fixed out the window.

A shout rang out behind them. Tommy frowned, glancing in the side mirror.

Jimbo waved his arms. "Tommy, wait!"

Tommy wound down the window. "What's up?"

"We're coming with you, dude."

Tommy stared at him, his brow furrowed. "What?"

"We're coming with you. To Philly. Me, Zero, Roxy."

Tommy shook his head. "But...but what about making a go of it here?"

Jimbo shrugged. "We're family now, dude. Family sticks together."

Tommy felt a lump rise in his throat as he swept his gaze across Jimbo, Zero, and Roxy's faces. "You best get your gear together then."

Jimbo let out a whoop. "Look out, Philly! The cavalry's coming!"

12. The Shipping Container

The sun hung low in the sky, casting a golden glow over the highway as Tommy guided the van towards Philadelphia. They were so close now.

Behind him, the others were quiet. Laila stared out the window, her face pensive. Jimbo and Roxy huddled together, their heads bent close in conversation. Zero sat in the passenger seat, his eyes scanning the road ahead.

They had been making good progress, despite the occasional detour around blocked roads or abandoned towns. But as they approached the outskirts of West Chester, the highway began to clog with abandoned vehicles once more.

Tommy slowed the van, weaving between the cars. Lone zombies shambled along the shoulder, their faces slack and empty. He swerved to avoid them.

A horde of zombies burst from the treeline. They swarmed towards the van, their rasping moans filling the air.

"Hold on!" Tommy stomped on the gas, the van lurching forward. But the zombies closed in around the vehicle, their hands scrabbling at the windows, their bodies thudding against the sides.

Tommy gritted his teeth, trying to ram through the horde. But the van shuddered and groaned under the impact, metal shrieking as it crashed into an overturned semi.

For a moment, Tommy sat dazed, his ears ringing, his vision blurred.

The zombies' moans cut through the haze, jolting him back to reality.

"Everyone out!" He grabbed his bat. "We have to run!"

They piled out of the van, their weapons already in hand. The zombies pressed in from all sides, their faces contorted with mindless hunger.

Tommy swung his bat in a wide arc, feeling it connect with solid flesh. Beside him, Laila lashed out with her tyre iron, caving in skulls with brutal efficiency. Jimbo and Roxy fought back to back, their weapons flashing in the fading light.

"We need to draw them away!" Zero slammed his rifled butt down on a zombie's skull. "Get them to follow us, give us a chance to get back to the van!"

Tommy nodded, his mind racing. He scanned the highway, looking for a way out, a path to safety. "This way!" He gestured with his bat. "Let's head to the overpass!'"

They broke away from the van, abandoning their supplies, their precious cache of guns and ammunition. All except Zero, who clutched his rifle tight to his chest.

Tommy ran, his feet pounding on the asphalt, the others following behind.

Every step sent a jolt of pain through his ankle. But Tommy gritted his teeth, pushed it down.

The zombies stumbled after them.

The overpass loomed ahead, a narrow strip of concrete and metal that stretched out over the highway.

Tommy put on a burst of speed, his lungs burning, his muscles screaming.

He reached the top of the embankment and whirled around, his bat held high.

"This is our best spot to fight," Zero said. "Use the higher ground to our advantage."

Zombies scrambled up the bank towards them.

Tommy swung his bat down, feeling it connect with something solid.

Beside him, Roxy let out a wordless battle cry, her machete slicing through the air, each swing leaving a trail of severed limbs and shattered skulls in its wake.

Zero dropped to one knee, his rifle snapping up to his shoulder. He sighted down the barrel, his eyes narrowing, his breath coming slow and steady.

He squeezed the trigger, the sharp crack of the shot echoing across the overpass.

A zombie's head exploded in a spray of gore, the body crumpling to the ground.

Zero lined up his next shot, his movements calm and methodical.

Laila and Jimbo fought as if in a trance, their weapons rising and falling in a relentless rhythm, tearing through flesh and bone with brutal efficiency.

Tommy lost himself in the fight, his world narrowing to the swing of his bat, the burn of his muscles.

He struck out again and again, each impact jarring up his arms, each zombie that fell only to be replaced by another.

The air was thick with the stench of decay, the coppery tang of blood, the acrid smell of gunpowder.

Sweat poured down Tommy's face, stinging his eyes, but he blinked it away, refusing to let his vision blur, refusing to let his guard down for even a second.

"We need to move!" Tommy shouted, his voice hoarse and ragged. "Back to the highway, now!"

The others didn't hesitate, didn't question. They fell back as one, their weapons still flashing, still cutting through the ranks of the undead.

Tommy brought up the rear, his bat smashing into the faces of any zombies that got too close, buying the others precious seconds to retreat.

They reached the edge of the overpass, the highway stretching out below them.

Tommy risked a glance over his shoulder, saw the horde surging forward, their moans rising.

Ankle throbbing, Tommy forced himself to keep pace with the others, his bat clutched tight in his hand, his eyes scanning the shadows for any sign of movement.

Tommy glanced back as zombies poured off the overpass, their bodies hitting the ground hard.

Some staggered to their feet, their milky eyes fixing on the fleeing survivors, their jaws snapping with mindless hunger.

Tommy half-limped, half-ran until the moans faded into the distance, until the only sound was the pounding of his own blood in his ears.

He stumbled to a halt, his chest heaving, his vision swimming. He looked around at the others. "Is everyone okay?"

Roxy nodded, wiping the sweat from her brow. "Yeah, we're good."

Zero grunted his agreement, his rifle still held at the ready.

Laila and Jimbo leaned against each other, their chests heaving, their faces drawn. But they were alive, and that was all that mattered.

Tommy took a deep breath, forcing himself to stand straight, to push down the pain and the fear and the bone-deep weariness. "Let's get this van back on the road before the dead-heads regroup."

Tommy moved quickly, retracing his steps back towards the wrecked van, his eyes and ears straining for any sign of the horde's return.

As he approached the overturned semi, the crumpled front of the van came into view, wedged against the larger vehicle's undercarriage.

Smoke wafted from the crushed hood, and the windshield was a spiderweb of cracks.

Zero moved ahead, slinging his rifle over his shoulder as he circled the wreck, eyes roving over the damage. He crouched down, peering underneath, his hands probing at the twisted metal.

Tommy watched on, hardly daring to breathe, clinging to a desperate hope that somehow the van could be salvaged.

Zero straightened up and shook his head. "It's no good. Frame's bent to hell, engine's shot. We're not going anywhere in this."

Roxy kicked at a tyre, cursing under her breath.

Laila closed her eyes, her shoulders slumping.

Jimbo just stared.

Tommy looked out over the highway, at the distant city skyline. Philadelphia. It had never seemed so far away, so utterly out of reach.

But what choice did they have?

To stay here was to die.

To go back was unthinkable.

The only path was forward.

Tommy swallowed hard, tasting bile at the back of his throat. He turned to the others. "We need to keep moving, We stick to the plan. We get to Philly, we find my family. We survive. Let's gather what we can, and move out."

The sun dipped lower on the horizon, painting the sky in shades of indigo and violet. Tommy walked at the head of the group, his bat resting on his shoulder, his shotgun strapped to his pack, his eyes constantly scanning the surrounding landscape for threats.

Behind him, the others trudged in silence, the only sounds the scuff of their boots on the asphalt and the occasional whispered word of warning. Fatigue weighed heavy on every face, etched into the lines around their eyes and the tight set of their jaws.

Tommy's own body ached with every step, his muscles begging for rest, his injured ankle throbbing in time with his pulse. But he pushed the pain aside, forced himself to keep moving. They couldn't afford to stop, couldn't risk being caught out in the open after dark.

Roxy, pointed to something in the distance.

Tommy followed her gaze, squinting against the failing light. There, shuffling along the side of the road, was a lone zombie.

He raised a fist, signalling for the others to halt. They clustered together, watching as the creature stumbled closer.

Zero unslung his rifle, bringing it up to his shoulder in one smooth motion. He sighted down the barrel, his finger hovering over the trigger.

The crack of the gunshot made Tommy flinch.

The zombie crumpled, its head snapping back as the bullet found its mark.

No one moved.

Tommy's heart pounded in his ears, his eyes straining to pierce the deepening shadows. But the road remained empty, still.

With a jerk of his head, he motioned for the others to keep moving. They fell back into their weary march.

The light continued to fade as they walked. In the distance, the silhouettes of buildings began to take shape, rising up out of the gathering gloom.

West Chester. The outskirts of the town loomed ahead.

Tommy raised a hand, bringing the group to a halt at the edge of town. They stood in the shadow of an overturned delivery truck.

Tommy peered into the streets ahead, his eyes straining to penetrate the darkness. Abandoned cars sat scattered along the road, their windows smashed, their doors hanging open. He could make out the dim shapes of storefronts and houses, their windows dark and lifeless.

But it was the silence that unnerved him the most. It pressed down on him like a physical weight, thick and oppressive.

Every instinct told him to turn back, to flee. But they had nowhere else to go, no other choice.

Slowly, he stepped out from behind the truck, his bat held low and ready and led the way through the darkened streets, his senses straining for any sign of danger.

Behind him, the others followed in silence. They needed to find shelter, and soon. Somewhere defensible, where they could rest and regroup, plan their next move.

Tommy scanned the buildings around them, looking for anything that might serve. Most were too exposed, too vulnerable to attack. But then, tucked away in a narrow alley, he spotted a shipping container, its metal sides rusted and dented, but still solid. It was half-hidden behind a dumpster, almost invisible in the gloom.

"There. Let's check it out. We might be able to hole up in that for the night."

Zero followed his gaze and gave a nod.

They approached the container, Tommy in the lead.

He tested the doors, found them unlocked.

Slowly, carefully, he eased them open, peering into the dark interior.

It was empty, save for a few scattered pieces of debris. The floor was cold metal, but dry.

He turned back to the others. "Lai, Rox, you two get inside, start setting up camp. Zero, you stand guard. Jimbo, you're with me. We need to check the perimeter, make sure we're secure."

Without a word, Laila and Roxy disappeared into the container, their flashlight beams cutting through the darkness.

He turned to Jimbo, jerking his head towards the alley entrance. "Let's go."

Tommy took the lead, his bat held low, his eyes scanning the shadows.

The alley was narrow, choked with garbage sacks and overturned trashcans. They picked their way through, stepping over broken glass and twisted metal.

At the mouth of the alley, Tommy paused. He peered out into the street, his heart pounding in his chest.

It was empty, the shops and homes dark.

Satisfied they were alone, Tommy turned back to the others. "Okay, let's—"

He froze, the words dying on his lips.

At the far end of the alley, he saw movement.

Two figures, pressed close together, their faces inches apart.

Zero and Roxy. Kissing.

Tommy stared, his mind reeling.

He knew he should look away, should give them their privacy. But he couldn't seem to tear his gaze from the sight, from the way Zero's hands cupped Roxy's butt, the way her fingers tangled in his hair.

It was wrong. It was a betrayal, a knife in Jimbo's back.

He had thought Roxy and Jimbo were together, had seen the way they looked at each other, the casual intimacy of their touches.

But this...this changed everything.

The pair pulled away from each other and slipped into the shipping container.

Tommy stood frozen, his mind still reeling.

"All clear on my end," Jimbo said. "Nothing but empty streets and abandoned cars."

Tommy started, nearly dropping his bat. He turned to face Jimbo, his heart racing.

He opened his mouth, the words on the tip of his tongue. He wanted to tell Jimbo, to warn him about Roxy and Zero.

But as he looked at Jimbo's face, he hesitated.

Was it really his place to say anything? And what would it do to the group's dynamic, to their chances of survival, if he brought this to light now?

Tommy swallowed hard and forced a neutral expression. "Good. That's...that's good."

Jimbo raised an eyebrow. "You okay, dude?"

"I'm fine. Just tired." He gestured towards the shipping container. "We should get inside before anyone spots us out here...or anything."

Tommy sat with his back against the steel wall, his eyes heavy with exhaustion.

Jimbo lay on a bedroll nearby, humming softly to himself. The familiar tune, some old punk song Tommy couldn't quite place.

At the small camp stove, Laila stirred a pot of canned soup, the aroma filling the confined space.

In the corner, Roxy and Zero sat close together as they cleaned their weapons, their heads bent low over their task.

An almost unbearable tension permeated the atmosphere. Tommy felt it pressing down on him, thick and suffocating. He knew a secret that could tear the group apart, and the weight of it sat heavy on his chest.

Every glance, every whispered word, seemed loaded with hidden meaning. He wondered how long they could go on like this before something had to give.

He looked across at Roxy, catching her eye. "Can we talk? Outside?"

Her eyes narrowed, but she stood. "Sure."

He turned on his heel and strode out, not waiting to see if she followed.

The night air raised goosebumps along his arms.

He heard her steps behind him, the scuff of boots on concrete. When she'd caught up, he whirled to face her. "What the hell, Rox?"

She cocked an eyebrow. "What, exactly?"

"You and Zero!" Tommy flung an arm back towards the container. "I saw you two. How could you? What about Jimbo?"

Roxy snorted. "Not that it's any of your business, but Jimbo knows about me and Zero."

Tommy recoiled. "What? That's...Jimbo would never—"

"Oh grow up, Tommy," she snapped. "Did it ever occur to you that maybe, just maybe, I can make my own damn choices about who I'm with? That I don't need or want you moralising about my sex life?"

Tommy gaped at her. "I don't understand. You and Jimbo—"

"Yes! Yes, Jimbo and I are together. And yes, Zero and I are together too. And Jimbo knows, because I don't sneak around or lie to people I care about. We have an understanding, all of us. Not everyone prescribes to your heteronormative, monogamous standards, Tommy."

"That's not...I wasn't..." He shook his head. "You have to know how this looks, Rox. How much it could hurt the group, if things went bad."

"Don't you think I know that? You think any of this is easy for me? For us? But it is what it is, and we're all consenting adults, so I'll thank you to keep your archaic judgements to yourself."

Tommy couldn't formulate a response to that, couldn't seem to kickstart his brain past the roaring tide of conflicting emotions.

"Just because the world ended doesn't mean we all stopped being human, stopped having needs and wants." She stepped closer, jabbed a finger in his chest. "I've fought and bled for this group, over and over, just like the rest of you. My personal life is my business. So you keep your nose out of it, before you do damage you can't undo. We clear?"

Without waiting for his reply, she spun on her heel and stormed back into the container, leaving him alone. He'd overstepped.

Whatever her choices, he owed her more than knee-jerk accusations.

He needed to make this right.

With a grimace and a curse, he walked back to the shipping container. He dreaded the conversation to come. But he couldn't bear the tension, the fractures in their group cohesion.

When Tommy slipped back inside the shipping container, the others were already settling down for the night. The interior was dim, lit only by the faint glow of a small lantern in the corner.

Jimbo lay sprawled on his bedroll, his soft snores filling the small space. In the far corner, Roxy and Zero were huddled together under a shared blanket, their forms indistinct in the shadows.

Laila sat up against the wall, her eyes following Tommy as he entered.

Tommy unfurled his bedroll, his movements slow and deliberate as his mind churned.

He was supposed to be a punk, wasn't he? Open-minded, progressive, challenging societal norms.

Yet here he was, thrown completely off-balance by the concept of polyamory. It hadn't even occurred to him as a possibility.

He glanced towards Roxy and Zero, then back to his bedroll.

Should he try to talk to Roxy again now? Clear the air before morning?

Tensions were still too high. They all needed rest, and he needed time to sort through his own thoughts.

As he lay down, Tommy couldn't help but feel a twinge of shame. He'd acted like the very authority figures he'd always railed against, passing judgement without understanding.

He'd have to make it right, but it could wait until morning.

They had enough to deal with without him stirring up more drama in the middle of the night.

He closed his eyes, willing sleep to come. But his mind continued to race, replaying the conversation with Roxy, examining his own reactions, and wondering how he could mend the rift he'd caused.

It was a long time before sleep claimed him.

Tommy emerged from the shipping container early the next morning, his eyes gritty, his body aching from a night spent on the hard metal floor. He stretched, wincing as his joints popped and his muscles protested.

Around him, the others were stirring, their movements sluggish.

Laila sat hunched against the wall, her knees drawn up to her chest, her gaze distant. Jimbo and Zero were packing up their supplies.

Roxy stood at the far end of the container, her back to him, her shoulders tense.

Tommy swallowed hard, steeling himself.

He had been wrong. Wrong to judge, wrong to lash out, wrong to let his own preconceptions cloud his view of the people who mattered most.

He crossed the container, his footsteps ringing on the metal floor.

Roxy didn't turn, didn't acknowledge his approach, but he saw the way her shoulders stiffened, the way her hands clenched into fists at her sides.

"Roxy. Can we talk?"

She turned to face him, her expression guarded, her eyes wary. "What do you want, Tommy?"

He took a deep breath. "I want to apologise. For last night, for the things I said. I was out of line, and I'm sorry."

She raised an eyebrow. "You're sorry?"

He nodded, swallowing past the lump in his throat. "I am. I let my own hang-ups get in the way of what's really important. And I hurt you in the process."

Roxy was silent for a long moment, her eyes searching his face. "I appreciate that. But I'm never going to apologise for who I am."

"I get that. And I want you to know, I support you. I support all of you, no matter what. We're in this together, and that's all that matters."

A small smile tugged at the corner of Roxy's mouth. "Damn right we are. And we're going to make it through this, Tommy. We're going to find your family, and we're going to build something new. Something better."

He returned her smile, feeling a weight lift from his shoulders. "I know we will."

"Hate to break this up," Zero cut in. "But we need to get moving. If we make good time, we should hit Philly before nightfall."

Tommy nodded, feeling a surge of excitement at the prospect of finally reaching their destination.

As the group bustled around, packing up their meagre supplies, he made his way over to Laila. "Can you believe it? We're almost there."

"Yeah. Great."

Tommy frowned. "What's wrong? Aren't you excited?"

Laila sighed, shaking her head. "What makes you think Philly will be any different from the rest of the country? America has fallen, Tommy. There's nothing left for us."

"That's not true. As long as we've got each other, there's something to live for. We can rebuild, start over."

"I wish I could believe that." She checked her handgun, then secured her tyre iron to her belt and pulled on her pack, "But I've seen too much to buy into false hope."

He wanted to argue, to convince her that things would be better, but the words wouldn't come.

As they filed out of the shipping container and set off on foot towards Philadelphia, the excitement of reaching their goal was overshadowed by a creeping dread, a sense that the worst was yet to come.

13. Lockdown

The grey sky churned overhead as Tommy trudged along the highway, his injured ankle throbbing with each step, but he gritted his teeth and pushed on.

Behind him, Zero, Roxy, and Laila lagged as they checked inside each vehicle they passed.

"Come on, guys," Tommy called over his shoulder. "We need to keep moving."

Zero straightened up from where he'd been rummaging through a battered sedan, his rifle slung across his back. "Slow down, Tommy boy. Rushing past resources isn't going to do us any favours in the long run."

"Resources won't mean anything if we're dead." Tommy stopped, leaning heavily against a rusted-out Chevy, his ankle screaming. "We're losing time. Every second we spend here, we're exposed."

Roxy slammed the trunk of a Honda. "Zero's right. We find a working car, it could cut hours off our travel time. Give your ankle a chance to heal."

"I'll heal when I'm dead. Getting to Philly by nightfall. That's all that matters now."

A distant moan carried on the wind. Shadows moved at the far end of the highway, just beyond the last abandoned car.

Tommy's pulse pounded in his ears, his hand tightening around his bat.

Zero wrenched open the door of a van and cursed, leaping back as a zombie lunged out at him, its jaws snapping. He brought his rifle up, smashing the butt into the creature's face once, twice, until it crumpled.

"This is what I'm talking about," Tommy said. "The dead are everywhere. We can't afford to—"

"Hold up, dudes." Jimbo stepped between them, his hands raised. "Pretty sure we can walk and search at the same time, yeah? Let's motor before we're the blue plate special."

The moans rose.

Tommy risked a glance over his shoulder and immediately wished he hadn't. The horde was close enough now to make out individual faces, rotted and twisted with mindless hunger.

"Truck!" Zero yelled. "It's gassed up and good to go!"

They converged on the pickup, throwing bags of scavenged goods into the rusted bed.

Roxy swung into the passenger seat as Zero slid behind the wheel.

Tommy, Laila, and Jimbo clambered into the back.

"Stay sharp." Tommy hefted his bat. "We're not out of the woods yet."

The engine roared to life. Zero slammed it into gear and stomped the gas. Tyres screeched and smoked as the truck leapt forward, bouncing and rattling over debris, the suspension shrieking.

Tommy clung to the side of the bed, his knuckles white, his injured ankle screaming as the jolts sent agony shooting up to his hip.

"Guys, I..." Tommy swallowed, tasting bile. "I'm sorry. You were right. I shouldn't have pushed so hard."

Laila stared straight ahead, saying nothing.

Jimbo clapped Tommy on the shoulder. "All in the past, dude. We're rolling now. That's what counts."

Tommy nodded, looking back at the receding horde.

But as the first drops of rain began to fall, splattering cold against his skin, he couldn't shake the feeling that their luck was running out. That it was only a matter of time before the death and ruin around them caught up and dragged them down.

He clutched his bat tighter and turned to face the road ahead. Towards Philadelphia. Towards home—or whatever was left of it.

Ten miles. That's all that separated them from Philadelphia now. Ten miles of uncertainty, of not knowing what horrors might await them.

Tommy's grip tightened on his baseball bat, the wood rough against his calloused palms.

Jimbo sidled closer. "How's that ankle holding up, dude?"

Tommy shrugged, wincing at the movement. "I'll live. Got bigger things to worry about."

"True that." Jimbo hesitated, his eyes searching Tommy's face. "You know, I just realised—I haven't seen you take a swig for a few days."

"Huh. Guess I've been too busy to think about it."

Jimbo clapped him on the shoulder, a grin splitting his face. "Proud of you, dude. Kicking the habit in the middle of the apocalypse? That's as punk as it gets."

Tommy glanced down at the 'X' tattoos on his hands and managed a chuckle. "Couldn't have done it without you, man. You've been there for me. That means a lot."

"Always will be."

The road curved ahead, a gentle bend that obscured the path forward.

Zero rounded the corner and cursed.

Zombies. Hundreds of them, a writhing mass of rotting flesh and grasping hands, spilling onto the road.

"Damn it!" Zero slammed the brakes. "Roxy, take the wheel!"

In a blur of motion, Zero stepped out of the cabin as Roxy took the wheel.

He clambered into the back and unslung his rifle, the barrel glinting in the watery sunlight. "Get ready." He took up position at the front of the truck bed as Roxy moved them forward. "This is going to get messy."

Tommy, Jimbo, and Laila fanned out behind him.

The truck bed felt impossibly small, a flimsy scrap of metal between them and the horde.

"Hold on!" Roxy called, her voice barely audible over the roar of the engine.

The truck surged forward, Roxy aiming straight for the heart of the horde.

Tommy's stomach lurched as they ploughed into the mass of bodies, zombies thudding against the grille, bouncing off the hood.

Zero opened fire, his rifle cracking.

Each shot found its mark, zombies crumpling.

The truck shuddered and bucked as it mowed through the horde, the crunch of bones, the squelch of rotten flesh.

Tommy swung his bat in wide arcs, the impact juddering up his arms as he shattered skull after skull.

Beside him, Jimbo's golf club whirled, caving in faces, sending teeth and flesh flying.

Laila's tyre iron flashed in the sun, finding eye sockets, throats, temples.

Tommy fought in grim silence.

Every breath was a gasp, every muscle screamed with exertion.

Roxy held the truck steady as she barrelled forward.

Zombies scrabbled at the doors, their fingernails screeching against the paint.

Zero fired methodically, each shot precise, calculated.

Brass casings clattered at his feet, bright against the blood-slick metal.

He reloaded, never taking his eyes off the road ahead.

As the horde began to thin. Roxy crushed the last few stragglers beneath the tyres, their bodies pulverizing into ruin.

Silence fell, broken only by the panting of the living, the hiss of the engine.

Tommy slumped against the side of the truck, his arms aching, his lungs burning. "Everyone okay? Anyone bit?"

Jimbo and Laila shook their heads. Zero gave a curt nod.

Tommy leaned towards the driver's window. "Rox, that was some damn fine driving." He turned to Zero. "And shooting. You saved our asses back there."

Roxy flashed him a smile in the rearview mirror.

Zero grunted, already scanning the road ahead. "We got lucky. Can't count on that happening again."

Tommy nodded. He tightened his grip on his bat and stared ahead, trying not to think about what awaited them in the city. Trying not to picture Niamh's face, Sean's smile, warped and twisted by the infection.

They were so close now, close enough that he could almost taste the acrid tang of home on the back of his tongue. But with each passing mile, each ragged breath, he couldn't escape the sinking realisation that it might already be too late.

Tommy closed his eyes, letting the rumble of the engine, the rush of wind, drown out his spiralling thoughts.

Beside him, Jimbo started humming under his breath, a familiar tune that cut through the gloom.

Tommy recognised it instantly—'I Fought the Law' by The Clash.

One by one, the others joined in, their voices ragged but defiant, a chorus against the endless drone of the dead.

And as he added his own voice to the mix, Tommy felt something flicker to life in his chest, fragile but fierce. Something that felt almost like hope.

Punk's not dead, Tommy thought, a grim smile tugging at his lips.

Not yet.

The skyline of Philadelphia loomed on the horizon, a jagged silhouette against the dying light.

They were so close now, so close to the city that held everything he'd been fighting for.

Roxy guided the pickup truck along the deserted thoroughfare. In the back, Tommy, Laila, Zero, and Jimbo remained on high alert, their weapons at the ready, scanning the surroundings for any sign of threat.

As they drew closer to the city, military checkpoints dotted the road, abandoned now, the barriers left open.

Banners fluttered in the breeze, their stark lettering announcing quarantine zones, warning of the danger that lay ahead.

Tommy leaned against the side of the truck, his gaze drawn to the stillness that had settled over the city. It was as if all life had been sucked out, leaving only a husk behind.

"Heads up," Zero called, pointing to a sprawling complex off to the side of the road. "FEMA camp, two o'clock."

Tommy followed his gaze, taking in the high chain-link fences, the military barricades that surrounded the encampment. It looked as though it had been abandoned in a hurry, tents torn and flapping in the wind, supplies scattered across the ground.

"Looks like it got overrun," Jimbo said. "Zombies or looters, take your pick."

Zero shook his head, his lips twisting in a sneer. "Probably some Globalist ploy to round up survivors."

Tommy frowned, turning to him. "What are you talking about?"

"Think about it, Tommy boy. There's more going on here than meets the eye." "Look." Zero pointed to a nearby lamppost, where the shattered remains of a surveillance camera hung. "See that? And there, on that building. Drones, military grade."

Tommy followed his gaze towards the sleek, black shapes perched on the rooftops. "What the hell?"

"Globalists," Zero spat. "They've been watching us, tracking us. This whole thing, the outbreak, the quarantine—it's all part of their plan. They engineered the virus, unleashed it on the population. And now they're using it to control us, to herd us like sheep."

High chain-link fences topped with razor wire came into view, encircling the entire city. Watchtowers loomed at regular intervals.

Roxy slowed the pickup truck as they neared a heavily fortified checkpoint. Concrete barriers and sandbags formed a narrowing path.

"This doesn't look good," Laila said.

Tommy leaned forward, squinting at the soldiers manning the checkpoint. They were clad in full riot gear, their faces hidden behind gas masks and visors.

Roxy brought the truck to a stop as a soldier stepped forward, his hand raised. "State your business," he said, his voice muffled by his mask.

Tommy swallowed hard. "We're trying to get into the city. I have family there, my girlfriend and my son. I need to find them."

The soldier shook his head. "No one in or out. The city's under strict quarantine until the outbreak is contained."

"Please. You have to let us through. I'm a resident, I have a home there."

"Until the infection is cleared, Philadelphia is off-limits to new arrivals. No exceptions."

"And how long is that going to take, huh? Weeks? Months? You can't just keep us out of our own city!"

The soldier's grip tightened on his rifle. "That's not my call to make. But I have my orders. No one crosses this checkpoint without express military authorisation. Turn your vehicle around and leave the area immediately."

Zero surged forward. "I knew it! This is all part of their plan, isn't it? The Globalists, the New World Order. They engineered this whole thing, released the virus on purpose so they could lock us all down, control us like sheep!"

The soldiers tensed, their weapons snapping up to aim at Zero. "Sir, I'm going to need you to calm down and step back into the vehicle."

Tommy grabbed Zero's arm, hauling him back. "Are you trying to get us shot? Now's not the time."

Zero shrugged him off, still glaring at the soldiers.

"Zero," Roxy called. "Come on. Don't fall for their trap."

Zero looked between Roxy and the soldiers then allowed Tommy to steer him back onto the truck.

Tommy turned back to the lead soldier, his hands raised in a placating gesture. "I'm sorry about my friend. He's just stressed, we all are. But please, there must be some way you can help us. Some way we can get into the city to look for my family."

The soldier's stance seemed to soften. But then he shook his head. "I'm sorry. But orders are orders. No outside civilians allowed past this point."

Tommy's shoulders slumped. They were so close, so damn close to where he needed to be. But it might as well have been a million miles away, with the military blockade standing in their path.

"Come on, T," Roxy said. "We're not going to get anywhere here."

Tommy took a shuddering breath, the fight draining out of him. She was right. Trying to force their way through would only end in disaster.

They needed to find another way into the city.

With a last, lingering look at the barricades, Tommy nodded to Roxy and climbed into the back.

Roxy put the pickup in reverse, backing away from the checkpoint.

As they retreated, Tommy couldn't tear his gaze from the skyline of Philadelphia. Somewhere beyond those fences, beyond the soldiers, Niamh and Sean were waiting for him.

Tommy shook his head, forcing himself to focus. "Okay, so how do we get inside?"

"We need to find a way past their perimeter without drawing the Globalists' attention," Zero said.

"Pull over up here." Tommy gestured to a side street. "We need a plan."

Roxy guided the truck to a stop, killing the engine.

For a moment, they sat in silence.

"Gather everything we can carry," Zero said. "Make sure our weapons are in working order. "

They set to work, dividing up the remaining food and water, checking their guns and melee weapons.

As they worked, Tommy felt a sense of grim determination settling over him. This was it, the final push. They were going to make it into the city, find his family, and get the hell out of there. No matter what it took.

When they were as ready as they could be, Tommy gathered them around, looking each of them in the eye. "Listen up. What we're about to do, it's not going to be easy. We're walking into a city that might be crawling with soldiers and who knows what else. But we're going to stick together, watch each other's backs."

There was a moment of silence, broken only by the distant groans of the undead.

Roxy stepped forward, her hand outstretched.

One by one, the others joined her, their hands coming together in a tight circle.

Tommy looked around at their faces, these people who had become his family, his reason for fighting. "Are we ready?"

The others nodded.

Shadows stretched across the abandoned streets, the darkness broken only by the faint glow of the moon and the occasional flicker of a distant fire.

The perimeter fence loomed before them. Watchtowers stood at intervals along the barrier.

Zero unslung his rifle, peering through the scope. "Looks like these towers are unmanned. But that doesn't mean they're not watching."

Tommy nodded. "We need to find a way in that doesn't take us through the main checkpoints. Somewhere less guarded."

"Over there." Laila pointed to a section of the fence that was partially obscured by overgrown vegetation and piles of debris. "Utility tunnels. They might lead under the fence."

Zero grunted. "Let's check it out."

Tommy crept closer, keeping low to the ground, his senses straining. As he drew near, rusted grates came into view, half-hidden by the undergrowth.

He and Laila set to work clearing the entrance, pulling away the tangled vines and shifting the rubble as quietly as they could.

The others kept watch, their weapons at the ready, their eyes scanning the shadows.

With a final heave, Tommy managed to wrench one of the grates open, revealing a narrow, dark passage that disappeared into the earth.

He shone his flashlight into the opening, the beam revealing a cramped tunnel lined with pipes and cables. "Looks clear. But we'll need to keep the light low. Don't want to attract any attention."

One by one, they lowered themselves into the tunnel, the damp air and the close press of the walls doing little to calm his nerves.

He took a steadying breath, forcing down the rising tide of claustrophobia that threatened to choke him.

"Watch your step. And stay close."

Tommy took point with Zero bringing up the rear.

The only sounds were the soft scuff of their footsteps and the occasional drip of water from the pipes overhead.

The tunnel seemed to stretch on forever, a labyrinth of twists and turns that made Tommy's head spin.

The air grew thicker, more oppressive with every step, the musty stench of mould and decay filling his nostrils.

Behind him, Laila's breathing grew quick and shallow.

Tommy reached out, giving her shoulder a squeeze. "We're gonna be okay. Just a little further."

Zero held up a hand, bringing them to a halt. He cocked his head, listening intently. "You hear that?"

Tommy strained his ears, trying to pick out any sound over the pounding in his skull. And then he heard it—a soft, rhythmic thumping, like footsteps on the ground above.

"Someone's up there," Roxy said.

"Or something," Jimbo said.

Tommy stood frozen, hardly daring to breathe as the footsteps drew closer, the thumping growing louder and more distinct.

Tommy's mind raced, imagining the worst—a patrol of soldiers, a horde of zombies, some new horror they hadn't yet encountered.

But then the sound faded away, receding into the distance until it was swallowed by the silence.

Zero let out a slow breath.

Tommy pressed on, moving faster now, driven by a growing sense of urgency.

The tunnel began to slope upward, the air growing fresher, tinged with the faint scent of smoke and.

Up ahead, Tommy's torch beam illuminated a rusted metal hatch. "That must be our way out."

They gathered around the hatch, Zero and Jimbo working to pry it open with the blade of Roxy's machete.

It resisted at first, the hinges stubborn.

But then, with a screech of metal, it gave way, swinging upward to reveal a small, dark room.

Tommy found himself in what appeared to be the basement of an abandoned building, the walls lined with shelves of dusty boxes and crates.

He moved to a small window set high in the wall, peering out at the street beyond. His breath caught in his throat.

The city was pockmarked with scars of violence.

The dead wandered, their bodies twisted and rotting, their faces slack and empty.

"So much for a quarantine zone," Jimbo said.

Zero sniffed. "Just like everywhere else."

Tommy didn't answer, his gaze fixed on the desolation outside.

Niamh, Sean—they were out there. They had to be.

"Are we inside?" Roxy asked.

Tommy nodded. "Looks that way."

"I think I know where we are," Laila said. "We shouldn't be too far from the Bell Telephone Exchange."

Tommy turned back to the others. "We need to keep moving. Stick to the shadows, avoid the main streets." He took a deep breath. "Let's go."

Tommy crept through the shadowed streets, his heart pounding in his chest, his every sense strained to the breaking point. Behind him, the others followed in a tight formation, their weapons held at the ready.

They moved like ghosts, flitting from cover to cover, using the gutted cars and crumbling walls to shield them from view.

Tommy led the way, his hand signals sharp and precise as he guided them through the city.

Windows gaped, their jagged edges glinting in the moonlight. Graffiti sprawled across every surface, the spray-painted words a jumbled mix of desperation and defiance. Distant gunfire echoed through the streets.

Tommy's gaze flicked from building to building, searching for any sign of movement, any hint of danger.

They were still a long way from the neighbourhoods where he and Laila had grown up, the places where their families had made their homes. But with every step, every breathless dash across an exposed intersection, they were getting closer.

As they turned a corner, Tommy threw up a hand, bringing the group to a sudden halt.

A military patrol was engaging a small knot of zombies, their rifles firing in short, controlled bursts.

Tommy crouched low, watching from the shadows as the soldiers made short work of the undead.

They moved with a grim efficiency, their fire disciplined.

In a matter of moments, the zombies were down, their bodies still on the blood-slicked ground.

The soldiers moved in, dragging the corpses onto the back of a waiting truck with a practiced ease. As they worked, Tommy heard snatches of their muffled conversation, the words distorted by their gas masks.

"...another sector clear...rendezvous at base...maintain quarantine..."

Then, the soldiers were gone, the truck rumbling away into the darkness.

Tommy turned to Zero. "See? They're trying to protect what's left of the city, not control it. They're doing their job, keeping people safe."

Zero shook his head, his eyes hard. "You're naive, Tommy boy. This is all part of their plan. The Globalists, the New World Order. They wanted control, and now it's all spiralling out of their grasp."

Tommy frowned, but he pushed his retort down, forcing himself to focus on the task at hand. They couldn't afford distractions, not now. Not when they were so close.

He signalled for the others to move out, and they slipped back into the shadows, picking their way through the ruins of the city.

Niamh. Sean. His family. They were so close.

Tommy's grip tightened on his bat, his eyes darting from doorway to alley, searching for any hint of movement.

Every step was a battle against the fear that clawed at his throat, the dread that coiled in his gut.

As they approached an intersection, Tommy held up a hand.

He peered around the corner, his breath catching in his throat at the sight of the empty street beyond.

He turned back to the group. "Looks clear. Zero, you're on point. Then Roxy, Jimbo, and Laila. I'll bring up the rear."

Zero nodded, his face grim. He hefted his rifle and darted out into the street, his footsteps echoing in the stillness. Roxy followed a heartbeat later, then Jimbo, and Laila.

Tommy took a deep breath, his grip tightening on his bat. He stepped out from the shelter of the buildings, every muscle tensed, every nerve singing.

A guttural moan ripped through the air.

Zombies poured from the alleyways, their rotting faces contorted in snarls of hunger.

Tommy shouted a warning, but it was too late. The zombies were on them, a tide of grasping hands and snapping teeth.

He swung his bat hard, feeling it connect with yielding flesh, the wet crunch of shattered bone.

Roxy hacked with her machete as Jimbo's golf club caved in skulls with every blow.

The zombies kept coming, an endless wave of putrid flesh. They pressed in from all sides, their sheer numbers threatening to overwhelm them.

Tommy fought with a savage intensity, his every blow fuelled by the desperate need to survive, to protect his friends, to reach his family.

A scream pierced the night.

Tommy whirled just in time to see Zero go down under a crush of zombies.

Zero flailed and thrashed, his rifle knocked from his grasp.

With a roar of fury, Tommy charged into the fray, his bat swinging.

Hands clawed at him, teeth snapping at his flesh, but he ignored them, his focus narrowed to Zero.

Roxy was there beside him, slashing with a berserker's fury.

Together, they tore the zombies away from Zero.

Jimbo and Laila fought their way to their side.

The last zombie fell, its skull pulped by a vicious blow from Tommy's bat.

Zero lay on the ground, his chest heaving, his face slick with sweat and gore.

Tommy dropped to his knees beside him, his hands shaking as he checked for bites.

"I'm alright. Just got the wind knocked out of me."

Tommy sagged, his head falling forward as the adrenaline drained from his system. "Jesus, Zero. I thought..."

Zero managed a weak chuckle, his hand finding Tommy's shoulder and gripping it tight. "Sorry, Tommy boy. Guess I got a little careless there."

Tommy shook his head, a mirthless smile tugging at his lips. "Yeah, well. Don't let it happen again. I don't want to have to explain to the others why I had to put a bullet in your brain."

Zero sobered. "You'd do it, though. If it came to that?"

Tommy met his gaze. "Let's hope it never comes to that." He stood, offering Zero a hand and hauling him to his feet.

The others gathered around, their faces drawn and ashen.

"We need to keep moving," Tommy said. "This way."

The first hints of dawn crept across the city as Tommy and the others approached the apartment block that had once been his home.

He moved slowly, his steps heavy with exhaustion, his eyes raw from the long night of fighting and running.

The building looked much the same as he remembered, the red brick facade weathered but intact, the windows dark and still.

He glanced behind him, the others trudging in silence, their weapons held at the ready, their eyes scanning the shadows.

They had been through hell together, had fought and bled and nearly died more times than Tommy could count. But now, in the face of this final destination, they seemed to draw into themselves, each lost in their own thoughts, their own fears.

As he approached the building, Tommy held up a hand, bringing the group to a halt. He scanned the area, his eyes searching for any hint of movement.

But the street was deserted, silent.

Tommy took a deep breath, steeling himself.

Then, with a jerk of his head, he led the way up the steps, his heart pounding in his ears with every footfall.

He fished inside his jacket, took out his key, and unlocked the door.

The lobby was dark and silent. Tommy paused on the threshold, his hand trembling as it brushed against the cool metal of the door frame.

How many times had he passed through this door, coming home from a gig or a practice session, his mind buzzing with new riffs and lyrics?

How many times had he bounded up these stairs, eager to see Niamh's smile, to hear Sean's laughter?

It all seemed like a lifetime ago now, a dream from another world. A world where the dead stayed dead and the living didn't have to fight tooth and nail just to see another sunrise.

He forced himself to take a step, then another, his boots echoing on the scuffed tiles.

The others followed.

No one said a word.

But there was no sign of danger, no hint of the horrors that had consumed the world outside.

The mailboxes stood lined up against one wall, the potted spider plants still green and thriving.

It was as if the apocalypse had never touched this place, as if the last remnants of Tommy's old life had been preserved, waiting for him to return.

He turned to the others. "My apartment's on the third floor. 33. That's where they'll be. If they're..." He refused to give voice to the fear that had haunted him since the day he left Berkeley.

The fear that he would come home to find an empty apartment, a bloodstained floor.

The fear that his family had been taken from him, just like everything else.

Laila stepped forward, her hand finding his in the gloom. "We're with you, Tommy. No matter what we find up there. We're with you to the end."

The others murmured their agreement.

Tommy nodded, his throat tight. He squeezed Laila's hand, drawing strength from her warmth.

Then, with a deep breath, he started up the stairs, the others falling into step behind him.

Every footfall seemed to echo in the stillness, each creak of the floorboards a gunshot in the silence.

Tommy's heart raced as they climbed, his palms slick with sweat on the worn wooden railing, the pain in his ankle driving him forward.

This was it. The moment he had been fighting for, the goal that had driven him across a thousand miles of zombie-infested wasteland. The moment when he would finally learn the truth, finally find out if his family had survived the end of the world.

He paused outside the door to 33, hands trembling as he fumbled with his key.

Tommy closed his eyes, his mind filling with memories. Niamh's laugh, the way her eyes crinkled at the corners when she smiled. Sean's chubby hands reaching for him.

But now, standing on the precipice of the truth, he was terrified of what he might find. Terrified that those memories might be all he had left.

He forced himself to take a breath, to steady his racing heart. He turned the key and pushed the door open, stepping into the unknown.

14. The Leaving Song

Tommy stepped into the apartment, his breath catching in his throat.

He stood there for a moment, his eyes scanning the familiar space, taking in every detail. The worn sofa where he and Niamh had cuddled on lazy Sunday mornings, the bookshelf filled with Sean's favourite bedtime stories, the faded band posters on the walls.

It was all just as he remembered it, untouched by the chaos and destruction that had consumed the world outside.

"Niamh?" His voice was hoarse, barely above a whisper. "Sean? Are you here?"

Silence.

He took a step forward, then another, his boots scuffing on the worn carpet.

"Niamh, please. If you're here, if you can hear me, answer me. Please..." His voice broke on the last word, a sob welling up in his throat.

He moved through the apartment in a daze, his fingers trailing over the familiar surfaces, the memories threatening to overwhelm him.

Sean's room was just as he had left it, the bed neatly made, the stuffed animals arranged on the pillow.

Tommy picked up a small teddy bear, its fur worn and matted from countless cuddles. He held it to his chest, inhaling the faint scent of his son, the tears flowing freely now.

There was no sign of a struggle, no indication that anything bad had happened here. But there was also no sign of life, no hint of where his family might have gone or what might have happened to them.

The uncertainty was worse than anything, the not knowing. It ate at him like acid, corroding his hope with every passing moment.

He sank to the floor, his back against the wall, the teddy bear clutched to his chest. The sobs wracked his body.

He had come so far, had fought so hard to get back to them. And now, to find nothing, to be left with only questions and fears and the aching, empty hole in his heart...it was more than he could bear.

"Tommy?"

He looked up, his vision blurred with tears. Jimbo stood in the doorway.

"They're not here. I don't...I don't know where they are."

Jimbo crossed the room, sinking down to sit beside him. He put an arm around Tommy's shoulders. "Listen to me. We don't know anything yet, okay? Just because they're not here doesn't mean...it doesn't mean the worst."

Tommy shook his head, his throat tight. "But what if it does? What if they're gone, Jimbo? What if I've lost them forever?"

"You can't think like that, dude. Look how far you've come, everything you've been through to get here. You can't give up now, not when we're so close."

Tommy looked at him, his eyes searching Jimbo's face for some kind of answer, some kind of hope. "I don't know what to do. Where to go. This was it. This was supposed to be it."

Jimbo squeezed his shoulder. "So we keep looking. We knock on doors, we call on friends. We do whatever it takes to track them down."

Tommy hesitated. "I can't...I can't leave. What if they come back and I'm not here? What if I miss them?"

"So we leave a note. Tell them where you've gone, that you're gonna be back. And we come back, every day if we have to, until they turn up."

Tommy took a shuddering breath, his mind racing. Jimbo was right. He couldn't give up, not now. Not after everything he had been through, everything he had sacrificed to get here.

Slowly, painfully, he got to his feet. He set the teddy bear on Sean's bed, his fingers lingering on the soft fur for a moment.

He moved to the kitchen, rummaging through the drawers until he found a pad of paper and a pen. He scribbled a hasty note, his hand shaking slightly as he poured his heart onto the page.

Niamh, Sean.

I'm alive. I'm here. I've been fighting my way across the country to get back to you. If you see this, please, please wait for me. I'll come back, every day, until I see you again.

I love you both, more than anything.

Tommy.

He left the note on the kitchen table, propped up against the salt and pepper shakers. It looked small and insignificant against the expanse of the wooden surface, but it was the best he could do.

He took one last look around the apartment, committing every detail to memory. The scuffed flooring, the faded curtains, the framed photos on the walls.

This had been his home, his sanctuary. And even if Niamh and Sean weren't here now, even if he didn't know where they were or what had happened to them, he had to believe that they would find their way back. That they would be a family again.

Tommy stepped into his and Niamh's bedroom and rummaged through the closet, his fingers brushing against the familiar fabrics of his old clothes. He pulled out a few t-shirts and pairs of jeans.

He turned to the others, who were gathered in the living room, sorting through their supplies. "Anyone want a change of clothes? I've got plenty here."

Zero and Roxy looked up, their faces brightening. "Hell yes," Roxy said, pushing herself to her feet. "I feel like I've been wearing these rags for a decade."

Jimbo chuckled, shaking his head. "Nah, dude. Thanks, but I don't think your skinny jeans would fit over my muscular thighs."

Tommy cracked a smile. He tossed a bundle of clothes to Zero, watching as he sorted through the offerings.

He held up a black t-shirt, the logo of Zero's band, Anarchy's Child, emblazoned across the front. "Hey, Zero. How about this?"

Zero took the shirt, his eyebrows raising. "You're actually a fan?"

Tommy shrugged. "What can I say? I saw you a couple of years back here in Philly."

Zero barked out a laugh, shaking his head. "Man, the idea of you moshing to our tunes...that's just too good." As Zero stripped off his blood-stained shirt, Tommy noticed a wicked-looking scratch running down the length of his forearm. The skin around it was red and inflamed, the edges of the wound ragged and torn.

"Whoa, what happened there?"

Zero glanced down at his arm, his brow furrowing. "Must have caught it on something when I fell during that last fight. It's no big deal."

Jimbo appeared at Zero's side, a first-aid kit in his hands. "Let me take a look at that, dude. We can't afford to let anything get infected."

Zero sighed but held out his arm, allowing Jimbo to clean the wound with antiseptic wipes.

"I don't like the look of this, Zee. It's deep, and the edges...they're not clean. Almost like..."

"Like what?" Tommy asked.

Jimbo met his gaze. "Like a zombie scratch."

Zero yanked his arm away, his face twisting. "No way, man. No freaking way. I would know if one of those things got me. I'm fine."

Tommy held up his hands. "Okay, let's just...let's not jump to conclusions. We'll keep an eye on it, make sure it doesn't get any worse."

Zero grumbled but allowed Jimbo to bandage the wound.

Tommy turned away, his mind racing.

He grabbed a bundle of Niamh's clothes, the soft fabrics feeling strange in his hands. He approached Roxy, holding them out to her. "Here. These should fit you."

Roxy took the clothes, her eyes softening as she ran her fingers over the material. "Thanks. Appreciate it."

Tommy nodded, swallowing past the sudden lump in his throat. It felt wrong, somehow, to be giving away Niamh's things. Like he was betraying her, erasing her presence from their home.

But it was necessary. Roxy needed the clothes more than the empty closet did.

He turned to Laila, who was sitting on the couch, checking her handgun. "Lai? You want anything?"

Laila shook her head, her gaze distant. "No point."

"It's fine."

"My place isn't too far from here."

Tommy nodded. He had been so focused on his own family, his own desperate search, that he had almost forgotten that Laila had people waiting for her too. Parents she loved, parents she was fighting to get back to.

As the others finished changing and gathering their supplies, Tommy took a deep breath, steeling himself for what came next.

Tommy led the way through the empty corridors of his apartment block. Behind him, the others followed.

They had started at the top floor, working their way down, knocking on each door, calling out to anyone who might be inside.

But every apartment was locked, every knock met with silence.

Tommy tried not to think about what might have happened to the residents, tried to focus on the task at hand. But with each empty apartment, each unanswered call, he could feel the hope draining out of him, replaced by a cold, creeping dread.

They reached the ground floor, the last of the doors yielding nothing.

Tommy stood in the lobby, his bat hanging at his side, staring at nothing. "They're not here. None of them. It's like the whole block just...disappeared."

Roxy laid a hand on his shoulder. "We keep looking. We check the other buildings, the houses nearby. Someone has to know something."

Tommy nodded and exited the apartment block, stepping out into the deserted street.

They moved from door to door, knocking, calling out.

But just like in the apartment block, there was no answer, no sign of life.

Laila's shoulders slumped as she sidled up to Tommy. "I just want to go home."

Tommy nodded slowly. "Okay, let's head to your place, Lai. Maybe we'll have better luck there."

They set off through the city, navigating the maze of deserted streets and abandoned buildings.

The silence pressed down on them, broken only by the occasional moan of a distant zombie.

As they walked, Tommy spotted a familiar house, the home of an old friend. He veered off course, bounding up to the front door.

He knocked.

But there was no answer.

He peered through the windows.

But inside, there was only darkness, the rooms empty and still.

Zero appeared at his side. "Haven't seen a soul except soldiers and dead-heads. Starting to think there's no one left in this whole damn city."

A zombie shambled into view at the end of the block, its movements jerky and uncoordinated.

Tommy tensed, his hand tightening on his bat. But the creature was too far away to pose an immediate threat. "Let's keep moving before more of those things turn up."

"Maybe the quarantine zone's to keep people out, not in," Jimbo said. "Maybe there's some sort of safe zone, and everyone's holed up somewhere, waiting for the all-clear."

Zero shook his head. "Or maybe they were all rounded up and taken to that deserted FEMA camp we saw. Herded like cattle, for God knows what purpose."

"There could be another camp," Roxy said. "I mean, not all FEMA setups would be abandoned, right? Maybe we should try talking to the soldiers, see if they know anything."

Zero scoffed, his lip curling in a sneer. "Right, because we totally didn't just sneak into this city illegally. I'm sure the soldiers will be thrilled to welcome us with open arms."

"We don't really know anything, do we?" Tommy said. "We've been out on the road, cut off from everything. Maybe Roxy and Jimbo are right. Maybe we're just looking in the wrong places."

"Can we keep going?" Laila asked. "I just want to go home."

Tommy nodded. "We'll get to your place, and we'll figure out our next move."

The group moved through the deserted streets, deep into the morning.

Tommy led the way, his bat held loosely at his side, his eyes scanning the alleys and windows for any sign of movement.

As they skirted the edge of a small park, a rasping moan drifted on the breeze.

Tommy froze, the hair on the back of his neck standing up. He held up a clenched fist, signalling the others to stop.

Shambling between the gnarled trunks and overgrown bushes, a small group of zombies lurched into view.

Tommy's grip tightened on his bat, his breath coming hard and fast.

With a jerk of his head, he motioned for them to fan out, to surround the undead before they could be surrounded themselves.

They moved quickly, Zero and Roxy breaking left while Jimbo and Tommy went right. Laila hung back, her tyre iron held loosely at her side.

The zombies turned towards Tommy and the others, their jaws slack and snapping.

With a roar, Tommy charged forward, his bat whistling through the air. It connected with the lead zombie's skull.

Beside him, Jimbo swung his golf club in a vicious arc, the heavy end pulping a zombie's face into a mess of gore and shattered teeth.

Across the clearing, Roxy's machete sliced through decaying flesh and muscle, severing limbs and heads with each devastating blow.

Zero took shots, his bullets ripping through heads and shoulders.

Tommy found himself surrounded, rotten hands grasping at his clothes. He lashed out, his bat connecting with yielding bodies.

A cry of pain off to his right.

Jimbo, his arm caught in a zombie's grip, its jaws stretching wide.

Tommy pivoted, swinging his bat, caving in the creature's skull.

Jimbo staggered back, clutching his arm.

Tommy had no time to check on him—more zombies were closing in, their moans rising.

He risked a glance towards Laila, saw her standing motionless at the edge of the clearing.

A zombie stumbled towards her, its grasping fingers inches from her face.

Tommy opened his mouth to shout a warning, but Roxy was there, her machete cleaving the zombie's head from its shoulders.

Another shot rang out and the last zombie fell.

Tommy stood amidst the carnage, his bat dripping with black ichor, his heart slamming against his ribs.

He looked around at the others, checking for injuries, for bites.

Jimbo was pale and shaken, but unharmed.

Roxy and Zero were splashed with blood and brains, but their eyes were clear, their movements steady.

And Laila still stood apart, her face blank, her eyes distant.

Tommy stormed over to her, his jaw clenched. "What the hell, Lai? Why didn't you help? You could have been killed, standing there like that!"

She looked up at him. "I just want to go home. I'm so tired, Tommy. So goddamn tired of all this."

Tommy opened his mouth to argue, but the words died on his tongue as he saw the depth of pain in her eyes, the utter hopelessness.

He reached out, gripped her shoulder. "I know. I know you're hurting. We all are. But we can't give up. We have to keep fighting, keep going."

Laila said nothing, just stared at him with those haunted eyes.

Tommy swallowed hard, trying to push down the fear that clawed at his throat, the sinking feeling that he was losing her, that she was slipping away into some dark place he couldn't follow.

He turned away, blinking back the sudden sting of tears.

Zero leaned heavily against a tree, his face pale and slick with sweat.

"You okay, man?"

Zero pushed himself to stand and nodded. "I'm good."

Tommy nodded.

They set off again, picking their way through the city.

Finally, they turned onto Laila's street, the neat rows of houses standing empty.

Tommy felt a pang of unease as they made their way up the driveway, the gravel crunching beneath their feet.

Laila paused at the front door, her hand resting on the knob. She turned to face the others. "I need to do this alone. Please."

"Okay," Tommy said. "We'll be right out here if you need us."

Laila nodded. "Thanks, Tommy."

Then she turned and disappeared into the house, the door clicking shut behind her.

Tommy and the others took up positions around the yard, their weapons held at the ready.

He glanced over at Zero, who was leaning against the porch railing, his head bowed. "Hey man, you okay?"

Zero looked up, his face ashen. He opened his mouth to reply, but before he could speak, a gunshot rang out from inside the house.

Tommy stood frozen, unable to comprehend what he had just heard.

Then he was moving, sprinting towards the door.

He crashed through the entrance, his bat raised, ready to face whatever horrors lay within.

"Laila! Laila, where are you?"

He moved through the house, checking each room. The kitchen, the dining room, the bathroom...all empty, all still.

And then he reached her bedroom.

He paused in the doorway, blinking.

Laila lay on the bed, her eyes staring sightlessly at the ceiling. A pistol dangled from her limp fingers, a neat hole in her temple.

Tommy felt his knees give out, felt himself sinking to the floor.

A scream tore from his throat, a wordless cry of anguish and despair.

Laila was dead.

He had failed her. He had failed his friend, his sister in arms.

He should have seen the signs, should have known how close to the edge she was.

But he had been too wrapped up in his own pain, his own desperate quest to find his family.

And now she was gone, lost to the darkness that had consumed so many.

He felt arms around him, hands pulling him to his feet.

He blinked through the tears, saw Roxy's face, Jimbo's.

They led him out of the room, out of the house.

He stumbled blindly, his mind reeling, his heart shattered.

They gathered in the back yard, huddled together.

No one spoke.

Tommy looked around at their faces, saw the same pain, the same guilt he felt reflected back at him.

They had all failed her, all been too caught up in their own struggles to see how much she was hurting.

"I'm sorry," he whispered, the words tearing at his throat. "I'm so Goddamn sorry."

Roxy shook her head, her face streaked with tears. "It's not your fault, Tommy. It's not any of our faults. We couldn't have known...couldn't have stopped her."

But even as she spoke, Tommy saw the doubt in her eyes.

Could they have done more?

Could they have saved her, if only they had paid closer attention, if only they had been there for her when she needed them most?

He would never know. And that, perhaps, was the cruellest thing of all. The not knowing, the endless cycle of what-ifs and might-have-beens.

They stood there in silence, united in their grief, their loss.

They couldn't let Laila's death be in vain, couldn't let the darkness win.

The afternoon sun hung low in the sky, casting long shadows across the yard.

Tommy felt numb, his mind reeling with shock and grief.

Laila was gone. And he had been powerless to stop it.

He shook his head, forcing himself to focus on the task at hand. They couldn't leave her like this, couldn't just walk away and let the undead claim her body.

She deserved better than that. They all did.

"We need to find a shovel. Something to...to dig with."

Jimbo nodded, his face grim. "I think I saw a garage around the front. There might be some tools in there."

They made their way to the garage, the gravel crunching beneath their feet.

Inside, they found a shovel and a spade, the metal blades dull with rust.

Tommy took the shovel, his hands shaking as he gripped the wooden handle. He led the way back to the yard, to a spot beneath the tree that Laila had once told him was her favourite place to sit and think.

They began to dig, the scrape of metal biting into earth.

Tommy worked mechanically, his body operating on autopilot, as if he watched himself at a distance.

Beside him, Roxy and Jimbo took turns, their faces streaked with sweat and tears.

Zero stood watch, his rifle held at the ready, his eyes scanning the street. But the neighbourhood remained quiet.

As he dug, Tommy couldn't shake the guilt that gnawed at his gut. He should have seen the signs, should have known, should have stopped her.

He thought back to all the times she had been there for him, all the moments of laughter and tears they had shared.

She had been his rock, his best friend, his confidante, the one person who understood him better than anyone else.

And now she was gone, and he would never have the chance to tell her how much she meant to him.

The hole grew deeper, the pile of dirt beside it rising.

Finally, it was done, a neat rectangle cut into the earth.

They returned to the house, to the bedroom where Laila lay.

Tommy couldn't bring himself to look at her, couldn't bear to see the ruin of her once-vibrant face.

He helped the others wrap her in a blanket, his hands trembling as he tucked the fabric around her still form.

They carried her out into the yard, laying her gently in the grave.

Tommy knelt beside her, his vision blurring with tears.

This was too much. Too damn much.

"I'm sorry. I'm so sorry, Lai. I should have been there for you. I should have...I could have stopped this."

Jimbo laid a hand on his shoulder, his grip firm. "It's not on you, dude. She was fighting a battle none of us could see. PTSD, it...it screws you up in ways you can't imagine."

Roxy nodded. "We're all fighting our own demons, Tommy. Sometimes, it's just...too much."

They had all been through hell, had all seen and done things that would haunt them for the rest of their lives.

Tommy cleared his throat, forcing himself to stand, forcing himself to speak. "Laila was...she was the strongest person I knew. She brought so much light into our lives. She was my friend, my sister...and I'll never forget her."

Roxy stepped forward and began to sing the words to 'The Leaving Song' by AFI.

As she sang, Jimbo bowed his head, his shoulders shaking with silent sobs. Zero stood rigid, his face a mask, his eyes fixed on some distant point.

When the song was finished, they stood in silence for a long time, each saying their own private goodbyes to the friend they had lost.

Finally, Tommy picked up the shovel, his hands shaking as he began to fill in the grave.

The others joined him, working together to put Laila to rest.

When it was done, they returned to the house.

Tommy couldn't shake the feeling of emptiness, the sense that something vital had been ripped away from him.

As they gathered their belongings, preparing to leave, Jimbo called out from the kitchen.

"Guys, come look at this."

They crowded around him, peering at a notice pinned to the fridge with a magnet, the text bold and urgent.

"Attention all residents," Jimbo read aloud. "Due to the ongoing crisis, the city of Philadelphia has established a designated Protected Zone for all survivors. Please make your way to Fairmount Park for safety and shelter." He looked up. "Dudes, do you know what this means? There might be other safe places out there. Places where people are still alive, still fighting." He met Tommy's gaze. "Maybe...maybe that's where your family went."

"Then that's where we're going."

Zero frowned. "Or it could be a trap. Another one of the Globalists' schemes to round us up like cattle."

Tommy shook his head, his jaw clenching. "I don't care. If there's even a chance that Niamh and Sean are there, I have to take it. I have to."

15. The Horde

Tommy stood on the porch of Laila's house, his bat dangling loosely from his hand as he stared out at the quiet street. The sun hung low on the horizon, painting the sky in shades of orange and purple, casting long shadows across the neat rows of houses.

It all looked so normal, so peaceful. As if the world hadn't ended, as if the dead weren't walking the earth, as if they hadn't just lost another friend to the darkness that had consumed everything.

Behind him, the others moved around inside, gathering their supplies, checking their weapons.

But beneath it all, there was a hollow silence, a void where Laila's presence used to be. Her laughter, her fierce determination, her unwavering loyalty—all of it gone.

Tommy's chest ached with the weight of it, with the guilt and the grief that threatened to swallow him whole. He had failed her, just like he had failed Micky, just like he had failed everyone who had trusted him to keep them safe.

The screen door creaked open behind him, and he turned to see Roxy stepping out onto the porch. Her eyes were red-rimmed, her face pale and drawn.

"We're almost ready," she said, her voice rough and hoarse. "Just need to do one last sweep, make sure we haven't forgotten anything."

Tommy nodded, not trusting himself to speak. He followed her back inside, his feet heavy on the worn carpet.

The living room was a mess of scattered supplies and discarded wrappers, the detritus of their hasty packing.

Zero sat on the couch, his rifle across his knees, his face slick with sweat. Jimbo leaned against the wall, his arms crossed, his eyes distant.

Tommy moved through the room, his gaze skittering over the familiar objects, the little touches of Laila's life. The framed photos on the mantel, the stack of well-worn paperbacks on the coffee table.

All of it meaningless now, all of it just another reminder of what they had lost.

He forced himself to focus on the task at hand, on the supplies they would need for the road ahead. Water, food, ammunition.

As he stuffed the last of the canned goods into his backpack, he heard Roxy's sharp intake of breath. He looked up to see her standing in the doorway to Laila's bedroom, her hand pressed to her mouth. "I can't. I can't go in there."

Tommy crossed the room to her, his hand finding hers, squeezing gently. "It's okay. We'll do it together."

He pushed open the door, steeling himself for what lay beyond.

The room was just as Laila had left it, the bed neatly made, the curtains drawn against the fading light. And there, on the nightstand, the gleam of metal, the dark stain of blood.

Tommy swallowed hard, his throat tight and aching. He forced himself to look away. They needed to gather anything useful.

But as he moved through the room, opening drawers and rifling through closets, he couldn't escape the feeling of wrongness, of violation. This was Laila's space, her sanctuary. And now it was just another tomb, another monument to the dead.

He stared down at the pistol, but couldn't bring himself to take it.

As they stepped back out into the living room, Tommy saw that the others had finished their own packing, their bags bulging with supplies.

Zero stood by the front door, his rifle slung over his shoulder. "We need to move. The longer we stay here, the more likely we are to attract attention."

Tommy nodded, shouldering his own pack. He took one last look around the room, one last moment to remember Laila as she had been—brave, fierce, loyal to the end.

Then he turned and followed the others out into the gathering dark, the screen door banging shut behind them with a dull finality.

The street was deserted, the houses silent and still. In the distance, the skyline of Philadelphia loomed, a jagged silhouette against the darkening sky.

Somewhere out there, his family was waiting for him, his reason for fighting, for surviving.

He led the way towards Fairmount Park, his bat gripped tight in his hand, his eyes scanning the shadows for any sign of movement.

Behind him, the others followed in silence, their footsteps echoing off the crumbling facades of the abandoned buildings.

Tommy's mind raced as he walked, his thoughts torn between the desperate need to find his family and the gnawing guilt that ate at his gut. Laila was gone, another casualty in this endless war against the undead. And he hadn't been able to stop it, hadn't been able to save her from the darkness that had claimed her.

He shook his head, forcing himself to focus. Fairmount Park. That was where they needed to go, where they might find some hint of Niamh and Sean's fate.

It was a slim hope, a fragile thread to cling to in the midst of all this chaos and despair. But it was all he had left.

As they turned a corner, Tommy held up a hand, bringing the group to a halt.

The street ahead was blocked by a tangle of abandoned cars. Tommy edged forward, his eyes straining to pierce the gloom beyond the makeshift barricade.

"I don't like this," Roxy said, her machete held low at her side. "It's too quiet."

Zero grunted, his rifle sweeping the surrounding buildings. "Could be an ambush. Hostiles, maybe. Or just a load of dead-heads waiting to jump out at us."

Tommy hesitated, weighing their options. They could backtrack, try to find another route around. But that would cost them time they couldn't afford to lose. And there was no guarantee the other streets would be any clearer. "We push through. Stick close, watch each other's backs. Anything moves, you call it out."

The others nodded, readying their weapons as they fell into formation behind him. Tommy took a deep breath. Then he stepped forward, easing his way between the bumpers of the stalled cars.

The metal was sun-warmed against his skin, the smell of gasoline and decay thick in his nostrils.

He moved slowly, his ears straining for any sound beyond the crunch of broken glass beneath his boots.

A low, guttural moan made the hairs on the back of his neck stand up.

He froze, his heart slamming against his ribs as he eyed the shadows.

In the dark maw of an alleyway, something moved.

He pointed with his bat. "Over there."

The others fanned out beside him, weapons at the ready.

For a moment, nothing happened.

Then the zombies shambled into view, dozens of them.

Tommy leapt forward to meet them, his bat crunching into the first zombie's skull. Black blood sprayed across his face, his arms.

All his focus, all his rage and pain and desperate terror, was poured into the swing of the bat, the crack of splintering bone.

Beside him, the others fought with savage intensity.

Zero's rifle boomed, each shot punctuated by the wet smack of a bullet striking rotten meat.

Roxy's machete flashed, severing limbs and heads.

And Jimbo crushed and battered his way through the press of bodies with his golf club.

Tommy's arms burned with the effort of swinging his bat. He could feel his strength flagging, his reactions slowing.

Roxy cried out, a sound of pain and fear that cut through the moans of the dead.

Tommy whirled to see her stagger back, blood pouring from her nose.

A zombie lurched towards her, its jaws wide and snapping.

Tommy lunged, throwing himself between Roxy and the monster.

His bat connected with the side of its head, caving in its temple.

It crumpled, but more surged forward, a writhing mass of grasping hands and gnashing teeth.

"Fall back!" Tommy shouted. "We have to get out of here!"

They fought their way back through the barricade, the zombies clawing at them from all sides.

Tommy's world narrowed to the swing of his bat, the burn of his muscles, the frantic pounding of his heart.

He struck out again and again, until his arms felt like lead, until his vision blurred with sweat and gore.

And then they were through, stumbling out onto the open street.

Tommy risked a glance back over his shoulder and immediately wished he hadn't. The zombies were pouring through the gap in the cars.

"Run!"

They fled through the darkening streets, the moans of the dead echoing behind them.

Tommy's lungs seared as he gulped down air, his feet pounding on the broken pavement, each step sending jarring bolts of pain through his ankle.

He had no idea where they were going, no sense of direction beyond the blind need to escape.

They careened around corners and sprinted down alleyways, putting as much distance as possible between themselves and the horde.

Finally, when Tommy felt like his legs were about to give out, they stumbled to a halt in a small courtyard, huddling in the shadow of a crumbling brick wall.

Tommy leaned against it, his chest heaving as he struggled to catch his breath. "Is everyone okay? Anyone bit?"

Roxy shook her head, her hand pressed tight against her bloody nose. "Dead-head caught me with an elbow or something."

Zero and Jimbo were battered and bloody but still standing.

Tommy let out a shaky breath, relief warring with the adrenaline still pumping through his system.

"We can't stay here," Zero said. "That horde could be right behind us."

Tommy pushed off from the wall. "Then we need to keep moving."

Roxy frowned, her gaze drifting towards the darkening sky. "Tommy, it's getting late. We're all knackered here. We need to find somewhere to crash, just for a few hours."

"She's right," Jimbo said. "I haven't slept in...I don't even know how long. And after that last fight..." He trailed off, shaking his head. "I'm not sure I've got anything left in the tank, dude."

Tommy's fingers tightened around his bat. "Fairmount Park is closer than my place. We can make it there before full dark."

Zero stepped forward, his rifle clutched tight to his chest. "Tommy's right. We stop now, we might not get started again."

Roxy sighed, her shoulders slumping. "Alright. If you're sure about Fairmount, then I'm with you. But we're no good to anyone if we're too exhausted to function."

Tommy nodded. "Okay. We stick to the side streets, the back alleys. Avoid the main roads, the open spaces. Anything looks off, we go around, find another way. And if we run into trouble..."

"We deal with it," Zero said.

Jimbo stood straight, his golf club held at his side. "Just promise me one thing, dude. When we get to Fairmount, I get first dibs on any beds they got. My back is killing me."

Tommy managed a tight smile, clapping Jimbo on the shoulder. "You got it, man. Now let's move. We're burning daylight."

They set off into the gathering dark, their weapons held at the ready, their senses straining for any hint of danger.

Tommy took point, his bat gripped tight, his eyes scanning the shadows.

Behind him, the others fell into formation, Roxy and Zero flanking him on either side, Jimbo bringing up the rear.

They moved quickly and quietly, darting from cover to cover, using the abandoned cars and buildings to shield them from view.

Tommy's heart pounded in his chest as the alley ahead filled with the shuffling sounds of countless feet, the air thick with the groans of the undead.

Shadows shifted within the narrow space between the buildings, growing denser, louder.

The stench of decay wafted towards him.

Tommy turned to the others. "Circle up! Watch each other's backs!"

Roxy and Jimbo moved closer to flank him on either side.

Zero maneuvered himself behind a fallen statue, using it as a makeshift sniper's nest, his rifle already sweeping for targets.

As the zombies began to pour out of the alleyway, the group tightened their formation.

Tommy met the milky eyes of the frontmost zombies as they staggered forward.

His bat swung with a ferocity born of desperation and fear, the crack of splintering bone echoing in the narrow space as he took down the first of the horde.

Each swing was a blow for survival, each connection a visceral crunch that sent sprays of coagulated blood into the air.

To his right, Roxy was a blur of motion, her machete slicing through the air. Limbs and heads fell at her feet as she carved a path through the advancing dead, her every move fluid and precise. Her breaths came sharp and quick, punctuating each strike with a fierce grunt.

On his left, Jimbo wielded his golf club like a war hammer, each heavy swing accompanied by a thud as the club connected with rotting flesh.

Behind them, the steady crack of Zero's rifle echoed between the buildings, his shots precise, each bullet finding its mark.

As the fight dragged on, Tommy felt the strain in his arms, the burn of his muscles screaming for rest.

They had to hold the line, to keep fighting despite the odds.

Each fallen zombie meant one less threat, but the horde seemed endless, each monster replaced by another. They pressed in from all sides, their jaws snapping, their fingers clawing.

"To the alley!" Tommy's voice cut through the moans and gunfire. "Force them in!"

He motioned towards the narrow passageway behind them, swinging his bat in wide, sweeping arcs to clear the way.

The others rallied at his call, each step backward hard-won as they struggled against the relentless press of decaying bodies.

As they retreated into the alley's confining space, the rank stench of the undead intensified, a pungent mixture of decay and blood.

Tommy felt the oppressive heat from the zombies' rasping breaths as he fought with desperate ferocity, his bat a blur of motion as he smashed through their faces.

Beside him, Roxy erupted into a fierce battle cry, her voice raw and powerful. Her machete moved with lethal grace, slicing through the air, splattering the bricks with dark ichor.

Jimbo swung with ruthless efficiency, each heavy thud a sickening crunch of pulped flesh and broken bone.

Further down the alley, they reached a narrow gap between two rusted dumpsters.

The tight space acted as a funnel, restricting the advancing horde to a single-file assault.

Tommy positioned himself firmly in front of the gap, feet planted wide, his bat cocked back over his shoulder, poised for the onslaught. "Come on, you bastards! Come get some!"

The zombies surged forward, their arms outstretched, their faces slack.

Tommy met them with a roar, his bat slamming into the lead zombie's chest, caving it in.

He kicked the corpse aside and swung again, the wood connecting with the next monster's jaw, snapping its head back at an obscene angle.

The heavy thud of Jimbo's club and the slicing hiss of Roxy's machete melded with the sharp blasts of Zero's rifle.

Each gunshot was followed by the thump of another zombie body hitting the ground.

Despite their efforts, the swarm seemed endless, each fallen creature replaced by another.

Exhaustion clawed at Tommy, his arms heavy from the relentless swinging of his bat, each breath he drew laden with the acrid stench of decay.

His muscles screamed in protest, his lungs burned with the foul air, and he felt his strength ebbing away, his reactions becoming sluggish.

A scream.

Tommy spun around just in time to see Jimbo overwhelmed, dragged down beneath a mass of writhing, decayed bodies.

Jimbo's club swung wildly.

"Jimbo!" Roxy's voice cut through the tumult as she fought her way towards him.

Her machete slashed at the encroaching zombies, but it was too late.

Jimbo's cries choked off abruptly, replaced by the sounds of the zombies feeding.

A visceral rage exploded within Tommy, a searing mix of grief and fury.

He charged forward, his bat raised in a blind frenzy, every swing fuelled by the raw need for vengeance.

His weapon smashed into skulls, crushed through bones.

His world narrowed to the simple, brutal need to destroy these creatures, to make them pay for the life they had ripped away from his grasp.

But his arms grew leaden, his vision blurring with exhaustion and blood.

Yet still, the zombies pressed forward.

His movements slowed, each swing less effective as despair began to seep through the fury.

From somewhere beyond the immediate chaos, he heard Roxy's screams, calling his name in a desperate plea.

Zero's voice joined hers. "We can't help him! Tommy, we need to move!"

But the voices seemed distant, almost unreal, against the backdrop of his overwhelming rage and the endless tide of the undead that continued to surge towards him.

He shook his head, tears and sweat stinging his eyes.

He couldn't leave Jimbo, couldn't abandon him.

But even as the thought formed, he knew it was hopeless.

Jimbo was gone.

With a cry, Tommy turned and fled, his feet pounding on the blood-slick pavement. Roxy and Zero were right behind him.

They ran, the moans of the horde dogging their heels.

Tommy's lungs burned, his muscles screamed in protest, but he pushed himself harder, faster.

They burst out of the alley and into another courtyard, this one ringed by tall, crumbling tenements.

Tommy skidded to a halt, his chest heaving as he scanned for an escape route.

But there was nowhere to go, no way out.

The zombies were closing in from all sides.

Zero took up a position at the edge of the courtyard, his rifle snapping up to his shoulder.

He fired, the shots cracking like thunder in the confined space.

Zombies crumpled.

Tommy and Roxy fell back to join Zero, their weapons held at the ready.

They fought with a desperate ferocity, their movements fuelled by grief and adrenaline.

Tommy's bat crunched into skulls, Roxy's machete cleaved through limbs, Zero's rifle barked and boomed.

But it wasn't enough.

The zombies kept coming, their numbers inexhaustible.

Tommy felt a hand close around his ankle. He screamed, his bat smashing down on the zombie's skull, pulping it to gory ruin.

Beside him, Roxy cried out as a zombie seized her arm. She wrenched free as Tommy struck down with raining blows.

Zero stood over them, his rifle spitting fire.

Tommy's vision blurred, his limbs growing numb. He could feel the darkness closing in, the world slipping away.

This was the end, he realised with a distant sense of clarity. This was how they died, torn apart by the horde, just like Jimbo, just like so many others.

He thought of Niamh, of Sean. He had failed them, had left them alone in this nightmare world. The grief and the guilt threatened to consume him, to drag him down into the abyss.

A sound cut through the moans of the dead.

Engines.

The zombies fell in waves, their bodies shredded by the hail of bullets. Blood and gore painted the walls.

Soldiers advanced, their faces hidden behind masks and visors.

Tommy stood frozen, hardly daring to believe what he was seeing. Beside him, Roxy let out a sob, her hand finding his.

"What the hell..." Zero's voice was barely audible over the roar of engines and gunfire.

Soldiers poured into the courtyard, their rifles sweeping the area.

A man in an officer's uniform strode forward, his eyes hard and assessing behind his visor. "Identify yourselves." He trained his rifle on Tommy's chest. "What are you doing in the quarantine zone?"

Tommy swallowed hard, his mouth suddenly dry. "We...we were trying to get to Fairmount Park. We got overrun..."

The officer's eyes narrowed. "That camp there was overrun days ago. There's nothing left but the dead."

Tommy felt as if the ground had dropped away beneath his feet.

Niamh, Sean...

The officer barked orders and the soldiers moved in, their hands rough as they yanked Tommy, Roxy, and Zero to their feet. They stripped them of their weapons and lined them up against the wall.

"Check them for infection."

A soldier approached Tommy first, his gloved hands probing at his neck, his arms, his legs.

The soldier moved on to Roxy, then to Zero.

Zero jerked away from the soldier's touch, his face twisting into a snarl. "Get your hands off me, you Globalist scum! I know what you're really after. I know what you're doing!"

The soldier tried to grab him, but Zero was too quick.

He lunged for his rifle, his fingers scrabbling for the trigger.

"Zero, no!" Tommy shouted.

Gunfire.

Zero staggered back, his hands clutching at his chest as a bloom of red spread across his shirt.

He looked down at the wound, then up at Tommy, his eyes wide with shock. "Tommy...don't let them...don't let them take you..." He dropped to the ground, his body twitching as the life drained out of him.

Tommy could only stare.

Zero had been with them since the beginning, had fought beside them through hell and back.

And now he was gone, just like that.

"This one's infected." A soldier kicked Zero's body with the toe of his boot. "Look."

Tommy followed the man's gaze and stared at the ragged, oozing wound.

The soldier turned to the officer. "Sir, what do we do with the others?"

The officer studied Tommy and Roxy. "Check them again, just to be sure. And then we'll take them in for processing."

Tommy tensed as the soldiers approached him once more, their hands roving over his body, probing for any sign of infection.

But they found nothing, no bites, no scratches. Just a body wracked with cuts and bruises.

They moved on to Roxy, and Tommy held his breath, praying that she too would be cleared.

After a long, tense moment, the soldier stepped back. "All clean."

The officer nodded and gestured for his men to take up positions around Tommy and Roxy. "Escort these civilians to the transport. We're moving out."

As soldiers marched them towards the waiting vehicles, Tommy turned to the officer. "Where are you taking us?"

The officer kept his gaze fixed on the road ahead. "You'll be taken to a secure facility for processing and questioning. After that, we'll decide what to do with you."

He wanted to run, to fight. But what choice did he have? They were outnumbered and outgunned, with nowhere else to go and no one else to turn to.

As they climbed into the back of the transport, Tommy caught a final glimpse of Zero's body lying on the ground.

A sob rose up in his throat, but he choked it back, forcing himself to be strong, to keep going for Roxy's sake if nothing else.

The doors slammed shut, plunging them into darkness as the engines roared to life.

He slumped against the wall, his head in his hands as the grief and the guilt threatened to overwhelm him.

Laila, Jimbo, Zero...they were all gone.

And Tommy was still here, still breathing, still fighting.

But for what?

Niamh and Sean were gone.

He had nothing left to fight for.

Nothing left to hope for.

What was the point?

16. Limbo

Tommy jolted awake, his heart pounding, his skin slick with cold sweat. For a moment, he was disoriented, the darkness pressing in on him from all sides. But then the events of the past few hours came rushing back, and he remembered where he was.

The military transport. The soldiers. The officer's cold, assessing gaze as he ordered them taken into custody.

He sat up, his muscles aching.

Beside him, Roxy stirred, her eyes fluttering open. She looked as exhausted as he felt, her face pale and drawn in the dim light filtering through the small window. "Where are we?"

Tommy shook his head. "I don't know."

The transport lurched to a stop, the engine cutting off. There was a moment of silence, then the sound of heavy boots on metal as the soldiers began to disembark.

The rear doors swung open, flooding the compartment with harsh, artificial light. Tommy squinted against the glare, his hand coming up to shield his eyes.

"Out," a gruff voice said. "Both of you. Now."

Tommy and Roxy exchanged a glance, then climbed to their feet. They stepped out of the transport and into a world of concrete and barbed wire, of armed guards and spotlights.

The base was a hive of activity, soldiers moving with precise, purposeful strides, vehicles rumbling past laden with supplies and equipment. Medics hurried by, their faces obscured behind masks.

A soldier approached them. "You two, come with me. We need to get you processed and cleared."

Tommy opened his mouth to protest, to demand answers, but the soldier cut him off with a sharp gesture. "Save it. You'll be briefed once we've determined you're not a threat."

The soldier led them across the compound, past rows of tents and prefabricated buildings. They passed through checkpoint after checkpoint.

At each stage, the security grew more stringent, the guards more heavily armed and wary. By the time they reached the final checkpoint, Tommy felt like a prisoner being led to execution.

The soldier ushered them into a stark, brightly-lit receiving area, all white tiles and stainless steel. A military officer stood waiting for them. "Separate them. Full decontamination protocol. I want them checked for bites, scratches, any signs of infection."

Tommy's stomach clenched. "Wait. You can't just split us up like this. We stay together."

The officer's gaze flicked to him, his expression unchanging. "We have to be sure you're not a threat."

Tommy opened his mouth to argue, but before he could speak, a pair of soldiers stepped forward, their hands closing around his arms.

He tried to pull away, but their grip only tightened.

"Tommy!" Roxy called after him as soldiers hauled her away. "Tommy, don't let them—"

But her words cut off as she was dragged through a door and out of sight.

"Where the hell are you taking her? You can't split us up like this!""

"Keep moving, sir. It's for security purposes. You'll be reunited with your friend once we've determined you're not infected."

Tommy wanted to fight, but he knew it was useless. Instead, he let the soldiers lead him away.

They took him to a small, brightly-lit room filled with metal tables and racks of equipment. A team of faceless technicians stood waiting for him, their hands gloved and their eyes hidden behind protective goggles.

"Remove your belongings," one of them ordered, his voice muffled behind his mask. "Step forward. Remain calm."

Tommy hesitated, his fingers clenching around the straps of his backpack. It was all he had left, the last remnants of his life before the world had gone to hell.

With a sigh, he shrugged off the pack and handed it over, watching as the technicians emptied it onto the table, sorting through the contents with clinical efficiency.

They patted him down next, their hands roving over his body with impersonal thoroughness. They checked his pockets, his waistband, the soles of his boots.

When they were satisfied, they led him to a medical tent, a cavernous space filled with the beep and hiss of machinery. Doctors and nurses moved among the rows of beds, their faces obscured behind masks and face shields.

A doctor approached him. She gestured for him to sit on a nearby exam table.

She shone a light in his eyes, checked his pulse and blood pressure, palpated his lymph nodes with gloved fingers. "Any history of illness or injury? Any allergies or medical conditions?"

Tommy shook his head, wincing as she probed at a particularly tender bruise on his ribs. "No. Nothing like that."

She nodded, making a note on her clipboard. "And have you had any exposure to infected individuals? Any bites, scratches, or other wounds?"

He hesitated, his mind flashing back to their countless battles with the undead. To Jimbo, dragged down and torn apart before him. "No. No bites or scratches."

The doctor eyed him, but didn't press the issue. She took a blood sample, the needle biting into his arm with a sharp, fleeting pain. Then she stepped back, stripping off her gloves with a snap. "You're clear. We can't take any chances."

Tommy nodded, his throat tight. He understood the need for caution, for vigilance. But the idea of being trapped here, cut off from the outside world was almost too much to bear.

The soldiers led him out of the tent and across the compound, past more checkpoints and guard stations, more rows of identical buildings and tents.

They took him to a small, bare room, little more than a cell with a bench along one wall and a barred window set high in the opposite wall. "Someone will come for you soon."

Tommy stepped inside, his heart sinking as the door swung shut behind him, the lock clicking into place.

He sank down onto the bench, his head in his hands, his mind spinning.

Where was Roxy?

What were they doing to her?

And what about Niamh and Sean?

If the camp at Fairmount Park was gone, if the city was lost...what hope did he have of ever finding them again?

How had it come to this?

How had everything fallen apart so quickly, so completely?

He thought of Jimbo and Zero, of Dee and Spike and Nix and Kim, of Laila and Micky.

All the friends he had lost, all the people he had failed.

But he couldn't let it consume him.

He had to stay strong, had to keep fighting.

For Roxy, for whatever slim hope remained.

He sat in the silence of the cell, his eyes fixed on the window, his mind racing with plans and possibilities.

Time dragged on.

His stomach growled, his throat dry.

He tried to distract himself, shifting on the bench, running his hands through his hair, but the discomfort in his gut was relentless.

He stood, the movement making his head spin.

He couldn't sit here any longer.

He started pacing, his boots scuffing against the floor, the sound almost rhythmic in the silence.

One, two, three steps to the wall, turn.

One, two, three steps back to the door, turn.

His body was in motion, but his mind was stuck, circling the same worries over and over.

Where was Roxy?

What were they doing to her?

What if she was infected?

What if she didn't pass their tests?

He could hardly stand to think about it, but the thoughts were insistent, pounding in his skull with every step.

He reached the door again and stopped.

The room felt smaller than before, more claustrophobic.

He pounded his fist against the door. "Hey! Is anyone out there? I'm starving! I need water!"

He waited, his ear pressed against the door, hoping for some response, any sign that someone was listening.

But there was only silence.

His breath came faster, his chest tightening.

He banged on the door again, harder this time, his fists slamming against the metal. "Come on! I know you can hear me! Let me out of here!"

Nothing.

He slumped back against the door, sliding down until he was sitting on the floor, his head resting against the cool metal.

His eyes drifted to the barred window.

Time blurred again, and Tommy didn't know how long he sat there, staring blankly at the window, his thoughts spiralling.

The lock clicked.

He scrambled to his feet.

The door swung open, and a soldier stepped into the room. "Follow me."

With a heavy sigh, Tommy nodded and stepped forward, his body aching.

The soldier turned and led him out of the room, down a dimly lit corridor.

As they walked, Tommy's thoughts returned to Roxy. He had to find her. He had to make sure she was safe.

But for now, all he could do was follow.

They came to a stop outside a nondescript door, indistinguishable from the dozens they had already passed. The soldier swiped a key card, and the lock disengaged with a soft click. He pushed the door open and gestured for Tommy to enter.

"Your quarters. You should get yourself cleaned up."

With a nod, Tommy stepped over the threshold and into the room beyond.

The door closed, leaving him alone once more.

A single bed stood against one wall, its plain blanket and pillow crisp and unwrinkled. A table and chair occupied the opposite corner, a closet tucked beside them.

He crossed to the small bathroom. A sink, a toilet, a shower stall.

He turned on the faucet, watching as the water flowed clear and steady, steam rising from the heat.

How long had it been since he had seen running water, since he had felt the simple luxury of a hot shower?

With trembling hands, he stripped off his filthy, bloodstained clothes, letting them fall to the tiled floor.

He stepped into the stall, the water cascading over him in a scalding rush.

For a long time, he simply stood there, his eyes closed, his face tilted up to the spray.

The heat seeped into his aching muscles, washing away the grime and sweat.

Tears pricked at the corners of his eyes, mingling with the water that streamed down his face. He couldn't remember the last time he had allowed himself to feel anything beyond the numb, relentless drive to survive.

But now, the emotions threatened to overwhelm him.

Grief, guilt, fear, and despair crashed over him in waves, leaving him shaking and gasping under the spray.

He stayed there until his skin was raw and wrinkled and the tears had run dry.

He turned off the faucet and stepped out, taking a towel from the neat stack on the shelf.

As he dried himself, he caught sight of his reflection in the mirror above the sink. He barely recognised the man who stared back at him—gaunt, bearded, and hollow-eyed, his skin pale beneath the scrapes and bruises. At least the tattoos remained the same.

Gone was the cocky, self-assured punk he had once been. In his place was a stranger, a broken shell of a man with nothing left to lose.

He turned away, unable to bear the sight of his own emptiness.

In the closet, he found a stack of fresh clothes—simple sweatpants and a t-shirt, a plain hoodie and a pair of sturdy boots, military issue.

He dressed slowly, savouring the feeling of clean fabric against his skin.

When was the last time he had worn clothes that weren't stiff with grime and sweat, that didn't reek of blood and decay?

With nothing else to do, he sat on the edge of the bed, his hands dangling between his knees.

The room was so quiet, the silence broken only by the hum of the air conditioner and the distant, muffled sounds of the base beyond the walls.

It was a mundane sound, a reminder of the world that had been lost.

The world of electricity and running water, of safe homes and soft beds.

The world where people didn't have to fight and scrabble for every scrap of food, every moment of rest.

But that world was gone now, swept away in the tide of the undead.

And in its place was this—this sterile, soulless limbo.

He reached for the water bottle on the bedside table and unscrewed the cap.

The water was cool and clean, and tasted of nothing.

He rose to his feet, pacing the small confines of the room. Four steps to the door, four steps to the window. Back and forth, back and forth, his mind racing with fragmented thoughts.

He tried to sleep, to shut out the chaos in his head. But every time he closed his eyes, he saw their faces—Niamh, Sean. Zero, Laila, Micky, and Jimbo.

Why hadn't he done more?

Why hadn't he been faster, stronger, smarter?

Why had he let them down?

He curled onto his side, his knees drawn up to his chest, his arms wrapped tight around himself.

Sobs wracked his body, tearing from his throat in heaving gasps.

He cried for the world that had been lost, for the people he had loved and the life he had known.

He cried for Niamh and Sean, for the family he had failed to protect, for the future they would never have.

And he cried for himself—for the man he had been and the man he had become, for the choices he had made and the ones he hadn't.

How long he stayed like that, he didn't know.

Minutes stretched into hours.

Finally, as if from a great distance, he heard the sound of footsteps in the corridor outside.

He sat up when the footsteps stopped outside his door.

With a soft beep, the lock disengaged, and the door swung open.

A soldier stood in the doorway. "Come with me."

The soldier led him through a maze of identical hallways, past door after featureless door.

Finally, they came to a stop outside a larger door, this one flanked by armed guards. The soldier swiped his key card, and the lock clicked open. "In here."

Tommy stepped inside. The room was larger than his quarters, with a long table and several chairs arranged in the centre.

An officer in a crisp military uniform sat at the far end of the table, his face hard and unreadable. "Sit down, please. We have a lot to discuss. State your full name and purpose for entering the Quarantine Zone."

Tommy swallowed, his mouth suddenly dry. "Thomas Merrill. I was trying to reach my family in Philly. I didn't know about any quarantine restrictions; we've been on the road since the outbreak started."

The officer's pen scratched across the paper as he took notes. "Describe the route you took to enter the zone."

"We found a gap near an old maintenance tunnel."

The officer's head snapped up, his eyes narrowing. "And you just walked in? Just like that? How did you manage supplies and evasion of the infected?"

Tommy shifted in his seat, the hard plastic digging into his back. "It's been challenging."

The officer's lips thinned. "It's alarming that civilians could enter a secure zone unnoticed. This speaks to a serious breach of our protocols." He leaned forward, his elbows resting on the table. "Were you aided by anyone inside the zone or given information prior to your arrival?"

Tommy shook his head, a bitter laugh escaping his lips. "It was just us. Bunch of punks evading the US military."

The officer sat back, his fingers steepled in front of him. "Have you had contact with the infected? Any symptoms or sickness?"

Tommy's throat tightened, images of Kim and Zero flashing through his mind. "We've been careful. Two of my group were infected. I fought when I had to, but managed to stay clear of getting bit."

The officer made another note. "I see. And your group, how many are you? Who else is with you?"

Tommy's shoulders slumped. "Originally? Ten, including me. Now...now it's just me and another friend, Roxy. We lost a lot of good people along the way." He swallowed hard. "I just wanted to get home. To find my family."

The officer's expression softened. "Your family? Who are they? What are their names?"

"Niamh and Sean. O'Reilly." Tommy's voice caught on the names, his heart clenching.

The officer wrote the names down. Then he closed the file, his hands folding on top of it as he met Tommy's gaze. "Your information will be reviewed. Stay in the designated area until you are contacted. The safety of this zone and its operations are paramount. Your breach is...concerning."

Tommy smirked. "It's not really my problem, is it? I didn't ask for any of this. I just wanted to find my family."

The officer's eyes hardened. "No, Mr. Merrill, it is very much your problem now. You and your friend have compromised the security of this entire operation." He nodded to the guards, who stepped forward to flank Tommy on either side. "Escort him to the mess hall. The man looks half-starved."

Tommy sat at a long table in the dining area, his stomach growling as he stared down at the steaming bowl of stew. It had been so long since he'd had a hot meal, since he'd tasted anything beyond the bland, canned rations they'd been living on for weeks.

But even as his hunger gnawed him, he couldn't bring himself to take a bite. His mind was too full, too caught up in the events of the past few hours.

Roxy appeared in the doorway, flanked by two armed guards.

Tommy rose to his feet as the guards led her to his table and gestured for her to sit.

"Rox! Are you okay?"

"I'm fine," she snapped. She sighed and rubbed a hand over her face. "Sorry. It's just...it's been a long day."

Tommy reached across the table to take her hand. "I know. Believe me, I know."

They sat in silence for a moment, the only sound the clink of utensils and the low murmur of conversation from the other tables.

The dining area was simple, just a few long tables and benches, with soldiers and personnel keeping to themselves.

"They asked about how we got into Philly," Roxy said.

"Same. I think us getting in must have spooked them."

Roxy shrugged. "It's got me thinking."

"About what?"

"About Zero. About his ideas."

"His conspiracy theories, you mean?"

"What if he's right? What if this whole thing, the outbreak, the quarantine zones...what if it was all orchestrated for some reason?"

"You think some evil cabal is behind this? "

Roxy shook her head, a bitter laugh escaping her lips. "I don't know. I don't know anything anymore. But think about it—the way they're questioning us, the way they're keeping us separated and confined. It's like they're trying to control the flow of information, like they're trying to keep something hidden."

Tommy opened his mouth to respond, but before he could speak, a soldier appeared at their table. "You two, with me. Now."

With a squeeze of each other's hands, they stood and followed the soldier out of the dining area and into the corridor beyond.

The soldier led them through a series of hallways.

"Where are they taking us?" Roxy asked.

"I don't know."

"You think they heard us back there?"

Tommy shrugged. "I don't know."

They emerged into the open air, the sudden brightness of the rising sun making Tommy squint.

The soldier led them to a landing strip. In the centre of the space, stood a Chinook helicopter, its blades whirring, the wind from its dual rotors whipping at their clothes and hair.

"Hurry," the soldier said. "On board. Quickly."

"What's going on?" Tommy yelled, trying to make himself heard over the noise. "Where are you taking us?"

But the soldier didn't answer. He grabbed Tommy by the arm and steered him towards the waiting helicopter,

Roxy following close behind.

They were helped on board, the soldier shoving them into seats and strapping them in.

Tommy's mind raced, trying to make sense of it all.

Were they being taken somewhere else?

To another base, another quarantine zone?

Or were they being flown out into the wilderness, to be abandoned and left to fend for themselves?

As the doors slammed shut, Tommy looked over at Roxy. She reached out, her hand finding his, squeezing tight.

The helicopter lifted off, the ground falling away beneath them.

Tommy watched as the base receded, the buildings and vehicles growing smaller and smaller.

"Where do you think they're taking us?"

Tommy shook his head. "I don't know. But wherever it is, we need to stick together, Rox. We have to."

"I know. I just...I'm scared, Tommy. I'm so scared of what might be waiting for us out there."

He swallowed hard. "Me too."

17. Ghosts

The rotor blades droned through the cabin as Tommy and Roxy soared over the vast expanse of the Atlantic Ocean.

They had been flying for what felt like hours, the monotony of the endless blue broken only by the occasional ship.

Tommy pressed his face against the window, his eyes straining to make out anything on the horizon.

The pilot's voice crackled through their headsets. "Approaching the destination. ETA, ten minutes."

Tommy straightened in his seat. He glanced over at Roxy, who was already peering back out the window.

A dark shape emerged on the horizon, rising out of the water.

Tommy squinted, trying to make out the details.

"It's an oil rig," Roxy said. "That's where they're taking us?"

Tommy didn't answer, his mind racing.

The rig loomed larger as they drew closer, a massive structure of steel and concrete rising from the ocean.

It was like an island, a fortress in the middle of nowhere, with cranes and derricks jutting into the sky, surrounded by a network of platforms and walkways, with helicopters and boats docked at various points.

The helicopter began its descent, circling the rig.

People moved about on the various decks, tiny figures going about their duties.

"Look at all this," Roxy said. "It's like a goddamn city."

Tommy nodded, his eyes wide as he tried to take it all in.

The helicopter touched down on a designated helipad with a gentle bump.

The door slid open, and a rush of salty ocean air filled the cabin.

Tommy and Roxy unbuckled their harnesses and stepped out, squinting against the brightness of the midday sun reflected off the metal surfaces of the rig.

A young military officer approached them, his hand extended in welcome. "Mr. Merrill, Ms. Delano. Welcome to Poseidon Base."

Tommy shook his hand, still trying to process everything he was seeing. "I didn't know places like this still existed. I thought everything was gone, that it was just *Mad Max* out there."

The officer nodded. "It's a common reaction. But as you can see, we've managed to keep some semblance of order, of normalcy. This rig is part of a network of safe zones, places where survivors can live in relative safety while we work to clear and secure the mainland."

Roxy stepped forward, her eyes narrowed. "And how's that going? The mainland, I mean. Last we saw, it was overrun. The cities, the towns...all of it."

"I won't lie to you, we are fighting a war. The infected are everywhere, but those behind it have been neutralised. We're making progress. Slowly but surely, we're taking back what's ours."

He gestured for them to follow him, leading them away from the helipad and into the heart of the rig. "We have a fully equipped medical centre. There are schools for the children, gardens, and hydroponics bays to grow our own food. We even have a desalination plant to provide fresh water."

Children played under the watchful eyes of adults, their laughter carrying on the salt-tinged breeze. People tended to communal gardens. Others went about maintenance tasks, repairing and reinforcing the rig's structures.

"How many people live here?" Roxy asked.

"Several thousand at last count. We've taken in survivors from all along the east coast. You'll get to meet many of them soon, but for now, let's get you settled in."

He led them to a large, modular building near the centre of the rig, the word "Administration" stencilled on the side in crisp, military lettering.

Inside, they were processed by a team of staff, their names and details entered into a database, their fingerprints and retinal scans taken for identification.

Then, finally, they were shown to their quarters. Tommy tried to stifle his surprise when the officer leading them stopped outside a block labelled "Couple's Quarters."

Tommy opened his mouth to protest, to explain that he and Roxy weren't like that, but something stopped him.

Maybe it was the fear of being separated from her. Or maybe it was just the bone-deep exhaustion, the need for any kind of comfort and familiarity in this strange new world.

Whatever the reason, he held his tongue as the officer handed them each a keycard and showed them inside.

The room was small but clean, with a double bed, a desk, and built-in storage.

Tommy stood awkwardly in the middle of the floor, unsure of what to do with himself.

Roxy offered him a smile. "It's okay, Tommy. We'll just...we'll figure it out."

He nodded, swallowing past the lump in his throat.

They took turns in the small attached bathroom, washing away the grime and sweat of the journey.

When he emerged, clean and dressed in a fresh set of clothes provided by their hosts, he found Roxy sitting on the edge of the bed.

"You alright?" he asked, settling beside her. "Something wrong?"

She shrugged, not meeting his gaze. "Everything. Nothing. It's just...it's a lot to take in, you know? This place, these people. It's not what I expected."

Tommy huffed a laugh. "Yeah, I know what you mean. I keep waiting for something to go wrong."

"But what if it doesn't?" She turned to face him. "What if this is real, if this is actually a chance for something better? What if we can actually have a life here? I think we can make it work."

Tommy stared at her. He wanted so badly to believe it, to embrace the possibility of a future beyond mere existence.

But the faces of the lost rose in his mind—his friends, his family. Everyone.

"I don't know, Rox. I don't know if I'm ready for that, if I can ever be ready. Not after everything that's happened."

She reached out, taking his hand in hers. Her skin was soft, her grip warm. "I know. Believe me, I feel it too. But we can't carry that weight forever. We have to find a way to live with it, to keep going. I need it to mean something."

He closed his eyes, letting her words wash over him.

She was right They owed it to the ones they'd lost to make their sacrifices mean something. Otherwise, what was the point?

But it was hard, so hard, to imagine a life beyond the unrelenting struggle for survival, beyond the daily grind of scavenging and fighting and running and just staying alive.

A chime sounded, startling them both.

Tommy looked up to see a small screen set into the wall flashing with a message: "Attention new arrivals. Please report to the main auditorium for orientation at 1600 hours. Attendance is mandatory."

Roxy sighed, releasing his hand, and standing. "Guess that's our cue. Time to go see what our brave new world has in store for us."

Tommy and Roxy found seats near the back of the auditorium, settling in among a dozen or so other new arrivals.

A broad-shouldered man in a crisp military uniform strode out onto the stage, his gaze sharp and assessing. "Good afternoon. I am Colonel Gonzalez, the commanding officer of this facility. On behalf of myself and all the brave men and women who serve here, I want to welcome you to Poseidon Base."

The Colonel began to pace. "I know you all have questions, concerns. You've been through hell to get here, seen, and experienced things no one should have to. But I want to assure you, you're safe now."

A ripple of applause swept over the auditorium.

"This base, this community, is a haven, a place where we can rebuild and reclaim what was lost."

He gestured to the screens behind him, which flared to life with images of the rig. "Here, we have everything we need to not just survive, but thrive. Food, water, medical care. Education for our children, work, and purpose for our adults. It is our chance to rebuild."

The images changed, showing scenes of the mainland, of cities and towns overrun by zombies, of desolate highways and burned-out homes. "But we cannot do it alone. Out there, beyond the safety of these walls, the world is still in chaos. The threat of the infected remains."

His gaze swept the room, his expression grave. "That is why we need you. Each of you has skills, knowledge, experience that is vital to our mission. Whether you were a doctor or a teacher, a soldier or a mechanic, a parent or a student—you have value, you have purpose."

The screens shifted again, now displaying lines of text, lists and organizational charts. "Tomorrow, you will be interviewed and assigned to your new roles, your new duties. Some of you will work in the greenhouses or the kitchens, helping to feed our population. Others will assist in the medical centre, or the schools, or the workshops. And some of you, those with the necessary aptitude and ability, will join our security forces, helping to protect and defend this base and all who live here."

Tommy shifted in his seat. The thought of taking up arms again, of fighting and killing, made his stomach churn.

Beside him, Roxy tensed, her hand finding his and squeezing tight.

"I know this is a lot to take in," the Colonel said. "But I want you to know that you are not alone. We are all in this together, all working towards the same goal—a future where our children can grow up safe and free, where we can rebuild what was lost and make it better than before."

He straightened, his eyes blazing. "It will not be easy. There will be challenges, setbacks, moments where it all seems hopeless. But we will persevere, because we must. Because the alternative is unthinkable."

With a final nod, he stepped back from the podium. "Thank you for your attention. You will be assessed for your assignments in the morning. Use this evening to think about what you can bring to our community. Your skills. Your specialisms. Until then, get some rest, take some time to explore your new home. And welcome, once again, to Poseidon Base."

As the Colonel left the stage and others began to disperse, Roxy turned to him. "I don't like this. It feels too...too perfect, too easy. Like they're selling us a dream, but not telling us the whole truth."

Tommy nodded. "I know. But what choice do we have? We can't go back, not now. We have to give this a chance."

She sighed, leaning into him. "I know. I just...I have a bad feeling about this place."

"We'll figure it out, Rox. But for now, let's just...let's just try to get through tonight, okay?"

She nodded and together they sat, watching as the last of the other new arrivals trickled out of the auditorium, until they were alone.

"What now, Tommy?"

He shrugged. "We wait it out and see what comes next. For the first time in a long time, we don't have to run anymore."

He reached for her hand, twining his fingers with hers and giving a squeeze. The contact grounded him, a physical reminder that they were here, together, alive against all odds.

Roxy shifted closer, wrapping her arms around him in a warm embrace.

Tommy responded in kind, pulling her close and resting his chin on the top of her head.

They sat like that for a long time, just holding each other.

"At least we're safe here, right? That's something."

Tommy nodded, his eyes closing as he let himself feel the truth of those words. Safe. It was a concept that had seemed so foreign, so unattainable for so long. "Yeah. It's more than we dared hope for, at times."

Tommy's mind drifted to Niamh and Sean, to Laila and Micky and all the others who hadn't made it. Their faces rose in his mind, so clear and vivid it was almost as if they were standing right in front of him.

But he pushed the images down, forced himself to focus on the present, on the warmth of Roxy in his arms and the steady thrum of the rig all around them.

They had survived, but he couldn't hold onto a past that no longer existed.

They had a chance, however slim, at something more than mere survival.

"We've got an opportunity here, Rox. A chance to figure out what living means now. It won't be easy, and it won't be the same as before. But it's something. It's a start."

Roxy pulled back slightly to look at him, her eyes shining. "I know. And I want that, Tommy. I want it so badly it hurts. But I'm so damn scared. Scared of losing this, of losing you. Scared that this is all just another false hope."

Tommy cupped her face, his thumbs brushing away the tears that had begun to fall. "I'm scared too. Terrified, if I'm being honest. But we can't let that fear control us."

She leaned into his touch, her eyes closing. "You're right. I know you are."

He pressed a kiss to her forehead. "But we have to try."

Roxy nodded, a small, tentative smile curving her lips.

Tommy gazed into her eyes, seeing a reflection of his own fears, hopes, and determination.

In that moment, he felt a shift within himself, a letting go of the past and an embracing of what lay ahead.

"Rox, we've been through hell together. You've been my rock, my constant. I don't know if I would have made it this far without you."

"Tommy, I—"

"Let me finish. I've been holding onto ghosts, onto a life that doesn't exist anymore. Niamh, Sean...they're gone. And it kills me to say that, to really accept it. But I have to. For my sake, for our sake."

He took a deep breath as he cupped Roxy's face. "I love you, Roxy. I think I have for a long time, but I was too scared to admit it, too guilty to let myself feel it. But life's too short, too precious to waste on fear and guilt. Whatever comes next, whatever challenges we face here, I want to face them with you."

Roxy's smile lit up her entire face. "I love you too. So much. And I'll be here, always, no matter what comes our way."

Tommy leaned in, his lips meeting hers.

He lost himself in the moment, the passion.

It was a promise, a new beginning, a defiance against the darkness that had consumed their world.

As they broke apart, Tommy rested his forehead against hers. "So, what do you say? Ready to build a new life here, together?"

Roxy nodded. "I guess we should go back to the room."

Tommy got to his feet and smiled. "We definitely should."

She reached out, taking his hand once more. "We're going to be okay, Tommy. We're going to make this work."

He nodded, squeezing her fingers. "I know we will."

Later that day, Tommy and Roxy entered the mess hall, the chatter of refugees filling the air.

"What do you think, Rox? Should I order the lobster or the filet mignon tonight?"

Roxy snorted, elbowing him in the ribs. "Oh, definitely the lobster. And make sure to ask for a side of caviar too."

They grinned at each other. As they inched forward in the line, Tommy scanned the room, taking in the faces.

And then he saw them.

Niamh and Sean, standing further ahead in the queue, a tall, broad-shouldered man beside them.

Tommy dropped his tray, the clatter of plastic on concrete drawing glances from nearby diners.

Roxy followed his gaze "Is that...?"

Tommy nodded, unable to speak. He stared at them, drinking in the sight of his partner and son, alive and whole. They looked different, thinner, but they were here. They were safe.

He took a step forward, then another, his feet carrying him towards them. "Niamh!" His voice cracked. "Sean!"

Niamh turned, her brow furrowing.

Then her eyes widened, her hand flying to her mouth. "Tommy? Oh my god, Tommy!" She ran to him, throwing her arms around his neck, her breath hitching in a sob.

Tommy held her tight, burying his face in her hair, breathing in the familiar scent of her.

Tears streamed down his face, but he didn't care.

She was here, in his arms.

Nothing else mattered.

Niamh pulled back, her hands cupping his face as she searched his eyes. "I can't believe it. We thought...we didn't know if you'd made it, if you were..."

Tommy shook his head, his throat too tight to speak. He looked past her to where Sean stood, clinging to the leg of the tall man beside him.

Sean peered out at Tommy, his expression wary, uncertain.

Niamh followed his gaze. "Sean, sweetheart. It's okay. It's your dad."

But Sean only burrowed deeper into the man's side, his small hands clutching at his legs. The man laid a gentle hand on the boy's head.

Tommy felt a rush of jealousy, hot and bitter in his throat. He turned to Niamh, a question in his eyes.

She sighed. "This is Chad. He's been with us since Philly. He helped us get here, kept us safe."

Tommy nodded, forcing a smile onto his face. "Thank you," he said, extending a hand to the other man. "For taking care of them. I can't...I can't tell you how much that means to me."

Chad took his hand, his grip firmer than was comfortable. "Of course. They're good people. They didn't deserve being abandoned."

There was a heavy silence hanging in the air between them.

Then Roxy stepped forward, her hand finding Tommy's once more. "I'm Roxy. I've been with Tommy since the beginning of all this. We've been through hell and back, let me tell you. He's been a good friend."

Niamh smiled. "I'm glad he had someone. I'm glad he wasn't alone."

Tommy swallowed hard, his gaze dropping to the floor. "Not everyone made it. Laila, Micky...we lost a lot of good people along the way."

Niamh's face fell, her eyes filling with tears. "I'm so sorry. I can't imagine..."

Roxy released Tommy's hand. "We all lost people. But we're here now. We're safe. That's what matters."

Sean suddenly let go of Chad's leg and ran to Tommy, throwing his arms around his waist. "Daddy, you came back."

Tommy dropped to his knees, gathering his son into his arms, holding him tight. "I'll always come back, buddy. Always."

They stayed like that for a long moment, the rest of the world falling away until it was just the two of them, father, and son, reunited at last.

Then Tommy stood, Sean's hand clutched tight in his own, and they rejoined the others in the meal line.

There was so much to say, so much to catch up on. But for now, it was enough just to be together, to know that they had all made it.

As they took their trays and found a table, Tommy couldn't help but smile.

So much had changed, so much had been lost.

But they were still standing, still fighting, still holding onto hope in the face of unimaginable darkness.

He looked around at Niamh, her eyes sparkling as she watched Sean chatter excitedly to Roxy. Chad, his expression guarded. And Roxy, his friend, his anchor.

Whatever lay before them, they were a family.

They had seen the worst of humanity, had stared into the abyss, and come out the other side.

But in that moment, everything had changed.

There were still so many questions, so many uncertainties.

But for now, those questions could wait.

For now, there was only this moment.

They would rebuild and they would heal.

Punks to the end.

THE END.

Want to know what happened to Niamh and Sean in Philly?

While Tommy fights his way across zombie-infested America, Niamh faces the collapse of civilisation with nothing but a baseball bat and her toddler son.

Get Humans Versus Zombies free when you join the newsletter.

Includes:

– Niamh's full story of survival

– More gripping tales from the outbreak

◈ joncronshaw.com/humansversuszombies[1]

Author's Note

P*unk's Not Dead* marks the end of Tommy's journey, and honestly, I'm not sure I'm ready to let these characters go.

When I started writing about this ragtag band of survivors in 2023, I never imagined how deeply their story would affect me. What began as a weekly serial for my patrons became something much more personal—a meditation on loss, resilience, and what it means to find family when everything familiar has been stripped away.

After spending years in fantasy worlds, I didn't think I'd return to post-apocalyptic fiction. The pandemic changed how I viewed stories about societal collapse—suddenly, they felt too close to home. But this idea of following a punk band through the zombie apocalypse wouldn't leave me alone. There was something about combining the DIY spirit of punk with the ultimate test of human endurance that demanded to be explored.

I've been publishing since 2017, starting with my post-apocalyptic Wasteland series before moving into fantasy. After four novels in that first series, I thought I was done with the end of the world. But sometimes stories choose us, and this one insisted on being told.

Tommy's struggle with addiction, his desperate journey across a ruined America, his evolution from a broken man clinging to the past into someone who could embrace an uncertain future—these themes resonated with me in ways I didn't expect.

The punk ethos isn't just about the music; it's about building something meaningful from nothing, about creating community in the face of systems that want to break you down.

That's what Tommy and his found family do throughout this trilogy. They refuse to let the world's ending define them.

Thank you for following this brutal, hopeful journey to its conclusion. If these books moved you, please consider leaving a review—even a few words help other readers discover these stories and keep indie fiction thriving.

If you enjoyed my mixture of gritty, character-driven dark fiction where hope bleeds but never dies, you'll probably enjoy my fantasy work as well. Check out *Guild of Assassins*, which tells the story of Soren, a sculptor's apprentice who finds himself embroiled in the Guild of Assassins to get revenge for his father's death. It's a dark, gritty tale of vengeance and transformation that explores similar themes of found family and moral complexity in a fantasy setting.

Thanks for being part of this journey. In the end, punk really isn't dead—it just evolves.

- Jon Cronshaw, August 2025

P.S. Turn the page to get a sneak-punk of *Niamh's Journey*, a *Punks Versus Zombies* side story.

1.

Niamh knelt beside the bathtub, her hands moving as she washed Sean, her three-year-old son. The water was only lukewarm—the ancient water heater in their third-floor Philadelphia apartment was temperamental at best—but Sean didn't seem to mind. He splashed happily, babbling to himself as he played with his favourite toy boat.

"And then the brave pirate captain sailed across the wild, wild sea," Niamh said. "He faced sea monsters and storms and all sorts of dangers, but he never gave up, because he knew that his crew was counting on him."

Sean giggled, his chubby hands reaching for the boat. Niamh handed it to him, watching with a smile as he crashed it through the shallow water.

Bathtime was one of Niamh's favourite parts of the day. It was a chance to slow down, to focus all her attention on her son and the simple joy of his imagination.

In these moments, she could almost forget the constant anxiety that gnawed at her—the worry over money, over Tommy's long absences, over the state of the world that seemed to grow more chaotic and uncertain with each passing day.

With a final rinse, Niamh lifted Sean from the tub, wrapping him in a fluffy towel and peppering his damp hair with kisses.

In the bedroom, she helped him into his favourite pyjamas, the ones with the faded dinosaurs marching across the front. Sean had picked them out himself at the thrift store.

As she combed his hair, working gently through the tangles, Niamh hummed an old lullaby her mother used to sing to her.

Sean's eyes were beginning to droop, but he fought against the pull of sleep.

"More story," he said. "More pirates!"

Niamh smiled, settling him into his small bed and tucking the covers around him. "Alright, my love. One more story, and then it's off to dreamland for you."

She spun a tale of daring deeds and narrow escapes, her voice rising and falling with the rhythm of the story. Sean listened, his eyes wide in the soft glow of the nightlight.

When the story was finished, Niamh kissed his forehead, whispering a goodnight. She lingered for a moment, watching the slow rise and fall of his chest.

Then, with a sigh, she pushed herself to her feet and set about tidying the apartment. She gathered Sean's scattered toys, stacking them in their designated corner. She wiped down the bathtub and hung the damp towels to dry.

When the apartment was clean and Sean was settled, she could almost pretend that everything was normal.

A quick glance at the clock on the wall reminded her that it was almost time for her nightly call with Tommy.

Niamh felt a flutter of anticipation in her stomach, mixed with a now-familiar pang of longing.

These calls were a lifeline, a chance to connect with her partner across the miles that separated them.

But they were also a reminder of how much she missed him, of how badly she wished he was here with her and Sean, instead of out on the road.

Sean burst into the living room, his plastic guitar clutched in his hands. "Mommy, look!" He strummed the brightly coloured strings, producing a series of tinny, off-key notes.

"Wow, Sean! You're really rocking out, aren't you?"

Sean nodded. "Just like Daddy!"

Before she could respond, her phone buzzed.

With a swipe, Tommy's face filled the screen.

She smiled at him. "Hey, how was it?"

"Killed it. The pit was insane," Tommy said, his voice full of the usual post-gig energy.

"Sounds like it was wild. I bet you had them eating out of your hand."

Tommy grinned, but before he could reply, Sean leapt into the frame, waving his guitar in front of the camera.

"Daddy! Look at me! I'm playing just like you!"

Tommy laughed.

"He's been shredding all day. Little guy misses his dad."

There was a moment of silence. Niamh saw the way Tommy's smile faltered, how his eyes clouded with that familiar sadness. It was the same feeling that tugged at her heart every time she had to tell Sean that Daddy wouldn't be home tonight.

"I miss you both too," Tommy said, his voice quieter.

Niamh wanted to reach through the screen, to touch him, to feel his warmth beside her. But all she could do was smile, trying to keep the mood light, for Sean's sake, if not her own. "Don't worry,. We're saving all the real fun for when you get back."

Tommy's smile returned.

They chatted a bit more, talking about the little things—how Sean had finally managed to eat his broccoli tonight without a fuss, how the weather had turned cooler, bringing with it the promise of autumn. But as always, the call had to end.

"Alright, my love, it's bedtime for Sean."

Tommy nodded. "Goodnight, Niamh. Kiss the little man for me."

"I will. Goodnight, Tommy. Love you."

"You too."

She lingered for a second after the call ended, staring at the blank screen. Then, with a sigh, she tucked the phone away, turning to where Sean was now sitting, strumming the guitar.

"Come on, rock star." She scooped him up into her arms. "Time for bed."

As she carried him back to his room, Sean's head rested against her shoulder, his small body warm and heavy with sleep. She tucked him in once more, brushing a kiss over his forehead. "Goodnight, my love. Daddy loves you. I love you. Everything's going to be alright."

She slipped out of the room, pulling the door closed behind her.

In the quiet of the apartment, her loneliness felt like a physical presence. She closed her eyes, breathing deeply through the ache in her chest.

This was her life now—long days and lonely nights. But she had Sean, and she had Tommy, even if he was far away. They were her anchor, her reason to keep going, to keep fighting for the future they had dreamed of together

She settled onto the couch, allowing herself a moment to unwind after the long day. Sean was asleep, the apartment was quiet, and she had a precious few hours to herself.

She grabbed her phone and leaned back into the cushions, scrolling through her social media feed out of habit.

Friends shared photos of their kids, their pets, their meals. Mundane status updates about work. A few memes made her chuckle.

A fellow nurse shared a post: "Violent Attacks Reported in Downtown Philadelphia - Police Suspect Drug-Related Cause"

She clicked on the link and scanned the article. It was vague on details, but the gist was clear - there had been a series of brutal, seemingly random assaults in the heart of the city, leaving several people critically injured.

Niamh shook her head. This was Philly, after all. Violence was nothing new, especially in certain parts of the city..

She kept scrolling. More and more posts about the attacks, some sharing eyewitness videos, others just expressing shock and fear.

Niamh watched a few seconds of one shaky clip, wincing at the screams and the confusion before she swiped it away.

Another headline caught her eye, this one from a national news outlet. "CDC Investigating Possible Viral Outbreak Linked to Recent Violence."

Reports of similar incidents in New York, Chicago, Los Angeles.

Videos of people attacking each other in broad daylight, their movements erratic, almost inhuman.

Frantic status updates from friends and family in other cities, warning people to stay inside, to lock their doors.

Niamh's mouth went dry, her fingers trembling as she kept scrolling, kept reading.

This couldn't be real. It had to be some kind of hoax, or a misunderstanding.

Things like this simply didn't happen.

Niamh stumbled upon a live video from a local news station, the feed choppy and pixelated. "...confirmed reports of infected individuals exhibiting extremely violent, erratic behaviour...advising all residents to shelter in place... "

The video cut out, the screen going black.

Niamh stared at it, her breath coming in shallow gasps.

What would she do if this thing, this infection or whatever it was, reached their neighbourhood?

How would she protect Sean?

Niamh shot to her feet. She needed to do something, to prepare somehow.

Her nursing training kicked into gear, her mind racing through the supplies they had on hand, the precautions they could take.

She strode to the kitchen, yanking open the fridge and scanning its contents.

They had enough food for a few days, maybe a week if they rationed carefully. She filled every container she could find with water, her hands shaking as she worked.

She dug out her first aid kit from the back of the closet. Bandages, antiseptic, a few basic medications. Not much, but it was better than nothing.

As she worked, she kept one eye on her phone, watching the news updates scroll by with increasing dread.

The situation was escalating rapidly, the number of reported attacks growing by the minute.

Niamh's heart clenched as she saw a familiar street flash across the screen, just a few blocks from their building.

She recognised the storefronts, the graffiti on the walls.

People ran and screamed.

Cars lay overturned and burning.

Dark figures lurched and lunged through the smoke.

She turned off the phone, unable to watch.

Her mind was reeling, trying to process it all.

She braced herself against the kitchen counter, her knuckles white as she gripped the edge.

She needed to stay calm, to think clearly.

Panic would only make things worse, would only put her and Sean at greater risk.

She closed her eyes, forcing herself to take deep, steady breaths.

An image of Tommy rose in her mind. His warm brown eyes, the curve of his smile, the strength of his arms around her.

She reached for her phone and tried to call Tommy, but the network was jammed.

With a shaking hand, she put the phone down.

She moved through the apartment, checking locks, blocking windows.

All the while, her mind raced ahead, spinning out scenarios and contingencies.

If the power went out, they had flashlights and batteries.

If the water stopped running, they had the jugs and bottles she had filled.

If they had to leave...

She shied away from that thought, not wanting to contemplate the possibility of abandoning their home.

She worked until her body ached and her eyes burned from exhaustion.

Only then did she allow herself to sink back onto the couch, her emergency preparations as complete as she could make them.

The apartment was quiet, the silence broken only by the soft ticking of the clock on the wall and the distant wail of sirens outside.

She hugged her knees to her chest, suddenly feeling very small and very alone.

She didn't know what the next hours would bring, let alone the next days or weeks.

But she was alive, and Sean was alive, and for now, that would have to be enough.

Read the full novella as part of Humans Versus Zombies.
Get your free copy at joncronshaw.com/humansversuszombies[1]
now.

---

1. https://joncronshaw.com/humansversuszombies

Follow Jon online

Amazon: amazon.com/author/joncronshaw[1]
Bluesky: @joncronshawauthor.bsky.social[2]
BookBub: bookbub.com/authors/jon-cronshaw[3]
Facebook: @joncronshawauthor[4]
Patreon: @joncronshawauthor[5]
Threads: @joncronshawauthor[6]
X: @jon_cronshaw[7]
YouTube: @joncronshawauthor[8]
Website: joncronshaw.com[9]

Search for Jon Cronshaw's Author Diary wherever you listen to your podcasts to follow the ups and downs of his writing journey, or download the episodes directly at anchor.fm/joncronshaw[10].

---

1. http://www.amazon.com/author/joncronshaw

2. https://bsky.app/profile/joncronshawauthor.bsky.social

3. https://www.bookbub.com/authors/jon-cronshaw

4. http://www.facebook.com/joncronshawauthor

5. https://patreon.com/joncronshawauthor

6. https://www.threads.net/@joncronshawauthor

7. https://twitter.com/jon_cronshaw

8. https://youtube.com/c/joncronshawauthor

9. http://www.joncronshaw.com

10. https://anchor.fm/joncronshaw

Acknowledgements

Thank you to everyone who made this work possible. Especially to my family and friends who've supported me in countless ways.

I've got a great team of people helping me get my books to the highest standard I can, so thank you to my street team, you guys rock!

I also want to thank the members of Why Aren't You Writing, Indie Fantasy Addicts, the Sci-fi Roundtable, and the Indie Fantasy Author Mastermind. Sometimes writing books can be a lonely business, so having that kind of support means a great deal.

Special thanks for all my Patreon supporters, especially GhostCat, Debbie Harris, Laura, Russell Witte-Dycus, G. Mark Cole, T Wolf, Kathi Barreras, Michael Cantrelle, and Valerie Jondahl.

This book was edited by Claire from cherryedits.com[1]

Covers by Christian made the cover. I think it's awesome!

---

1.   https://cherryedits.com

About the Author

Jon Cronshaw writes fantasy and speculative fiction brimming with adventure, escapism, and an exploration of life's big questions.

He lives with his wife and son in Morecambe, England.

Read more at https://joncronshaw.com.

Printed in Dunstable, United Kingdom